Zydeco Queen and the Creole Fairy Courts
Leah Cutter

Also by Leah Cutter
Paper Mage
The Caves of Buda
The Jaguar and the Wolf
Baker's Dozen
Clockwork Kingdom

Zydeco Queen and the Creole Fairy Courts

Leah Cutter

Knotted Road Press

Zydeco Queen and the Creole Fairy Courts

Copyright © 2012 Leah Cutter
All rights reserved.
Published 2012 by Knotted Road Press
www.KnottedRoadPress.com

ISBN: 978-1477572115

All the characters in this book are fictitious,
and any resemblance to actual persons,
living or dead, is purely coincidental.

Knotted Road Press
www.KnottedRoadPress.com

Dedication

To Mom, Dad, and Claire. Though they're not here anymore, I have no doubt they're proud of me.

Chapter One

Francine waited and waited and *waited* all through supper. She didn't ask Aunt Noella to stop telling stories about the crazy white lady she sewed for, or tell Uncle Rene to stop asking for another round.

Normally, she loved eating with all her cousins, aunts, and uncles all squished together in the kitchen, everyone scooted up close to each other, but today was her birthday.

Presents wouldn't come until after everyone was done.

Though Francine wasn't supposed to look, she'd still managed to stand on her toes and peek at the brightly wrapped packages on the table out front. The soft squishy one she knew was from Aunt Lavine, maybe another T-shirt from her store, done up in pink and white rhinestones. The big plain bag probably held another hand-carved wooden puzzle from Uncle Leroy.

But in her quick look she hadn't seen the long package Mama and Papa had been fighting about last week; the one she knew had to be hers.

She was old enough, a whole five now. It was what she wanted most of all.

Finally, everyone had their fill, though Uncle Leroy did tease about making coffee first. Mama hushed him and they all strolled into the front room.

Francine felt like a princess with her court assembled: all her aunts, uncles, and cousins scattered in a circle around her. Papa sat in his big recliner, smiling at her like she was his sun and his moon.

Mama handed Francine each present. She carefully opened it and then always jumped up to hug the giver. She'd guessed right about the shirt and the puzzle. There were also coloring books, games, school clothes, and a tiny silver bear from Uncle Rene.

But nothing from Mama and Papa.

When Francine looked at Mama, expectantly, Mama just looked at Papa.

"Charles," she drawled, sounding a little impatient.

Papa tried to look like he didn't know what Mama was asking for.

Francine could see a smile hiding at the corners of his mouth.

"Papa?" Francine asked.

"Very well," Papa said.

He reached down beside him. The package had been hidden there—long, sleek, and black.

Francine reverently took it from his hands, running her fingers across the nubby grain.

"Now, you know what this means?" Papa asked seriously.

"We get to play together!" Francine exclaimed as she finally opened the case and looked at her first fiddle. It was just her size, with gleaming metal strings and softly glowing wood.

Everyone laughed, but Francine didn't mind. The dusty smell of the instrument caught her. She rubbed a finger along the smooth veneer, tracing the scrolled cutouts.

"It's so pretty," she breathed.

"It's not a toy," Papa warned.

Francine gave him an exasperated sigh.

"I *know* that, Papa."

She looked at his empty hands.

"Where's the bow?"

Uncle Rene cleared his throat.

Francine turned toward him expectantly.

He bowed and pulled it out with a flourish from behind his back.

Francine had never seen a bow so white. Papa's was worn to beige with age and use.

"Made this special, just for you," Uncle Rene said, handing the bow to Francine in the same way a king would give a knight a sword.

"The hairs are from a horse's tail. I plucked 'em myself on midwinter's eve, in the cold and the dark, without a light shining."

Francine took the bow cautiously. It was so pretty. She held out her finger and balanced it carefully, finding the middle point exactly where it should be.

"Thank you so much," she whispered, entranced. She couldn't wait to learn how to play with it properly.

"Can we start now, Papa?" Francine asked, unable to tear her eyes away from the best gifts she'd ever received.

"Tomorrow," he promised.

And tomorrow and tomorrow and tomorrow: Francine heard in her head what Papa was really saying. They'd be making music together, every day, for the rest of her life.

* * *

Francine stood in the middle of the living room, arms crossed over her chest, her toes dug into the thick brown rug. The smell of warm toast and coffee floated from the kitchen, remnants of what had been an anxious breakfast for Francine.

"Won't go back," she said stubbornly, as she made her stand against her papa.

She'd spent all night sitting by her window, casting wish after wish on the moon, praying for it to stop in its tracks so morning would never come. She knew Mama would be shocked by her blasphemy, but Francine didn't care.

She was never going back to that private academy. Even if the local high school wouldn't actually teach her anything about music. She'd learn on her own.

"Yes, you will," Papa said, still standing in the kitchen doorway. His voice cut through the room, flat and cold, bouncing off the wooden walls. He glared at Francine; even without coming closer and looming over her, the power of his stare pushed against her like a summer storm.

When she'd been little, those storms had made her hide her head under her blankets. Now that she was fourteen, they just riled her up more.

"We jumped through more hoops than you can imagine to get you a scholarship to a good high school so you'd have a chance of a better life. You *will* be going back."

Francine shook her head.

"You didn't hear what those kids called me," she said, trying to make her voice hard like Papa's, but it came out with a quiver.

"Gator-bait. And that I had swamp stink. And muck growing between my toes. They even said I'd marry my brother. I told them I didn't have a brother, so they said I'd marry my cousin."

While the words had hurt, the looks had stung more, like Francine was worse than the swamp she lived in.

Mama appeared beside Papa in the doorway, wiping her hands with a dishrag.

"Now Francine, do you not like your teachers?"

Francine bit her lip and looked down at her bare toes. She actually did like them. If pressed, she'd also admit to liking her classes, particularly her music class.

While Papa had taught her to play fiddle, and Uncle Rene had taught her zydeco and the blues, blowing his sax, this class had opened up new worlds of music to her. Her old school had nothing like it.

"Charles, you and Francine are going to Uncle Rene's on Saturday, right? So Francine can see her relations and learn more fiddling?"

Papa couldn't hold his glare against Mama's hard look.

"Yes," he said softly.

"So, Francine, if you go to school for the week, Papa will make sure you get some fun on the weekend. Does that sound fair?"

Francine shook her head.

"That's four whole days," she complained.

Four days where she'd spend hours in the afternoon on a stinky school bus instead of in the woods out back, the only place she felt like she could breathe these days—that was, when she wasn't making music.

Mama looked thoughtful for a moment.

"I'll pack cornbread in your lunch every day," she said.

The offer tempted Francine. If this had been the regular high school, the one down the road and not the private one miles away, she would have been able to trade that cornbread for just about anything at lunch. The kids she'd grown up with knew her mama baked the best cornbread in Pointe Coupee parish.

These kids, though, bought their lunches. They'd called her a charity case because she brought a packed meal every day.

"And Papa will pick you up at least twice this week," Mama volunteered.

Even though Francine was still mad at Papa for making her go to the private academy, time alone with him was precious.

"Deal," she said, grinning. That also meant she'd get home early enough to spend time with the trees out back.

"Deal?" Papa grumbled.

Francine knew enough not to be bothered by his grumbling. Mama sometimes called him a big old bear 'cause he growled like one.

"It's only fair, Charles. Your daughter is giving up some of her time for you. You should give up time for her, as well," Mama pointed out reasonably. Then she told Francine, "You know what you should do? Get Aunt Noella to sew a gator patch to your bag. Then tell those kids that anyone who messes with you is gonna get bit."

Francine giggled. While the kids might tease her for being from the woods, even they knew better than to mess with swamp magic.

Papa pressed his lips together like he didn't think that was a good idea, but he still nodded.

"Fine."

"Now, since you've already missed the school bus, and since I owe you some cornbread, come back into the kitchen and help. Charles will drive you in later."

"Yes, Mama," Francine said, relieved that she didn't have to ride the bus again. It was always better when Papa took her to school.

Before Francine could join Mama in the kitchen, Papa stopped her, laying a warm hand on her shoulder.

"You study hard," he told Francine. "You need to learn more than just fiddling music. Want you to do me proud."

"I will, Papa," Francine promised. She'd do just about anything for him.

* * *

Francine felt a slight impact on the back of her head, as though someone had tapped her lightly with their fingers. But no one stood beside her.

Mainly, she heard the wet *splat*.

With a hesitant hand, Francine reached back and brushed the slimy mess with her fingertips.

Bewilderment filled her. Why would someone spit at her? In her hair? How could someone do that?

Anger slammed through Francine, washing away the confusion. Damn them. Damn them all.

Francine shoved herself out of her desk and stalked toward the group of smirking boys sitting at the back of the classroom. Without warning, she slapped Billy McGyvner as hard as she could. His head snapped to the side with a satisfying *crack*.

After a second of shocked silence, Billy's pals started laughing and hooting.

A rush of white noise filled Francine's head. She felt as though her blood literally started to boil. Billy's friends all laughed, some giving her grudging congratulations. Billy's face grew red as he surged to his feet.

"I'm gonna kill you," he promised as he launched himself at Francine.

Francine howled in return and reached for Billy as well.

However, instead of aiming for her face, he hit her in the tits, which hurt so much it shocked a yelp out of her.

As well as made her furious.

Francine clawed at Billy's face, his arm, any part of Billy she could reach, her hands curled like talons. She scored his cheek, but then he punched her in the stomach hard enough to make her double over and stagger back, her breath gone.

Francine struggled to straighten up before Billy hit her again. Then hands were pulling her back. She tried to throw them off, but they held on.

Finally, Francine heard Mrs. Sinclair yelling, shouting both her name and Billy's.

With an effort, Francine drew herself up. She shrugged her arms and the people holding onto her let her go. She smiled a tight smile as she drew herself up straight, at least a head taller than the kids surrounding her.

Mrs. Sinclair appeared beside them. "What happened here?"

"She just attacked me!" Billy proclaimed. "I didn't do anything!"

Francine looked at Katy and Sue, Linda and Keesha, the girls who were at least friendly to her.

None of them would meet her eyes. No one said anything.

They knew—they all knew. However, none of them stood up for her.

"He spit in my hair," Francine said. She turned to show the teacher the wet mess still there, still obvious against her black hair.

No one seconded her claim.

"Wasn't me," Billy said stubbornly.

"You were sitting directly behind me," Francine pointed out.

"Spit's just attracted to you." A couple of Billy's friends laughed quietly.

"Enough," Mrs. Sinclair said. "You both have detention."

"What?" Francine said. "He should be suspended for bullying!"

"We'll talk about it in Principal Martin's office," Mrs. Sinclair said smoothly. "I'm escorting both of you there. In the meantime," she added as she cast a frosty glance over the rest of the class, "straighten up these seats and be ready to discuss section ten. There may also be a quiz."

The other students groaned. Francine nearly joined them. Her hands shook with the release of her adrenaline. Her stomach hurt, and the other places Billy had hit were making themselves known.

As Billy walked out of the classroom, he threw a look at Francine so venomous it made her stumble.

It suddenly occurred to Francine that not only had she fought him, she'd humiliated him in front of his friends with that first slap.

No matter what happened, Billy McGyvner would never forgive Francine for that.

And he'd make her life a living hell forever more.

* * *

"What's that?"

Francine barely heard the words over the clatter of lockers and students making their way from one class to the next. "What's what?" she asked, turning around.

A dark-skinned girl with tight braids stood midstream—a newcomer, Francine figured—kids pushing around her on both sides.

"On your shoulder," she said, pointing.

Francine twisted, trying to see her back, afraid that Billy or Laura had taped something to her (again) or that maybe someone had drawn on her. She didn't have time to make it to the bathroom and then upstairs to her English class.

"No, that scar. On your shoulder."

Now Francine twisted the other way. All she saw was her birthmark, high on her left shoulder.

"This?" she asked, pointing, relieved.

The girl nodded solemnly.

"I was born with it," Francine said, running her fingertip along the crescent-shaped mark.

She'd wondered about it herself, standing with Mama's hand-mirror in one hand, examining it in the bathroom mirror behind her. It looked like a hoof-print to her, though Uncle Rene had said it was more like a sliver of the moon. Both Mama and Papa swore it was a birthmark and not a scar, though it was still shiny and smooth, like new skin.

"Oh," the girl said. She looked up and down the hall before shrieking, "It's a swamp stamp!"

A group of kids—including Billy and Laura—burst out laughing at the end of the hall.

Francine felt punched in the gut. She'd been tricked, yet again. She pushed down on her shame and let her anger rise.

"You think so?" she said, making her voice low and mean. She took a pair of scissors out of her bag. She'd spent the previous night at her cousins' house, and Aunt Noella had given them to her to give to Mama.

When Francine walked toward the girl, she stopped giggling and backed away.

"What are you doing?"

"Gonna take a braid of your hair," Francine said. She opened and closed the scissors twice, the slicing sound clear in the crowded hall.

"Gonna put a curse on you so it all falls out."

Aunt Noella had told her that if they were teasing her about being from the swamp, she might as well use it to her advantage.

"See? I told you she was swamp scum," Billy said, coming up to protect the girl. A tight knot of kids formed around them, all watching, wondering what was going to happen next.

Francine knew better than to hope that any of them would protect her.

"You better watch yourself, too, Billy McGyvner," she warned. "Or toads are going to start falling from your lips. Your mama's already sick."

That made Billy pause.

"Don't you talk about my mama," he hissed.

"Your mama's done spit on the crossroads," Francine said spitefully. The way his face paled made her feel powerful for once.

"When she dies, it'll be the horseman taking her away, not the angels."

The circle of kids surrounding them stood shocked-still. No one ever wished someone's mama to Hell that way.

"You take that back," Billy said, moving just an inch away from Francine, looking up at her, angry and quiet.

All the hairs pricked up on the back of Francine's neck.

"Or what?" she asked, raising the scissors.

She already had to sit at the back of the class so Billy and his pals wouldn't spit on her, she'd had to put plastic over the vents in her locker to stop them from spraying oil on her books, and she couldn't count the number of times she'd been knocked down or over. She'd only ever fought Billy the once, but she'd be happy to do it again, right here, right now, her anger boiling up.

"What's going on here?" Mrs. Beaumont's strident tones carried over their heads. She was Principal Martin's secretary. No one messed with her. Papa called her the real power at the school.

"She was threatening me!" Billy exclaimed, turning to Mrs. Beaumont, his eyes wide.

Billy should get an Oscar for the act he put on.

"She was going cut me up and feed me to the gators!" His voice even trembled.

"Is that true, Francine?"

"Naw. Gators wouldn't touch his slimy hide," Francine said.

When Mrs. Beaumont held out her hand, Francine reluctantly put the scissors into it. Now both Mama and Aunt Noella were going to be angry with her.

"I think you both should come with me down to Principal Martin's office," Mrs. Beaumont said. "And the rest of you should get to your classes."

"It wasn't my fault!" Francine complained as she slammed her locker closed. The principal would call Papa, which meant everyone was going to be against her at dinner that night.

"Whether or not that's the case, you know better than to threaten another student, Francine," Mrs. Beaumont said. "Unless, of course, it was self-defense," she added when Billy started smirking.

Francine shrugged. It wouldn't matter to Papa or anyone else in her family. They'd all blame *her* for fighting. Again.

* * *

Francine paused on the trail, listening again.

None of her cousins followed her.

None of them could.

Still, she waited another few moments in the deep woods, listening to the trees and wind whisper around her, before she lifted the fallen branch, slipped under it, and stepped into the fern house.

A nest of leaves and weather grass waited for Francine in the back of the space. Moving quickly, Francine made herself comfortable there, knowing the ferns, trees, and bushes would hide her from all eyes. Only then did she close her eyes and rest her head against the trees that made up the back of the fern house.

She wasn't looking forward to going back to school come Monday. But she'd survived a whole year at the academy, and she'd be a sophomore now. Soon enough she'd graduate. It was the only thing she could focus on. It seemed a lifetime away, but somehow, she had to get through it.

The summer had helped, hanging out with her friends and her cousins every day, making music and laughing far into the night.

Finally, the peace of the woods seeped under Francine's skin and she felt herself relax, forgetting the fights at school to come and the homework that would be piled on. She opened her eyes and looked around, seeing the damage the last storm had caused. Some of the younger, more frail trees had tilted over, while the older trunks remained untouched.

The fern house wasn't really a house overgrown with ferns and moss, but Francine always thought of it that way. Ages ago two trees had fallen in on each other, their trunks and branches forming an A-frame entrance. Sweet shrubs with their fragrant red flowers still blooming ran along one side, while creeping figs and hollies made up the other. Once Francine was inside, she could easily pretend all the greenery formed walls.

None of Francine's cousins or friends knew about this place.

She kept it from them by running faster through the trees, as well as going much further into the woods behind Uncle Rene's walled backyard than they dared.

When she'd been younger, she'd assumed they were scared, and it bolstered her pride. It wasn't until she was older that she realized they couldn't see the trails through the woods that she could. They blundered when they walked, snagging their jeans on briars and thorns Francine would never have walked into.

The paths obvious to her were hidden to others.

The woods seemed still in the soft afternoon light, a golden-green moment that stretched on and on. Francine wished she could always stay here, safe and secure, the trees her only companions.

Music to fit the scene drifted through her mind, a sweet, quiet tune that danced with the green light filtering through the leaves. The droning insects made a steady rhythm for the piece coming alive in her head. Her fingers moved on imaginary strings, already feeling the buzzing notes.

"Francine!"

Without conscious thought Francine rolled to her side and crawled out of her haven. She sprinted a few yards away, then stopped, waiting for Papa, to see how close he was.

Francine hadn't seen Papa walking through the woods

before. However, it didn't surprise her that while her cousins couldn't find a path even if they tripped over it, Papa walked confidently between the trees. He gave her a big smile when he saw her.

"Don't have to worry about you sneaking off with some boy, do I? You still have notes dancing around your head."

He looked beyond her, over her shoulder, obviously curious where she'd been.

Francine refused to turn around and even glance at the fern house. That was hers and hers alone.

"Papa, I do like boys," she protested, just not the awful ones at school.

Papa chuckled and shook his head, turning to go back to Uncle Rene's house, taking the path that was most direct, that no one knew except Francine.

"You really didn't notice your cousin Zeek's friend, did you?"

"Who, Petie? Why would I notice Petie?" Francine asked, wrinkling her nose at the thought. Petie was her age, true, but he had horrible acne and was so shy he couldn't even look her in the face.

"Oh, no reason," Papa said in that irritating manner that adults sometimes had.

"I swear you are worse than Aunt Lavine trying to match me up with boys," Francine grumbled.

Papa's laughter rang through the trees.

Francine paused. She could almost see it, those happy notes sliding through the soft sunlight shining through the trees.

"We gotta get going," Papa said, cutting through Francine's thoughts. Though he smiled, he seemed as tense as when Reverend Steeps came by, asking for a donation when it was the end of the month and payday was still half a week off.

"Your kin won't hold back, you know. All of Uncle Rene's

hush puppies will be gone by the time we get there."

"Hush puppies? Why didn't you say that earlier?" Francine teased. She walked up to Papa and he slung one arm over her shoulders.

"That's my girl," Papa said, relaxing more, giving her a brief hug before insisting Francine walk ahead of him. Every time she glanced back at him, he was looking around. Once, he made a warding motion with his hand, the kind Grandma Guiscard used to make to keep evil away.

When Papa glanced up, he smiled at Francine.

"Old habit," he said.

But his smile seemed brittle, and more than anything else, Francine didn't want Papa to be unhappy.

* * *

That night, when Francine came to say goodnight to her papa, he took her hand and asked her, "You go into those woods by yourself often, don't you?"

Francine nodded, not wanting to lie.

"You know they're not safe. I worry about you walking through them all on your own."

"Papa, I'm not three."

She knew about the gators, snakes, and everything else in the woods. As far as she was concerned, they were safer than the halls at the academy.

"I know you're not. That's the problem." He sighed.

Francine looked down at her hands in his. Though her hands were strong from playing the fiddle, and big because Francine was tall, they still looked small and frail in Papa's palms.

"I'm not going to ask you to promise me not to go back in the woods alone, or not go as deep. I wouldn't ask that of you. I know it means too much."

Francine nodded, a strange lump forming in her throat. What had Papa so scared? He seemed so sad, too, as if he'd lost something important.

"You just have to be careful. Watch yourself, and you come *running* back home if you ever see something strange out there."

Francine winced at the tremor in his beautiful, deep voice.

"Can you promise me that, darling?"

"Of course, Papa," Francine said. "I'll be extra careful."

"That's my girl."

Papa kissed Francine's forehead goodnight and he let her go.

It took Francine a long time to fall asleep that night. For the first time in Francine's life, Papa looked scared. And that scared Francine more than any warnings about the woods.

* * *

Francine started cursing under her breath as she drew closer to her gym locker. Old women used fox urine to keep critters out of their gardens. It smelled like someone had dumped a whole bottle against her locker. It stank worse than swamp gas, making Francine's eyes water.

Before Francine could touch her locker, she had to get a towel to wipe off the sticky surface. She had to stop cleaning more than once in order to step back and take a couple of deep breaths before she could continue. The anger coiled deep in her stomach, making her keep on.

"What happened?" Coach Beaker asked as Francine opened the locker.

"Someone did something they thought was funny," Francine told her. Her books were in her other locker, so at least they hadn't been doused. Her fiddle was always in the music room. However, her street clothes were ruined.

"Do you have something to change into?"

"No," Francine said with gritted teeth. She was going to have to wear her sweaty, stained gym clothes for the rest of the day. No wonder Karyn had knocked her down, making sure she'd be muddy.

"Who did this?" Coach Beaker asked as Francine reached in with the towel and picked up her favorite jeans.

"What does it matter?" Francine asked, scowling at the ruins.

"We're supposed to report all incidents of bullying," the coach said softly.

The coach was new, hired only that spring. Still, Francine was angry enough to ask, "Why? So you can feel good and tell each other you've done all you can? If only that poor girl would help herself?"

She slammed her jeans into the garbage can and went back for her shirt.

"You can't help."

"I still need to report it—"

"Blame it on me, then," Francine said as she tossed her shirt. Even her sandals were ruined.

"I'll get the janitor to clean up the rest," Coach Beaker said. "I can also write you a note, excuse you for the rest of the day."

Francine paused, tempted. But she had a test in history last hour, and no one who could pick her up, even though Cousin Franklin did get his permit recently. She shook her head. "But thanks," she said.

When Francine got back to her locker, Billy and Laura stood near by, camera in hand. "For the yearbook," Billy told her as he snapped a shot.

Francine just rolled her eyes. She knew that for people like Billy and Laura, high school was supposed to be the best years of their lives. For her it was just hard time. She was counting the days before she left this academy in her dust.

When Francine opened her locker she saw a bag that she'd forgotten about. Aunt Lavine had given her more clothes from her tourist shop. The jeans weren't her style, but they were decent enough, and would cover the mud on her shins.

The shirt...Francine looked down at her stained gym shirt. It would be better than what she was wearing. Maybe. Had Billy known she had extra clothes with her? Francine shook her head. He wasn't that clever.

Francine went into the restroom and quickly changed. When she walked out of the stall Laura stood there, waiting for her. She whistled when she saw Francine. "That's some mighty fine sparkle."

Francine glanced down at the shirt. It was charcoal gray, with the words "Zydeco Queen" emblazoned across it in purple, green, and gold rhinestones—Mardi Gras colors.

"Just letting my swamp flag fly," Francine told her proudly.

Laura giggled, and for a second they were just two girls sharing a joke.

Then Laura snapped another picture and said, "Definitely going into the yearbook."

Francine had to laugh.

"Oh honey. You ain't seen nothing yet."

* * *

For the Junior-Senior prom at the end of the school year, the gym had been decorated with banners and streamers, and a silver disco ball threw squares of light across the floor. The usual gym smells of waxed wood and sweat mingled with the scents of hairspray and cheap cologne. A band played up on stage, trying to please everyone with the range of music, from country to rock, even some hip-hop.

Francine had gone to Aunt Lavine for her dress. She planned to outshine everyone else there, literally.

She got her wish.

The bodice had blue, pink, and gold rhinestones across the bust. The hem held a good three inches of silver sparkle.

A rich hunter-green satin made up the rest of the gown. It had an iridescent glow to it, and changed colors subtly to a lighter blue-green as Francine walked.

Francine hoped that the sparkle of the dress would distract people from noticing that it was sleeveless. It mostly covered her birthmark, but she knew if she reached forward for something, the scarred skin would show. She had a shawl she draped across her shoulders, but it kept sliding off as she danced. People stared, but people always stared. She'd gotten used to ignoring them.

Francine's shoes hurt her feet early so she took them off, ignoring her mama's voice in her head about what people would think.

She only had one more year to go then she wouldn't have to think about high school ever again.

Finally, the band took a break and Principal Martin picked up the microphone. The spotlight made his pale face ghostly.

Francine rolled her eyes as he talked about how proud he was of the graduating class, knowing he was glad to get rid of some of the troublemakers. She clapped politely when Billy and Laura were announced the Junior king and queen, completely unsurprised. Laura had done her hair up perfectly so the tiara would fit.

"I want to thank everyone who voted for us," Billy started off once he had the mike.

Francine snorted softly. Billy sounded like a sleazy politician running for re-election. He'd never get her vote.

"Now, as some of you already know, we added a special title for tonight, for another lucky lady who's about to be queened."

A shiver of fear ran down Francine's spine when Billy called her name, asking her to come up on stage. Francine dragged her feet, dreading what was about to happen.

They weren't clever enough to dump pig's blood on her,

like in that movie, were they?

Up on the stage, the spotlights struck her rhinestones. Flashes of light bounced into the audience, and more than one person covered their eyes and called out that she was blinding them. Francine kept her chin up and head held high. She'd chosen to wear the dress. No way to make a different choice—or as Mama would say, to push the rain back into the sky.

She wished, though, that she could really blind the kids staring up at her, sniggering.

"As ya'll know, Francine here plays a pretty mean fiddle," Billy said. "So we'd like to present her with a special title that we made just for her. Please give a big round of applause to our new Zydeco Queen!"

One of Billy's cohorts came onto the stage bearing a crown bigger than the tiara Laura wore. A toy violin stood on its end in the front. Lines of white rhinestones swooped down from it. Cheap plastic crawfish decorated the sides.

If Francine's cousins had made this crown, she would have been proud to wear it. But Billy, Laura, and the others had come up with the idea in the spirit of meanness.

Francine still easily bowed her head to be crowned, enjoying her height and how Billy had to reach up to place it on her head.

She knew it would be the only title she'd ever receive.

The crowd whooped and Billy stepped back, asking for Francine to take a bow, saying how proud everyone at school was with her. Angry tears suddenly came to her eyes. The title didn't mark her as special to them—just different—*other*.

However, Francine couldn't escape. The entire court had to stay on the stage as Principal Martin announced the Senior king and queen, then have pictures taken. Francine was certain her cheeks must have glowed redder than Uncle Otis' nose after he'd been dipping in the Sidel moonshine.

She just wanted to die, for the earth to open and swallow her whole. Not only had she been embarrassed in front of the entire school, this picture would live forever with the framed pictures of the court.

Francine wished all of them to Hell a dozen times. She couldn't quit school as much as she might want. She didn't know what she could do for revenge. Some day, though, she'd get back at all of them.

* * *

Francine felt like her insides were all wiggly, more so then when she auditioned for the new jazz band at the academy. It was the first real gig for the band she and her friends had formed that summer. They hadn't gotten it themselves—they were opening for Uncle Rene's band, playing at Slim's as a favor to him.

Still. It was the first time Francine had ever played live with a band made up of her friends and not at school.

It was their music, the music they'd written together, though Francine had made up most of the tunes.

A few tables still sat open when Francine and her band got on the stage. Not many, though. Once Uncle Rene's band started the place would be filled, and the dance floor, packed. Still, it was a decent crowd for a brand new, unknown band.

Of course, they weren't completely unknown. Relatives of all three band members sat in the crowd, as well as their friends. A frisson of fear coursed through Francine. Her relations might say she did fine, but she knew them well enough to tell if they were lying. It would be worse than if she messed up at school, because she'd have to see these people for the rest of her life.

Francine lifted her chin. She wasn't about to mess this up. None of them were.

The microphone squealed when Francine picked it up,

the feedback instantly killing all the conversation.

"Wow," Francine said into the microphone. "I think that was a C-sharp."

A quiet chuckle passed through the crowd.

"We're The Zydeco Chicks," Francine announced. "And it's time to dance."

They started into their first number, a fast piece called "The Gator Waltz." Francine at first kept her gaze on her fingers, or the floor, scared of the people in front of her. Finally, though, she glanced up.

To her surprise, people were dancing.

Francine looked back at her bandmates—Simone on the accordion and Muriel on the washboard. They chased behind her musically as she took off, twirling the tune up on some arpeggios. Then the tune wove back tightly together in the middle and they all played off each other. They ended with a short improv between the fiddle and the accordion, neither willing to give the other the last note.

The second piece ran into the first one, a slower number. Francine heard people clapping along with the beat. She beamed at the crowd, riding on the wave of energy they built, and then she fed it back to them, making her notes brighter and sharper.

People glided by on the dance floor, quick on their feet.

A rush of power thrilled Francine. *She* controlled their movements. *She* directed the dance. She wanted it to go on and on. The music set Francine flying—her fiddle was part of her arm, her fingers dancing, and the tune part of her soul. However, eventually, the song drew to a close.

After stopping for sincere applause, Francine announced their third and final number, "Zydeco Queen." More dancers came onto the floor until it was as packed as it would be later for Uncle Rene's band. Francine danced with them on the stage, happier than she could ever recall being. She looked up and beamed, wanting to share her joy with everyone: They were all now her family.

That's when the strangers at the back of the bar drew Francine's attention.

They were tall, very tall, like Francine and her papa. Some had dark hair and pale skin like them, too. Others were darker, like Uncle Rene. One proud African American woman with white hair caught Francine's eye and smiled at her.

Francine couldn't help but smile back.

It was odd. She'd never met these strangers, but they looked familiar, like cousins she hadn't met yet.

Francine gestured that they should come closer, pointing at the dance floor with her fiddle. The woman with the white hair merely smiled and shook her head.

That seemed like a challenge to Francine, so she played her hardest, even going through the refrain a second time. However, the strangers stayed near the door and didn't join the other dancers.

The music ended to thunderous applause. Francine felt as though it was strong enough to lift her off her feet. She and her bandmates took their bows, though Francine wished she could play longer. She never wanted to stop making music, pouring everything out and getting it all back twofold.

She also knew if she could play another song, maybe two, she could get those newcomers onto the dance floor.

"That was so amazing!" Francine exclaimed as they got backstage. She hugged both Muriel and Simone.

Uncle Rene came up and gave all three of them a hug as well.

"You girls just stole the show," he said with a grin.

Francine knew that wasn't true—people out in the bar wanted to see Uncle Rene and his band. But she knew they'd done well.

Still buzzing with excitement, adrenaline coursing

through her, Francine made her way back out front. She ignored her family and their waves, weaving her way to the back of the room, to where the others had been standing.

No one waited there for her.

Francine tried to contain the disappointment she felt. She'd really wanted to talk with them. She didn't understand why, but she'd felt drawn to them.

She walked back to the table where Papa sat. Mama waved at her from a few tables over where she sat with her sisters.

"That was wonderful, darling," Papa told her, obviously proud, giving her a big hug.

"It was so much fun! I wonder if we can come back next weekend."

Francine looked around the crowd, still seeking those others.

"Now, you know how I feel about you playing in bands," Papa said.

Francine knew. She'd heard all her life how she was supposed to do something more.

"Who you looking for?" Papa asked.

"Some people came in. They kinda looked like us," Francine said, indicating herself and her papa. "Tall and dark-haired. I've never seen 'em before but they looked familiar."

Papa looked around the room quickly.

"They're gone now," he said evenly. "And you stay far, far away from them."

"Who are they?"

"People you don't need to know," Papa said grimly. "We should go."

"But—"

Francine wanted to talk with her aunts, uncles, and cousins. Her blood still buzzed with the energy from playing. Plus, she wanted to hear Uncle Rene and his band play.

Papa wouldn't be stopped.

"Home. Now."

Francine angrily went backstage and packed her fiddle away. Who had those people been? Why wouldn't Papa let her talk with them? It wasn't fair of Papa to keep her other relations separate.

She was determined to find them.

Chapter Two

The smell of sweet onions frying in butter filled the air in the kitchen. Though Francine had just finished breakfast, it still made her mouth water. Instead, she concentrated on chopping celery for Mama's mustard sauce, using her favorite cutting board—made by Uncle Leroy—and Mama's best knife, honed to a deadly edge once a week by Papa.

Mama peeled mushrooms next to Francine, humming softly under her breath, a soft counterpoint to the dripping rain outside. The cornbread was already finished and resting on the counter. They'd both start deveining shrimp next. The family was gathering at their house for this week's Sunday dinner.

It was just the pair of them. Mama liked to joke that while Papa was good at eating food, he was worse than useless in a kitchen.

Francine didn't want to bring anything into this cozy place that might ruin it. But she had to *know*.

"Mama, do I have any cousins I haven't met yet?" she asked.

"There's your Aunt Justine, who married that Yankee up in Montana, of all places. I don't think you've met her kids."

Mama shuddered.

"She sends us Christmas cards every year with pictures of all of them standing in the snow."

"No, I meant here," Francine said.

"Why?" Mama asked.

Francine looked up at the flat note in Mama's voice. It sounded like a warning, but Francine wanted answers.

"Last night while I was playing, some people came in to listen. They just looked familiar, I guess."

Mama sighed.

"Papa told me they'd stopped by. Now, don't you go looking for trouble. You stay away from those people, you hear me?"

"But Mama—"

"No. You will walk away if any of them ever comes up to you, Francine Adelaide Guiscard. Have I made myself clear?"

Francine swallowed around the lump in her throat.

"Yes, Mama," she said quietly.

She didn't understand. Mama rarely raised her voice or got angry, and never over something as small as this.

Mama sighed.

"I worry about you," she said, turning back to her mushrooms. "You're just like your papa. Headstrong and more stubborn than Mississippi mud. Hotter than Tabasco with that temper, too."

"I'll be fine, Mama," Francine assured her.

"I know you will be. I still worry. Now, are you ready for the shrimp?"

Francine let the topic drop, though she didn't stop thinking about it. She could take care of herself. She'd been doing that at the academy for years.

But no matter what warnings Mama or Papa gave her, she wasn't going to stop looking for her lost cousins.

* * *

Francine stared at the letter in her hand, the rest of the mail lying forgotten on the floor under the mail slot. She ran her fingers over the embossed symbol of the Louisiana Music College, then across the stark black signature at the bottom. Sunshine streamed through the windows behind her, but she could no longer feel its heat. The words ran together and Francine struggled to read the letter a second time:

Dear Ms. Guiscard,

I saw you perform last week at Slim's. I'd hoped to talk with you afterward but missed my opportunity. I learned from your uncle that you are a high school senior at Oak River Academy. I sincerely hope that you'll keep our school in mind when you're looking to further your education. We have more than one music scholarships that you could apply for.

Please don't hesitate to call if you have any questions.
Sincerely,
Frank Kitridge
Dean, Jazz Music Program

"Mama! Papa!" Francine shouted. When they both came running from the kitchen, she handed them the letter with a shaking hand.

"Is it real?"

Mama nodded while Papa took the envelope from Francine's hand and looked at it, holding it up to the sunlight and peering through it. He gave the letter the same treatment.

"Seems like," he said gruffly. "Has a fancy watermark and everything on the paper."

"Oh darling," Mama said, pulling Francine in for a big hug. "I'm so proud of you!"

Francine's arms shook and she held onto her mama for a long moment, drinking in the comfort. She looked up, thinking that her papa would join in. But he stood apart, his arms over his chest.

"Papa?"

"You shouldn't be thinking about going to some music school. You need to learn a trade, get a real job."

"Charles," Mama scolded.

"We sent you to that fancy academy to have a better life. Not to end up playing in bars, trolling for tips."

"I know, Papa, but this could be a chance to do something else with my music."

"What, writing songs for other people?" Papa said dismissively.

"I thought you liked my music," Francine said, stung.

"Of course, baby girl," Papa said quickly. "And I love playing with you. But life on the road is no life."

Francine shook her head. There were other things she could do if she could get into a college like this.

Maybe become a studio musician, or teach.

"Now, Charles," Mama said harshly. "You apologize to your daughter for being an old stick-in-the-mud. You should be happy other people recognize her talent."

Papa stuck out his chin mulishly.

"Too many have already noticed her talent."

"You mean my lost cousins," Francine said hotly.

"You stay away from them," Papa said, glaring at Francine.

"I'll talk with them if I want," Francine said, glaring right back. She hadn't found them yet; it hadn't even been a week. But she would.

"You will walk away from them," Mama said with quiet steel in her voice.

"I am seventeen years old," Francine said. "I will do what I want."

"Not in my house, young lady," Papa said, his tone flat and mean. "And right now, you need to go to your room. Or you'll learn you aren't too big to be laid over my knee and spanked."

For a long moment Francine and her papa stared at each other, both smoldering in anger.

Mama sighed and said quietly, "Both of you. Behave."

"Your room. Now," Papa said.

"Fine," Francine said. She snatched the letter out of his hand.

"It's not fair!" she complained as she stomped down the hall to her room.

"Not fair at all!" she added as she slammed the door shut.

For a second, Francine was afraid that both Papa and Mama would storm in after her, yelling at her for such behavior. She threw herself onto her bed, telling herself that she didn't care. They were wrong about everything.

However, Francine couldn't hold onto her anger. She found herself crying into her pillow.

How could Papa be so hateful? Why didn't he understand?

Francine loved making music. It was the only time she felt alive. Life on the road would be tough—she'd heard Papa and Uncle Rene's stories about it often enough. She *knew* that.

But the rewards were sure to be as great.

Finally, Francine finished crying. She carefully smoothed out the letter, putting it on her desk, determined to apply for those scholarships.

Then, defiantly, Francine got out her fiddle and started playing.

She'd show them.

* * *

Francine took down the oldest photo album from the shelf in the living room. The house was quiet. Golden dust motes danced in the corner, shimmering in the afternoon sunlight. Mama and Papa both napped in the heat of the day, the air hot and heavy despite the constantly blowing AC.

As quietly as she could, Francine took the album to her room and closed the door. It had been over a month since the gig at Slim's, but she still hadn't found her lost cousins. She hoped the old pictures would give her a clue because she couldn't talk with Mama, Papa, or any of her relations about it; everytime she tried, they just ended up either fighting or not talking to her.

The smell of musty paper greeted Francine as she opened the album. She flipped through the first few pages, then went back and looked through them again.

It was as she'd remembered. There weren't any pictures of Papa from when he'd been a boy, though there was at least one or two of everyone else.

Where exactly had Papa grown up? He knew those lost cousins, Francine was certain. He'd never denied them as family, either.

But there were no pictures of them.

The earliest pictures of Papa were of him as a young man, probably from when he'd first met Uncle Rene, when Uncle Rene and his family had claimed Papa as their own.

Francine was just going to have to get answers somewhere else. She turned to stare out the window of her room. The first line of trees stood just across the yard. Though it was hot as blazes outside, they promised shade and escape. She couldn't smell the woods, but she knew the scent by heart: baked bark and earth, a little sweet mulch, the heavy undertones of the nearby open water.

No one would notice if Francine slipped out for a while. Besides, no one had told her to stay in. They'd just assumed she'd nap like they were.

Heart pounding, Francine opened the window slowly,

silently. She wouldn't be long, she promised herself. Then she slipped into the liquid heat of the afternoon, closing the window behind her.

Francine walked quickly to the woods, ducking under the promised shade. Only then did she take a deep breath, smelling the heated leaves and a trace of smoke from one of the cabins deeper in the trees.

No matter how cautious Papa had told her to be, Francine wasn't worried: The woods always protected her.

It didn't take long for Francine to walk to Uncle Rene's. He lived alone in a small cottage, right on the main road. At one point, the house had probably been cute, but Uncle Rene had never painted it. The carved wood curlicues around the windows were gray and peeling. Moss covered the roof and crept up along the foundation. It looked like a bachelor pad, that kind of place where young bucks stopped by and shot the breeze with the older men.

No one was visiting, and the front porch swing sat empty.

When Francine knocked, Uncle Rene called out from the back, "Come on in if you're a friend!"

Francine let herself in, saying, "What if I'm a swamp witch come here to steal your spices?"

Uncle Rene appeared in the kitchen doorway, wiping his big hands on a dishtowel. His bright red and yellow apron said, "Kiss the Cook," which Francine did, on both cheeks. He wore his usual green hat, cocked to the side.

"Then it's lucky I have myrtle wreath hung over the door, now isn't it?"

Uncle Rene peered at Francine.

"You look like someone's stolen your favorite fiddle. Come on back to the kitchen. You eaten yet? I have some crawfish pie just frying up."

It wouldn't have mattered to Francine if she'd eaten or not—she'd never turn down Uncle Rene's food.

"You must have known I was coming."

"Maybe yes, maybe no," Uncle Rene said with a smile.

Francine made herself comfortable on the old white stepstool in the corner as she watched Uncle Rene flip over the first slice of pie, then put in a second. Francine fidgeted on her seat. On one hand, she didn't want Uncle Rene angry with her, particularly not with the promise of fried pie. However, she still had to know.

"Do I have any cousins I haven't met?"

"What you talking about, darling?" Uncle Rene said after a pause, lifting the corner of one of the slices, checking to see if it was ready.

Francine explained about the others she'd seen at her first gig.

Uncle Rene merely listened, nodding.

Then only the sound of the sputtering oil filled the kitchen.

Francine shivered and felt cold despite sitting in a boiling hot kitchen, dread filling her gut while her uncle flipped the pie pieces again, weighing them down now with a meat iron.

Finally, Uncle Rene nodded, as if he'd come to a decision.

"I'll tell you something about them. But you have to promise me you won't talk about them again, not with your Papa or your Mama. Not ever."

"I promise," Francine said, eyes wide. It wasn't going to be a difficult promise to keep. Every time she brought them up, she got in trouble.

"Let's finish up in here first. Then we'll go out back and talk."

Francine nodded solemnly.

Out back meant private stuff.

Usually, when Francine came over, she sat out front with everyone else. She'd only been out back a few times that she could recall. Mostly when people came over, they sat out front or in Uncle Rene's tiny kitchen.

While Uncle Rene served up the slices of pie, Francine made lemonade in his pale green pitcher, then helped Uncle Rene carry it out back.

The heat struck Francine as she walked outside, even though the kitchen had been hot as well.

Uncle Rene had a mist fan that he started up, blowing moist air on both of them.

The garden smelled of fresh earth and pungent herbs. Colored bottles hung from the trees. Waist-high iron rods stuck out of the earth, each with a piece of shiny glass, porcelain, or painted clay balanced on top. Kudzu came down over the wall and covered the trees on the far side, a gentle carpet of green.

Francine remembered the first time she'd been back here as a child. Lights were strung up on poles, circling the chairs. Fireflies had blinked beyond the circle, next to the trees, calling to her.

Uncle Rene had told her that only inside the circle of lights was safe.

Francine believed him: The shadows had danced to their own tune in his garden.

Now, in the soft summer afternoon, Francine still stayed inside the circle of lights. The trees watched them, drowsing in the heat of the day.

Uncle Rene's pie was as heavenly as any Francine had eaten: The outside was crisp; the inside, soft and tasty. She'd had crawfish pie at the school cafeteria once. She couldn't believe the academy kids thought it was better than the food she brought for lunches. Uncle Rene's piecrust melted on her tongue, and the filling was spicy enough that she had to quench it with a swig of cool lemonade.

After they'd both finished their slices and had put the dishes to the side, Uncle Rene finally started to speak.

"I'm sure that in that fancy school of yours they've taught you about Louisiana Creoles, right?"

"People descended from the French, Spanish, and slaves who stayed here," Francine said.

Uncle Rene nodded.

"Very, very simply put, yes. However, it wasn't just the French, Spanish, African, and American people who got mixed when they came over to the new land. Others came with them. Your mama and I told you stories about the others when you were young—about the elves, the dwarves, the goblins and the fairies. They all came as well, with the French, Spanish, and African people, and mixed with the native spirits already here."

"What are you saying?" Francine asked, shivering suddenly despite the heat.

"There are other types of Louisiana Creoles," Uncle Rene said. He looked out across the garden at the trees. There was no wind, and the garden lay quiet and still.

"Those others you saw, they were tall, weren't they? Dark hair. Couldn't keep your eyes off 'em."

Francine nodded slowly.

"And they seemed familiar. Like family."

"Yes," Francine said.

"We knew they'd come calling when you were born with their mark. Knew you were like them."

"Mark?"

"Your birthmark, on your shoulder."

Francine thought for a moment, taking a sip of cool lemonade.

"The kids at school called it a 'swamp stamp,'" she said, her feelings about it all mixed up.

"They're only a little wrong," Uncle Rene said, staring out across the yard.

"It means you belong here, in these woods. They're part of you, in your blood. Like they're in your papa's."

"But who are my lost cousins?" Francine said, wanting Uncle Rene to spell it out.

Uncle Rene turned and smiled at Francine, his shark smile, the one he used when he was playing cards in the back room at Slim's.

"Not who, darling. What."

"Uncle Rene, are you really saying there's some kind of *other* in our family?" Francine asked derisively.

This *had* been the uncle who'd sworn up and down on a stack of Sundays that there was a half-gator boy just down the road. Now he was claiming she had *Féerie* blood in her veins?

"What do you think?" Uncle Rene said, gesturing toward the trees at the far end of the garden. "Can you hear them talking?"

Francine wanted to deny what her uncle was saying. It was hard enough being from the country side of the parish and go to school on the other side. However, Francine couldn't deny there was something special about these trees. It was why most people were never invited into Uncle Rene's backyard. The trees didn't allow it. The kudzu in the corner covered more than just branches and trunks: It gave Francine the impression of a curtain hung over a door.

Something magical and dangerous lived beyond those leaves.

"It's why your papa had only you," Uncle Rene said quietly. "Though your mama wanted more children, she agreed to just one. They knew you were mixed. Your papa knew you'd be torn, wanting those woods and something more, like he was. He didn't want to bring another child into the world only to have her hurt that way."

"So why doesn't Papa want me to meet my cousins?" Francine said. "Why did Mama tell me to walk away if they came calling?"

"Do you think those trees are safe?" Uncle Rene challenged.

Francine looked out again, lips pressed together hard as she thought. The trees weren't cruel, that much she knew. But they weren't innocent either. They had their own thoughts and deeds; different than the puny humans they towered above.

They fascinated Francine as much as they made her uneasy.

"So my lost cousins—"

"Are just as foreign, frightening, strange, and fascinating as those trees."

"Huh," Francine said. She wanted to go take a closer look, but she wasn't about to leave the safe circle of lights. She knew once she stepped outside and went under those branches, there would be no going back.

"I know that look," Uncle Rene admonished. "You have their scent now, and you're curious as a cat with a hot radiator."

"Yeah," Francine admitted.

"Will you at least trust me when I say that you're not ready yet? That you should run when they come calling again? Because they will."

Slowly, Francine nodded.

"I do trust you. For now," she added.

"And will you tell me when they do?"

"Maybe," Francine said slyly. "Depends on what you bribe me with."

"Cornbread waffles," Uncle Rene said with a grin. "With bacon, grits, and bread pudding."

Then he leaned over closer.

"One other thing you should know: If you go with them, you'll leave all cooking behind."

Francine turned to stare at Uncle Rene. "Really?"

"Southern gentleman's word."

"Then why bother?"

"Exactly," Uncle Rene said. "We got it good here."

Despite the rest of her last year of school looming, Francine agreed.

"Yeah, we do."

* * *

Sniggers greeted Francine as she pushed open the door of the high school. She told herself she was a senior, only a few more months left. The perennial smell of wax and whiteboard markers made her nauseated. She braced herself as she walked around the corner, spying her locker easily.

Someone had "decorated" it for her—purple and gold glitter proudly proclaimed her "Zydeco Queen."

Francine's breath suddenly grew short. Darkness edged her vision. She hated this—this torture, this constant reminder of how different she was from the rest of them. She spun and raced for the girl's bathroom, barely making it to a stall to vomit up her breakfast.

Pale and shaking, Francine finally made her way back to her locker. Her first impulse was to scrub the words off, but she stopped herself. They would just do something worse.

Francine tried to think of how to get revenge. She considered asking her cousins for help. They would come running. Aunt Lavine's eldest boy had a truck; they could all hitch a ride into the city, then find Billy and put him down, hard. They wouldn't touch Laura—she was a girl. Francine would have to find some other way of getting to her.

But hurting Billy that way would get her cousins in trouble. And Billy had brothers. Francine didn't want to start a feud.

As lunch ended, Mrs. Beaumont, Principal Martin's secretary came into the cafeteria, calling Francine's name. Francine hurried over to her, worried that Billy and the others had already escalated their attacks.

"Would you come with me?" Mrs. Beaumont asked Francine, leading her to her locker. Principal Martin stood there, along with Billy, Laura, Karyn, and a few of Billy's other buddies. They were all looking down or away, anywhere but at Francine as she walked up.

"Is this your locker?" Principal Martin asked, his eyes pale and watery behind his thick glasses.

"Yes, sir," Francine said, drawing herself up, thankful again for her height. She crossed her arms over her chest and looked sternly at the principal, holding herself to hide her fear. Would he blame her for this?

"Did you do this?"

"No, sir."

"Did you ask these gentlemen to do it for you?"

Francine gave an unladylike snort.

"No."

At Mrs. Beaumont's look, Francine added, "No, sir. Ma'am. I wouldn't ask these gentleman for a drop of water even if we were standing in the middle of the Mississippi."

Principal Martin and Mrs. Beaumont exchanged a look.

"I attended some interesting workshops this summer," the principal said. "While this academy has always had a 'No Bullying' policy, it hasn't always been enforced."

He paused, cleared his throat, staring hard at Billy.

"From now on, this academy has a zero-tolerance policy regarding bullying. Billy McGyvner, you are suspended for the rest of the week."

"What?"

Billy's head snapped up and he stared in outrage at the principal.

"Furthermore, if I hear of any more of this behavior, I'll be advising the staff not to write you any recommendation letters, which will make it difficult, if not impossible, to get into the colleges you're applying for."

Francine couldn't believe what she was hearing. Was this year finally going to be tolerable? Was the staff finally going to do something?

"And you, Francine Guiscard. If I hear of any sort of retaliation, I'll advise the teachers to do the same. Which means no Louisiana Music College for you."

Francine gulped, surprised that he knew about the offer or her plans. She nodded.

"In addition, I want you to start seeing the school counselor, Mrs. Delacroix, once a week."

"What? Why? I'm not crazy," Francine protested.

Billy sniggered.

"I'm not suggesting you are," Principal Martin said, glancing at Billy, who abruptly schooled his expression into something more innocent.

"But you've been under intolerable stress," he said to Francine, while still looking at Billy. "It would be good for you to talk with someone. Plus, that way you'll have a regular dialogue with the staff and an easy avenue for airing grievances."

Francine barely stopped herself from rolling her eyes. She knew the stilted phrases came straight from whatever workshop Principal Martin had attended.

She decided she would never tell the counselor anything. She wasn't a snitch.

Then she glanced at Billy and her heart sank.

Billy's glare was pure hatred. He was never going to forgive her for this, even though she wasn't the one who started it, wasn't the one responsible for his punishment. He was going to make her life hell, even worse than it had been.

And there wasn't a thing she could do about it.

* * *

The week dragged on. Francine flinched every time she saw Laura or Karyn, certain they were plotting revenge with Billy. The next week was worse, once Billy returned. His friends all acted like he was a hero and being unjustly punished.

Francine, in return, spent a very uncomfortable thirty minutes with Mrs. Delacroix, replying to all her probing questions with, "yes," "no," or "I don't know."

The following Friday, Mrs. Beaumont pulled Francine out of her chemistry class. Mama sat in the stiff-backed visitor's chair in the principal's office. Principal Martin sat behind his desk, his thin, nervous fingers folded together but still twitching. The lights had been turned off and the shades drawn against the afternoon sunlight.

Francine sat down on the edge of her seat, too scared to sit back. It wasn't the first time she'd been brought in here, but it was the first time she didn't know what she'd done.

"You've been accused of cheating," Principal Martin told Francine bluntly.

"I've never—"

"That's what I told him," Mama interrupted.

"Parents don't always know what happens at school," Principal Martin said mildly. He steepled his fingers for a moment, stilling their action.

"Did you know that Francine has been bullied almost every day since she started attending the academy?"

Francine looked down at her feet. The principal was making it sound like she always needed rescuing or something. She gave as good as she got.

"I knew she was fighting—"

"She's been a *victim*, and now that the pressure is off, she's falling into bad habits."

"I'm doing what?" Francine asked, confused.

"I've never cheated. Not once."

Her grades were good because she worked hard.

"Francine," Mama warned.

"Whatever the case may be, now you've been accused of cheating." Principal Martin pulled out two papers.

Francine recognized them. They were the first papers required for history that week.

"As you can tell, they're practically identical."

One was Francine's. Joseph, a fellow band member, had written the other. As far as Francine knew, he wasn't friends with Billy or any of the others.

"I didn't cheat," Francine said exasperated. "I don't know how he copied my paper. But I didn't cheat."

"Why isn't this young man in here?" Mama asked reasonably.

"He turned in his paper before Francine."

"But he's in my class!"

"According to Mr. Frazier, he still turned it in before you did."

"Mama, I didn't cheat," Francine said earnestly, facing her mother. "I swear to you, I didn't."

"What do we have to do to prove she didn't?" Mama said, reaching out and taking Francine's hand.

"Mr. Frazier has assigned you another paper. Due Monday," Principal Martin said. "If you can produce original work with this one, we'll assume the other was some type of error."

"Will you pull Joseph in here and accuse him of cheating if I write you a good paper?" Francine demanded.

"She'll write you a good paper. I'll make sure of it," Mama replied, glaring at Francine.

Francine sat back in her chair, folding her shaking arms over her chest, while Mama and Principal Martin talked about her assignment. She was too angry to pay attention. None of this had been her fault. It was all so unfair. And, as always, she was powerless to do anything about it.

* * *

Francine stared at the red C at the top of her paper. She knew Mr. Frazier would be mean and give her a bad grade, no matter how good a paper she did for him to prove she hadn't been cheating.

Billy McGyvner had something on Mr. Frazier, and Francine would never find out what.

Joseph, the tall, reed-thin boy who swallowed too much when he was nervous could no longer meet Francine's eye. He had a new oboe that he showed off in class the next week, much fancier than what his shoes and hand-me-down coat said he could afford.

But that was history. This was English. Francine had always done well in English. She wrote A papers. What she had in her hand was an A paper. Why had Mrs. Anthony given her a C?

Mrs. Anthony continued to hand out papers to students, calling their names alphabetically. Francine could barely hear her through the sound of rushing blood in her head.

Had Billy gotten to Mrs. Anthony as well? Was there no teacher Francine could trust to be fair?

When Mrs. Anthony finished handing out papers, she gave the next assignment. Francine copied it down, word-for-word, to make sure she didn't mess up again. The bell rang just as Mrs. Anthony finished, and Francine made her way to the teacher's desk.

"I don't understand why you gave me a C on this," Francine said, anger giving her the courage to just ask.

"It wasn't up to your usual quality," Mrs. Anthony said gently. "You didn't form one of your references correctly, your point wasn't clear in the second paragraph, and your conclusion wasn't formed accurately."

Francine just stared at her teacher. Her last paper, which had received an A, had two references incorrectly done and a number of other concerns. She didn't understand why she was suddenly handing in C-quality work.

"It's because of Mr. Frazier's accusations, isn't it?"

"Now Francine, you know I don't believe you'd ever cheat. But your work has been slipping."

The look Mrs. Anthony gave Francine was one of sincere concern. It took Francine only a moment to put it together.

Francine *wasn't* slipping. She was doing the same level of work she'd been doing. But because of the accusation of cheating, the other teachers now looked at her differently.

For a moment Francine's vision wavered. She felt as if she were underwater, everything blurry and moving at slow speed. She was drowning with no way to swim against the current.

"You should go to the nurse," Francine finally heard as she came back.

"I'm fine," Francine assured Mrs. Anthony.

"No, really," Francine added when Mrs. Anthony just stared.

"And the next paper, you'll see. It'll be perfect."

Mrs. Anthony beamed at her. "If anyone can do it, I know you can."

Francine walked out of the classroom, barely able to pay attention to where she was going. She didn't know how she was going to create a perfect paper. She already worked harder than everyone else. But she had to try. Billy and his pals weren't going to win.

* * *

Mrs. Delacroix's office smelled like old gardenia perfume. The furniture was all brown and beige, as dull as the rest of the school. The only spot of color was the orange lamp on the side table, seemingly out of place, with a pile of bright parade beads curled up around the base.

The counselor had a pinched mouth and gray eyes the same color as storm clouds. Her voice, though, was gentle, as she asked Francine, "Why are you so hated, child?"

Francine shrugged. That was her standard response to most of Mrs. Delacroix's questions.

"I see I'm talking to myself again today," the counselor said with unexpected humor.

"I keep thinking it isn't because you're not from these parts, but because you're too much from here."

Francine shrugged again. The way things were going, she'd never be able to leave here, either.

"These boys and girls, their parents have filled their heads with stories about how while it's good here, it's gotta be better somewhere else. And it may be, for some of them. But most of them are stuck. They're always going to be looking outside, and away. You show them the things they've been told they don't want. Family and roots and belonging here."

"So?" Francine asked.

It wasn't as if she was ever going to change.

Mrs. Delacroix fiddled with a pencil, running her fingers along it, then tapping it on the end.

Francine recognized the gesture—the counselor wanted to light up a cigarette but smoking wasn't allowed in the school.

"Talk about wanting to leave as well," Mrs. Delacroix finally said. "Let 'em know you're stuck, too. It's the only thing you'll ever have in common with them."

"I don't want to have anything in common with them," Francine said, scowling. "Besides, it won't work. They already know about the music college."

Mrs. Delacroix tilted her head to the side, peering at Francine. "As hard as they push, you push right back, don't you?"

"So? If I don't push back, they'll run all over me."

"Sometimes you need to make a peace," Mrs. Delacroix said softly. "Find a way to bridge that gap between ya'll."

Francine pressed her lips together and looked out the window. How could she find a peace when no one wanted it? She stopped listening to Mrs. Delacroix until the phone in her office shrilly rang.

When the counselor put down the phone, she had tears in her eyes.

"It's your mama," she said softly.

Chapter Three

"Darling," Mama drooled.

Horror filled Francine but she made herself walk forward, into Mama's hospital room. It stank of false pine and bleach. The beige walls sucked all the color out of the room, even the white of the sheets on Mama's bed.

"Hey Mama," Francine said quietly, taking her right hand, her *active* hand.

The left half Mama's face was slack, her left eye wide and staring, her left side still as death.

Francine swallowed down her bile and finally asked, "Stroke?"

"No, no," Mama sighed. "No stroke."

"Then what?" Francine asked.

Mama shrugged, one shouldered. "Don't know yet."

"Where's Papa?"

"Gone to get the paper," Mama said. She squeezed Francine's hand.

"You're going to have to be strong for him, you know. Keep him safe. Keep him home."

"Okay," Francine said, though she didn't understand.

Papa came back in. He walked directly to the windowsills

beyond the bed and placed twisted branches on both of them.

"Rowan," he said quietly.

Francine shivered, wondering if it was to keep out her other cousins, or something worse.

Then Papa walked back to Francine and gathered her into his arms, giving her a strong hug.

Francine melted into it, leaning on Papa's strength and warmth. It almost shook loose the hard place deep in her heart, but she held on, with dry eyes and a clear voice.

"What's wrong with Mama?"

"The doctor's aren't sure. But it wasn't a stroke," Papa said, giving Francine one last hard squeeze, then letting her go.

Before Papa could sit down, a squat man with black, square glasses and a white coat came in.

"I'm Dr. Palaquin," he introduced himself.

Francine and her family introduced themselves, all shaking hands.

When they finished, Dr. Palaquin added, "I'm with the oncology staff."

"Cancer?" Francine asked, her voice squeaking, the edges of her vision darkening. She suddenly sat on the edge of Mama's bed, her hand flailing until it found Mama's again, grasping it tightly.

"Mrs. Guiscard has small cell lung cancer."

"What stage?" Papa asked.

Francine was grateful that he was able to think critically. The word *cancer* had just swallowed her world.

"I'm afraid small cell lung cancer has no stages, not like regular cancer. It's either crossed the bilateral line of the body or it hasn't. And, I'm afraid, that for Mrs. Guiscard, it's already crossed."

"What does that mean?" Francine asked, her voice small and unrecognizable.

"The cancer originated in a lump in her left lung. It's crossed to the right side of her brain, and infected her spinal cord. Hence the stroke-like effects."

The room reeled around Francine. *Cancer* rippled through everything, like floodwaters, swamping her home with rain and bad news that just kept coming and wouldn't stop.

Her heart beat hard in her chest as Papa asked the question Francine needed to hear, asking about how to treat it.

The pause the doctor gave made Francine's heart skip.

"Of course, you could chose to treat it. However, the cancer is so advanced, I'd advise against it. We need to focus on making Mrs. Guiscard comfortable."

"How long?" Mama asked, her voice raspy and weak.

"We can never really say—"

"You will give me a number," Papa growled. "I will not sue you or hold you to it. But you *will* give me an amount."

"I can't really—"

"Days or weeks?" Papa asked.

Mama added in, "Please. Days? Weeks?"

Francine hoped the doctor would tell them they were wrong, that Mama still had months or years.

"Weeks," the doctor finally admitted. He continued on with some weasel words that Francine didn't pay any attention to as tears pricked her eyes. She couldn't hear what else the doctor and Papa discussed. Only two words inhabited her entire existence.

Cancer. And *weeks*.

* * *

Golden charms the cousins had bought hung on brightly colored yarn off the wooden headboard of Mama and Papa's bed. *Gris-gris* voodoo dolls made for tourists from Aunt Lavine's store sat on the beautiful caved bedside table that

Uncle Leroy had made. Braided Rowan branches lay on the windowsills.

The room—the whole house, really—smelled stuffy like church, full of incense and candle oils.

They were all useless, of course, but they helped Francine and her relatives feel like they were doing something.

Mama lay in the center of the bed, resting her eyes. She'd grown skinny in just a month, her color ashen. Francine sat on the old rocker beside the bed, sliding back and forth, trying not to think on how Mama couldn't be left alone anymore, not even for a minute, and how the change had come in less than two weeks.

"Let's have spider holes for dinner," Mama announced suddenly.

"How do you fix spider holes?" Francine asked. She hated her mama's aphasia as much as anything else. Her mama had always had the right word or phrase. It was so unfair how much of her they'd lost in such a short time.

Mama looked at Francine as if she was slow.

"You cut them into thin slices and fry them, then serve them with dirty rice and mustard sauce."

"You want sausage for dinner?" Francine guessed.

"Yes, that's what I just asked for," Mama said impatiently.

Francine knew better than to argue.

"Sure, Mama. I'll fix that in a bit."

She checked the clock—only 4:15 P.M. She was certain there were sausages in the fridge, along with crawfish pie, sweet-and-sour corn soup, cabbage salad, and pot roast. All her relatives kept bringing over food, as if that could somehow make things better. They also sat with Mama, so Francine could take a break.

"Francine, you know both Papa and I love you, right?"

"Yes, Mama," Francine said. Mama told her that often,

as if she was afraid Francine didn't know.

"I've always been so proud of you," Mama added. "No matter what you do, I'll always love you."

Francine looked sharply at Mama. She wasn't normally this lucid.

"I'll always love you, too, Mama," Francine replied, reaching over to squeeze Mama's good hand.

"Papa, too?" Mama asked suddenly unsure, her hand lax in Francine's.

"Papa, too," Francine assured her, not necessarily lying, though doubt had set in. Papa wasn't there, not even as often as Uncle Rene, as if he'd already given up.

A part of Francine understood—it was *hard* to see Mama this way.

A part of her would never understand. This was *Mama*.

"Papa, too," Mama said, taking a deep breath, settling further into her pillows, and closing her eyes again.

"Papa, too," Francine said, as if trying to convince herself as well.

* * *

Grief choked the house like kudzu, invasive and omnipresent. Sunlight glared harshly through the front windows. Usually Francine welcomed the fall weather. Now, it amplified how she felt, cold and bitter.

Every time an aunt or uncle told Francine, "At least she went quick," she felt like screaming.

It wasn't fair.

Mama hadn't ever been sick a day in her life.

Francine didn't like admitting that Mama had been in horrible pain at the end, that it was good she didn't suffer for years. Still. It just wasn't fair.

Fresh-baked dishes overflowed the refrigerator and the pantry—gumbo, fish stew, cornbread, and chicken soup. When Francine sat very still on the living room couch, afraid that if she moved, she'd break, whatever aunt, uncle, or cousin was sitting with her would suggest she eat something.

Francine couldn't decide if she was grateful that she and Papa weren't left alone those first days, or if it was why she always felt like screaming.

Papa insisted that the funeral happen at noon. It wasn't until later that Francine wondered if that was to make sure her "other" relatives didn't come.

Francine sat in the fireside room next to the sanctuary as people filled the church. She heard her cousins, uncles, and aunts chatting, talking, not laughing, but living.

It hurt Francine so much that they still had their lives while hers was over. She hadn't died, but her old life had.

Papa sat beside her, still as a stone. His face looked gaunt and haunted. He stared at his hands or at the dull brown carpet, and barely spoke two words.

Francine didn't know how to bring Papa back. It was as if he was already following Mama into the grave.

The preacher brought the family into the front pew as the music started. Francine held onto Papa's arm, her eyes blinded with tears. Uncle Rene, Aunt Lavine, Aunt Noella, and others all sat there, ready to hold them.

Francine couldn't stop crying. Grief overwhelmed her, pain swallowing her heart whole. Francine didn't hear what the preacher said, though everyone told her later it had been a beautiful service.

Toward the end Francine finally tamed her tears enough to say a few words.

"Mama played peacemaker all her life, between me and Papa, between more than one of you," Francine said, looking at Aunt Lavine, then at Uncle Gilbert. Of all her relatives, they fought the most.

"She wasn't meek, or mild. She had that spirit. A bite. As did her cooking."

She paused as people chuckled and Francine almost smiled.

"I'm going to miss her more than I can possibly say. I'm going to make her proud of me. I hope she's in peace now."

A solemn line of cars wound down country lanes to the graveyard. The cemetery was pretty, and the grass was well watered and green. It wasn't fair for the sun to be so bright and the grass so green and alive.

Francine waited beside the car as Uncle Rene organized the musicians. In the tradition of New Orleans, they played a slow dirge as everyone walked to where the preacher waited for them at the top of a slight ridge, two lone trees casting shade behind them. Mama's own Mama and Papa would be right beside her.

The sad music tugged at Francine's heart, and she cried so hard Aunt Lavine had to lead her to the gravesite.

After the casket was lowered, the band struck up a happy tune, full of joy. It had a beat that made even Francine want to move.

It was time to celebrate Mama's life.

Everyone gathered at Francine's home that evening, telling stories about Mama and their life together. Francine still couldn't eat, but she tried hard to listen and remember every word. She only went to bed when she found herself nodding off in the middle of a story.

The next morning, when Francine opened her eyes, everything seemed flat and colorless. Cold settled into the air, seeping into the house. Francine wrapped herself in a sweater, sweatpants, and a thick bathrobe before going out to the kitchen.

No one waited for her.

For the first time since Mama's diagnosis, Francine sat alone in the house. The trees outside quietly talked together, and the old house creaked now and again.

After making herself eat a little, Francine went back to

her room and picked up her fiddle. She hadn't played in a while, refusing to use that hateful word *weeks*. She tried to play a dirge, something to express how heartbroken she felt. Her fingers fumbled and she found herself blinded with tears. Then she tried to play a happier piece, to cheer herself up. The melody came out tinny and her chords turned bitter.

Francine quickly escaped the house, but even the woods couldn't comfort her.

That night, when Papa finally came home, Francine told him over dinner, "I'm going back to school."

Papa nodded.

That was the only thing they said to each other all night.

* * *

"Fiddlesticks," Francine fumed as she rushed into the kitchen and turned off the burner under the forgotten, smoking pan.

"*Broken* fiddlesticks."

She would have used stronger language but Papa was standing right there.

"It's ruined, Papa. Everything's ruined."

She felt tears pricking her eyes and she didn't try to stop them as she picked up the pot.

"Thanksgiving won't be Thanksgiving without Mama's cream sauce."

"It'll be okay—"

"No, it won't," Francine said, slamming the pot back down.

"Nothing's right anymore."

She looked over her shoulder at Papa, standing all the way across the kitchen next to the door. She knew better than to ask for his help: He couldn't cook, and since Mama had died, he'd avoided going into the kitchen when he could.

Francine picked up the pot and brought it to the sink.

"Call Uncle Rene. Tell him we'll be late," she said over the hissing as the water hit the heated metal.

"We're already late," Papa pointed out. "We'll just make do with whatever gravy Uncle Rene has."

Francine shook her head and started scrubbing out the burnt gunk at the bottom of the pan, scalding her fingers and working blindly as her tears flowed.

An unexpected touch to her shoulder made Francine jump.

"Leave it," Papa directed.

Francine sniffed and wiped at her tears with her dry forearm. She trembled both inside and out, feeling like she was shaking apart.

"Papa," she said softly.

She wanted so hard for him to hold her like she was a little girl.

But Papa mere squeezed her shoulder and stepped back.

"It'll all be fine," he repeated, retreating again, out the kitchen.

"Pack up what you have and let's go."

Francine took a couple of deep breaths, forcing herself to swallow past the pain in her throat, will her tears to dry.

It wasn't fine and never would be again.

* * *

Though Uncle Rene's house wasn't as large as Francine's, or even Aunt Nicola's, they always held Thanksgiving there. A wave of sound crashed into Francine when Papa opened the door—kids squealing, Aunt Lavine laughing, the roar of everyone talking at the same time.

Francine made a beeline for the kitchen, pushing through the crowd of people. It was slightly less chaotic there, with only half a dozen of her relatives squashed together. The rich smell of turkey filled the air.

"I'm sorry, I'm so sorry," Francine blurted as soon as she saw Uncle Rene.

"I ruined Mama's cream sauce and there wasn't time—"

"It's all right, darling," Uncle Rene said, taking the potatoes from Francine and kissing her cheek.

"There's extra white gravy, as well as brown."

Before Francine could ask, Uncle Rene had her filling water glasses on the table, organizing the kids to gather at the smaller side table, then carrying in the feast of food. Francine sat next to Uncle Rene, who only patted her hand and didn't ask how she was doing. It hurt that Mama wasn't there, that Papa was mostly gone, too.

After dinner and before dessert, everyone pushed back their chairs and looked to Uncle Rene for the entertainment.

"Francine," he called, drawing her to her feet.

"And Charles."

Uncle Rene pulled out his golden sax, the alto one that was taller than the youngest cousin. Papa and Francine gathered their fiddles and went to stand near the front door.

Francine felt herself smiling, really smiling, at the two rooms crowded with tables and people, all looking expectantly at her. She'd always loved to perform. She followed Uncle Rene's timing, coming in three measures behind him. Papa was supposed to come in three measures later.

When Papa missed his entrance, Francine turned to look at him.

Papa stood with his fiddle clenched in his hand, his face ashen.

Francine felt the tune sliding away, diminished by Papa's sadness.

"I can't," he said softly as Uncle Rene stopped.

"I just can't."

He turned and walked out the door, leaving his fiddle behind.

"*Merde*," Uncle Rene swore under his breath. "He hasn't played since your mama passed. I thought—never mind. Something softer, eh?"

Uncle Rene started another tune and Francine followed, willing the music to fill her heart as it had before. These were her people; she wasn't going to let them down, no matter how betrayed she felt.

* * *

Francine sat outside on the porch swing, wrapped in a blanket against the cold afternoon air. Dust covered the grass next to the road. Even the trees had no advice for her, standing muted and bare.

Since Thanksgiving the week before, Papa had only been home for one day before he'd rushed back to work.

Christmas without Mama—Francine couldn't even bear to think about it. She wished she could howl her loneliness to the moon, but she was afraid that if she started screaming, she'd never stop.

Muriel saw her from the road and came up to join her.

"Vincent quit the band," she said as she sat down heavily next to Francine.

"I'm sorry. I know you really wanted that to work out."

Francine had quit the Zydeco Chicks when Mama had gotten sick. Muriel had started a new band on her own.

Mama, Papa, and even Uncle Rene had warned Francine about dating musicians, particularly the ones you played with. But Muriel had been in love.

When Vincent and Muriel had broken up, the band didn't stand a chance.

"We had a gig at Slim's and everything," Muriel complained.

"Week before Christmas. Now that Vincent's gone, the others will leave, too."

Francine suddenly sat up straighter.

"You could form a new band, you know," she said softly. "Different people."

"How am I going to do that in such a short time? I could maybe get another accordion player, but—" Muriel stopped and looked at Francine.

"Really?"

Francine paused. It had been a while since she'd played, really played. She'd been going through the motions at school, at home, throughout her life. She needed something, and soon, or the holidays would drive her crazy with grief. She nodded.

Muriel hugged Francine, hard.

"Bless you! You are an angel of mercy, come here to save me from myself." She stood up. "Come on. We need to practice."

Francine laughed as she dropped the blanket, feeling like she'd just lost her shroud.

"Let me grab my fiddle and leave a note for Papa."

Muriel was already on her phone, calling other musicians. She managed to talk two others into playing with them that night, Simone on the accordion and Layton on the guitar. Though it was the first time they'd ever rehearsed, they played well together, something gelling as the music became more than just the notes.

They named themselves Sticks and Stones. They wanted their band to be more than just words.

Francine practically danced back to the house after practice, smiling and feeling warm for the first time that fall.

"Papa!" she called as she came in, surprised to find him in the kitchen.

He sat at the table there, drinking a beer, his work reports spread out before him.

"Francine. Didn't we talk about bands?" Papa said disapprovingly.

Francine took a step back. Why wasn't Papa happy for her?

"It's to help out Muriel," she stammered. "And to make the holidays better," she added defiantly.

Papa had the grace to look ashamed at that.

"I know you miss Mama. I miss her, too. But a band isn't the answer. It's time you started looking for a real job instead."

"A job?" Francine asked, hating the way her voice became shrill.

"Do you know how hard it is to get a job here? At least with a gig I'll get some money."

Francine didn't mention the fancy music college. Her grades had suffered too much, first from the accusations of cheating, then Mama's death. She might be able to pull through it, and her music teacher was still willing to write her a recommendation.

However, it felt like just a dream, much like her comfortable life with both Mama and Papa had been.

"Not every roadhouse is like Slim's," Papa said stubbornly.

"Most bar owners will try to rob you. Charge you more for drinks than you'll bring in, so you end up paying them."

It sounded like a story from when Papa had been on the road, playing with Uncle Rene.

"I don't care!" Francine said. "At least it's doing something I love. At least it's living. Not hiding and wishing I was dead."

"It isn't much of a living," Papa argued. "It's a scramble, with only pennies in your pocket day-to-day. It eats your soul, more than living here will."

"Making music makes me happy. You just don't want me to be happy," Francine accused Papa.

"I want you to be successful," Papa said sternly.

"Little kids are happy when they're playing in the dirt.

You can do much more than just that."

"Making music is not the same as playing in the dirt," Francine said, stung. "It makes other people happy, too."

Papa set his lips in a thin line, but he finally nodded.

"Go. Make your music. We'll see how good it actually is."

Francine turned on her heel and raced to her bedroom, slamming the door.

She'd show him.

She stubbornly got out her fiddle and practiced for the next three hours, until her fingers cramped and her back ached. She'd been rusty that night, the others supporting her.

Fortunately, her fingers remembered.

She wasn't quite as quick as she'd been before Mama had died—the music didn't flow like it should—but by the time they played their first gig, she'd be ready.

* * *

Because they needed the practice, Sticks and Stones played at a smaller club later that week as a warm-up band. The bar had the same feel as Slim's, with the same cheerful neon signs and a big dance floor.

After they set up, Francine and the others waited in a small room off the service entrance, chatting with the barmaids and laughing nervously at each other.

As the bar was the next parish over, not as many relatives showed up as for the gig. The crowd wasn't interested in them—they were waiting for the "real" band. They talked through the start of their first song, and only politely applauded.

Francine didn't blame the people sitting out there, waiting to be entertained. She knew the band could play better. They just had to gel again, like they had that first night.

The next song on their playlist was supposed to be a slow

waltz. Francine asked Muriel to skip ahead to a later song that had a driving beat and catchy tune.

The crowd started listening, and a few got up to dance.

Francine kept pushing the band and the dancers, trying to inject more energy into the crowd.

When Papa came in, Francine relaxed a little. She nodded to him from the stage as they did a double-time two-step.

He sat down at a table right in the center, stretched out his long legs, and stared up at them.

Then Papa didn't move.

He didn't tap his fingers or move his feet. He just looked bored.

Francine couldn't believe that Papa would try to sabotage her like that. It was just mean. She knew she couldn't make him do anything, not here, so she divided her time on the different sides of the stage, trying to go around him, to push the dancers in the rest of the club to listen and kick up their heels.

She didn't think she'd ever worked so hard, not even when they formed a bucket trail bailing out Uncle Gilbert's house that one spring flood.

When the band took a break, Francine stormed out to Papa's table.

"What are you doing?" she hissed, so mad she could barely speak.

"You call that music?" Papa sneered.

"I think we wasted all that money sending you to academy if that's how you play."

The room grew darker and the cold from outside suddenly snuck in, licking at Francine's bones.

"Papa, how can you say such things?" she asked, hurt beyond reckoning.

She wished wildly that Mama would suddenly show up and make things better between them, because the road she saw before her looked awful and lonely.

"How did you get this gig? Did you pay the barman?"

"Papa, you don't mean that," Francine said. She felt as hurt as she had that first day of school, with the kids calling her "gator-bait." However, even if this was her Papa, she wasn't going to take it from him, either.

"Take it back."

"'Take it back'?" Papa scoffed. "I can see you're still in high school, aren't you? Maybe you should just go back to school and stay out of bars and clubs, making music you don't understand."

White fury lined the edges of Francine's sight. How dare he be angry with her for her age? She couldn't help how old she was—she was growing up as fast as she could.

"I hate you," Francine said.

"I wish you'd died instead of Mama."

She stalked away, shaking with anger, marching into the back where her bandmates waited.

Papa only stayed for a short while into their second set. It didn't matter. Francine was on fire, using her anger to fuel her playing, skipping niceties and playing a dirty, strong fiddle.

Toward the end of the second set someone else came and sat at the table Papa had vacated. At first Francine didn't pay much attention; she was too busy getting the crowd to kick up their heels like they never had before.

Finally something caught her eye—maybe his dark hair, or his pale skin, or the fact that he sat in the same position as her papa had, all stretched out. But instead of scowling at her, he was smiling and tapping his feet, moving his fingers as if he wanted to get up and join her making music.

After they finished the second set to thunderous applause, Francine went back out into the bar. She dripped sweat and the music still hummed in her blood, but she wanted to enjoy the crowd, their congratulations. Eventually she made her way to the familiar stranger's table.

"Nice playing," he drawled, standing as she drew near.

Most men only came up so high on Francine. With this one, though, she was the one to tilt her head up. His eyes were the same washed-out gray color as hers and her papa's. His skin shone pale and white in the dark club, and his black hair had blue highlights.

"Thanks," Francine said, feeling a strange fluttering in her chest.

The young man smiled at her, showing his city-white teeth, all clean and straight.

"You can call me Pierre, *ma chérie*," he said, taking her hand, bending over it, and kissing the back of it. Pierre's accent wasn't French or Cajun, but something else.

The ghost of his lips against Francine's skin sent chills like winter moonlight through her blood.

"You can call me Francine," she said.

Warnings about dealing with the *Fée* that Mama and Uncle Rene had told her came rushing back. *Never give one your name. Just something to call you by.*

"How you doing tonight?" Francine asked, pulling back her hand. She wanted to hide it under her arm, scratch off the tingling that lingered. Her heart took up a fast beat, like it was dancing.

"Very glad I came out to hear you," Pierre said. "Tell me about the bridge for that last song—did you go into a minor key for part of it?"

"Yeah, it isn't in the original, but it felt right," Francine replied, startled.

Pierre asked another question and they quickly fell into discussing music, talking about their favorite pieces, as well as difficult pieces and working hard to get that slide from one note to the next just right.

When Muriel made a thumping noise on the mike, Francine jumped, startled. She hadn't meant to spend the entire break talking with this strange relation, but time had slipped away so quickly.

"I'll see you later," Francine promised, racing back to the stage before Pierre could say anything else.

For the last set, Francine concentrated on mixing technique with passion, trying to impress Pierre, racing through arpeggios and adding harmonics.

Muriel rolled her eyes but grinned. During one of the guitar solos she leaned over and said in Francine's ear, "You know what they say about dating musicians."

Francine shook her head, shy and a little embarrassed.

"Not dating," she said.

She'd never been on a real date. And she couldn't assume Pierre was interested in her like that.

"Not yet. I saw how he looked at you."

Francine was glad the lights were low enough so no one could see her blush.

When they finished, the crowd rose to their feet and applauded. Francine bowed and smiled so hard it felt like it would break her face. This time, Francine hung out for a while backstage, talking with her fellow musicians, sharing the incredible high of their first real performance. They made plans for at least two rehearsals before their next gig, on Midwinter's Eve the following weekend.

Finally, Francine slipped away and out into the crowd.

Of course, Pierre was gone.

She swallowed her disappointment, and instead talked with the people who came up and congratulated her, not accepting any beer or whiskey. She was still underage, and while she'd had a drink now and then, she didn't want to get the owner of the bar in trouble.

As the crowd settled back down for the second band, Francine stepped outside into the cool night. A half moon shone down on her, coating everything in silver.

"I really liked that set."

The words came out of nowhere, making Francine jump and turn.

"Thank you," she replied as Pierre stepped out of the shadows. She would have sworn he hadn't been there a moment before.

"I know some others who would love to hear you play," Pierre said, stepping closer.

The feel of magical moonshine swept across Francine's skin. She understood now why all her relatives had warned her against talking with these lost cousins.

Pierre was mesmerizingly beautiful, as well dangerous.

"I don't know." Francine hesitated. She should talk with Uncle Rene first. She'd promised him she would.

"Please," Pierre said. "I'll have my fiddle there as well. We could play together."

That tempted Francine more than just meeting her lost cousins.

"Unless you think your papa wouldn't approve…"

Anger stiffened Francine's back.

"Where do you want to meet?" she asked flatly.

Papa had lost the right to tell her what to do.

"At the crossroads, Bellechasse and Dryades," Pierre said, giving the streets the old names that Francine's grandparents had used.

"I'll be there."

"At midnight," Pierre said as he stepped backwards off the porch and out into the moonlight.

Francine's breath caught in her throat.

The dark of the bar had hidden much about Pierre, making him appear much more human. The true light of the moon made his eyes shine overly bright, liquid and expressive. A ghostly pall coated his skin, making it glimmer. He waved his fingers through the air in an impossible pattern, as if they had extra joints.

"Midnight," Francine said, making a pact with herself as

much as with the others.

* * *

Francine sat through the next set nervously. She danced when people asked her, laughing when one of the older men swung her around the floor like he was her age, solemnly holding the hands of a pimple-faced boy who shyly asked her and then couldn't stop tripping on his own feet.

They weren't her people—she didn't know anyone here. But they were from the same background and they understood dancing and having a good time.

When it drew close to midnight, Francine told Muriel she was going to the ladies' room and would be right out. Once there, Francine wrote a quick note and gave it to one of the other girls to take to Muriel at the end of the next set.

"Sneaking off to see a boy?" the girl asked with a sly smile.

Francine shrugged. "You know how it is."

"Honey, I sure do. You don't have to pay me none. I'll do it for free."

"Thanks."

Francine slipped out the back, heart pounding as she made her way up the road, her fiddle strapped to her back. The woods on either side called to her, the wind talking through the branches. Everything else lay quiet and still. Even with the moon half-hidden behind the clouds, Francine easily saw every bump in the road. That was another thing she shared with her papa, and maybe these others.

A group of people had gathered at the crossroads. Clouds covered the moon so Francine couldn't see them clearly as she walked forward.

Someone whispered, "She's here."

The crowd parted and a tall African American woman stepped out.

Francine recognized her from the first gig. She wore her white hair piled high on her head, and was clothed in a simple blue shirt, jeans, and boots.

"Welcome, cousin," she said, holding out her hands.

The moon came out of hiding.

She had gator eyes.

Chapter Four

Francine froze in fear and surprise.

Uncle Rene's words came back to her, about how the *others* had mixed with the native spirits here. She hadn't believed him, not really, not until now.

She looked around at the people surrounding her. The moonlight brought out donkey snouts, feathered arms, glinting rock bodies, and tall woven-weed frames.

The same blood flowed in Francine's veins.

After only another moment's pause, Francine moved forward, taking her cousin's strong hands and kissing both her cheeks.

At the academy, she'd been called a freak, or worse, every day. Though she loved her cousins, she knew that she was different from them.

These people were her true kin.

"You can call me Yvette," the woman with the gator eyes said graciously, bowing her head. The smile she gave Francine warmed even the air between them.

"And you can call me Francine," Francine replied.

"Pierre said you can play," Yvette said, indicating the other fiddler should join them.

Pierre came up, carrying a black fiddle.

"Let's see if we can get them to move," he said with a conspiratorial wink. His extra-nimble fingers ran up and down the strings, plucking random notes.

Francine laughed and pulled out her own instrument.

"You're on," she said as she tuned up.

Pierre started the melody—a sweet and easy waltz.

Francine followed after he played through the verse and chorus once, the tune simple enough to understand. They stepped to the side as a tall thin man with the beak of a pelican took Yvette's hand and led her in a courtly two-step. The others joined in, coasting in polite circles around the intersection of the roads. Trees murmured to themselves in the distance, as if discussing the dancers. The air shone with silver dust motes, with more rising as the dancer's feet kicked them up.

"Now that we've got the warmed up," Pierre murmured at the end of the song, picking up the pace, heading directly into the next song.

Francine recognized the tune and took the lead, leaping up an octave and making it double-time.

Pierre looked surprised but followed, laughing and stealing the melody back.

They played well together, instantly gelling.

The heat of the music wasn't all that warmed Francine's belly, her eyes lingering over Pierre's face, watching his hands.

They divided their attention between each other and the dancers, prodding them this way and that, provoking them to extra flourishes and kicks.

Magic spilled out over the dancers like parade confetti. More than one couple took to the air, leaping with inhuman grace. Joy wrapped around Francine, making her fingers dance as well. Pierre sparred with her, flinging and catching notes; they chased each other up and down runs. They whirled around each other, adding to each other's work. She'd never played like this before, so in tune with another musician. It was the best music she'd ever made.

And it was only the first time she'd played with Pierre.

One song flowed into another. The dancers gave back everything Francine offered to them, and more. She proudly partnered with Pierre, surprising him as often as he surprised her with technique and tricks. Francine felt as though she could play all night.

A hard hand landed on Francine's shoulder.

"What are you doing?"

"Papa?"

Francine blinked the fairy dust out of her eyes. Shadows swallowed the dancers as they scattered. Exhaustion slammed into Francine. Her legs trembled, as did her arms. She stiffly flexed her fingers, aware of her body for the first time in hours.

"What did I tell you about them?" Papa asked, arms crossed over his chest. He looked furious.

He also looked different.

Moonlight frosted Papa's hair, making it as pale as Yvette's. His eyes changed from steady gray to black and liquid, and his ears sharpened, almost growing to points. Papa had always been tall; now he loomed over Francine. His nose took on a beak-like shape, making him even more fierce.

"Charles," Yvette drawled, the word a lazy caress. She came and stood next to Francine.

"How lovely to see you again. It's been a pleasure getting acquainted with your daughter. You should have brought her to court."

"Her mama's human," Papa said, transferring his glare to Yvette.

"She's more us than you," Yvette said smugly.

Francine looked at her hands. Was she? She didn't look

any different in the moonlight. When she looked up, Papa stared at her as well—like she was a stranger, someone to be afraid of—no longer kin.

"That's not true," Papa said hotly.

Even Francine could hear the lie in his voice.

"Why did you keep me from them?" she asked, shivering. They were as much her flesh and blood as her human cousins. Maybe more so.

"They're not what you think," Papa said. "It isn't always dancing and magic."

"It isn't always what he thinks, either," Yvette chimed in. "All bickering and infighting, polite smiles while someone stabs you in the back."

They held identical poses of anger, glaring at each other in the center of the crossroads.

Francine wondered how closely they were related.

"We're going home," Papa announced, taking Francine by the elbow.

"You know, you always have a place with us in the *Féerie* realm," Yvette said. "I'd love for you to play for my court. Both of you."

She turned and disappeared into the shadows.

Francine stood alone with her papa in the middle of the crossroads.

"You're not to seek them out again. Ever." Papa stood with his arms akimbo, glaring at Francine.

Francine mutely picked up her case and started putting her fiddle away. All the magic of the night had faded, gone more completely than any dream. Francine trembled inside, the changes buffeting her.

"Do you hate them that much?" she asked quietly.

When she looked at herself, she didn't seem changed. But she'd also seen how Papa had looked at her.

She was *different*, now, in his eyes.

For the first time, Papa lost his rigid stance, bowing his

head and putting his hands in his pockets. —and

"It isn't that easy," he said. "It isn't just love or hate."

"I don't understand." It sure seemed like he hated them.

"The cliques at the court—they're worse than at your high school. Trust me," Papa said. "There's backstabbing and infighting. Yes, sometimes there's dancing, magic, and amazing music. But it's like life. It isn't always some grand ball. Most of the time they're inhuman. Cruel and uncaring."

Francine flinched. Was Papa accusing her of that as well, with her mixed blood?

Papa continued. "The longer you're in the *Féerie* court, the more you forgive their hard ways. You'll lose yourself and your humanity."

They walked in silence all the way home. Francine swallowed down her words several times. How could she ask if Papa still loved her? What if he didn't?

On the front porch, Papa finally said, "You're grounded until Christmas."

"But I have a gig—"

"You're not playing at any bar between now and then, and that's final!"

"I can't let down the band," Francine said stubbornly. "They're depending on me."

"Find another fiddler," Papa said. "It shouldn't be too hard."

Stung, Francine fumbled with the lock. Papa really thought that little of her playing?

Of course he did.

Francine wasn't fully human, not like Mama.

Papa hated Francine's mixed blood, hated who and what she reminded him of. No wonder he was never home anymore.

Maybe Francine would just have to leave, too.

* * *

"Can I see you after class for a few minutes?" Mr. Frazier asked as he handed Francine her paper.

Francine dumbly nodded, still staring at the A emblazoned across the top of her latest paper. Despite her best efforts, Mr. Frazier had consistently been giving her Cs.

She knew the change couldn't be good, not given her luck.

"I just wanted to congratulate you on your effort," Mr. Frazier said, staring intently at Francine as the other students all shuffled out. "I knew you had it in you to do this level of work."

"Thank you?" Francine said, still puzzled by his change of heart.

"With your continued effort, you should finish the year with an A, Mr. Frazier stated boldly. "If you're still interested in attending that music college, I'd be happy to write you a recommendation."

Francine swallowed around the lump in her throat.

"Thank you," she said more strongly. She'd never thought to approach Mr. Frazier before about a letter—one or more coming from teachers outside of her music class would be really helpful.

Maybe she did have a chance of playing music all the time, doing what she loved.

"Now, about the next assignment—" Mr. Frazier rattled off a few more details. He looked so earnest, as if he really wanted her to succeed.

Francine nodded and promised she'd remember before walking out, dazed. She had no idea what had just happened. She quickly calculated her GPA.

Maybe it would be high enough.

Finally, Francine realized that the noise levels in the hallway were dimming and she needed to hurry if she was going to make it to English on time.

After changing books at her locker, carefully folding away the precious paper, Francine paused. She always took the front staircase. It was wider and better patrolled by teachers.

But she was late, the back staircase was closer to both her locker and her next class, and it *had* been safer for her since the start of the year.

She decided to risk it.

Heart pounding, Francine took the stairs two at a time. She was thinking of excuses to give to Mrs. Anthony, watching her feet so she didn't slip. She didn't look up until she was directly in front of Billy.

"Why the hell did you do that?" he said angrily, pushing her.

Francine, already off balance, grabbed for the handrail, catching herself after only stumbling down a few steps.

"Do what? Try to get to class on time? Moron," Francine gathered herself together, ready to run past Billy if necessary.

"No. Tell the principal I'd bought my last paper."

"What?" Francine asked, confused. She quickly recovered. "Now you know what it feels like to be accused of something you didn't do."

A look of guilt crossed Billy's face.

"What, so you did buy a paper? Idiot. You deserved to get caught."

"You're gonna pay," Billy hissed at Francine.

"I didn't do it," Francine said, taking first one step, then another. Though she was still one step below Billy, she could almost look him in the eye.

"Doesn't matter," Billy muttered. "It's only what you deserve. Swamp slut."

Francine kept walking, brushing past Billy. When she finally reached the top step, she looked back.

Billy was gone but his threat remained.

With heavy feet, Francine made her way to her English class, already dreading whatever was coming.

* * *

Francine threw her backpack onto the couch when she came home, a habit she'd gotten into since Mama had died. Though Papa had grounded her, she still thought about walking down the road to talk with Uncle Rene.

Papa appeared in the doorway leading to the kitchen. "Is that where that belongs?"

"No, sir," Francine said, surprised. Papa hadn't been home when she'd gotten back from school since Mama had gotten sick. She slowly picked her pack back up.

"Is everything okay?"

A look of guilt flashed across Papa's face.

"Everything's fine. You should go to your room, start your homework. Dinner will be in an hour or so."

Francine nodded, now catching the scent of some kind of soup reheating on the stove. "Okay," she said, not quite trusting this disruption, though it was nice that Papa was home, that she wasn't all alone.

"I got an A on my history paper today," she told him as he turned back toward the kitchen.

"That's wonderful, darling," Papa said. He actually paused and smiled at her.

"Mr. Frazier said if I keep doing well, he'll write me a letter of recommendation."

As soon as the words were out of her mouth, Francine wanted to take them back.

Papa's expression went from gentle happiness to stony coldness.

"Now, Francine, you know how I feel about you continuing with a music career."

"Yes," Francine hissed, her temper rising fast. "And I don't care."

"Well, music isn't going to feed you, and I'm not, either," Papa declared. "Go to your room."

"I hate it here; I hate you!" Francine said. "Someday, I'm not going to my room. I'm walking out that door, and you're going to regret it," she added as she stomped down the hallway. She slammed the door to her bedroom after her, seething with rage.

Her violin sat on her bed, her only solace and escape.

It could be an escape, too, Francine realized. If not the music college, then the fairy court.

Francine sat down on her desk chair as the thought fully sank in.

She did have an out. Finally. She could escape. Pierre would welcome her. As would Yvette. She shivered, remembering how wonderful playing for the fairies had been, how the music, magic, and moonlight had all spun together, shining with potential.

Did Francine really want to go? That was the question.

Though Papa had grounded her, and had now sent her to her room, he hadn't taken her phone. Francine slid her violin case to one side of the bed and flopped down on her back, calling Uncle Rene.

"Yeah?" Uncle Rene always sounded as if he were in a hurry on the phone, so different than his usual way of talking.

"I saw them," Francine told him with no preamble.

"Ah," Uncle Rene said. He took a deep audible breath and let it out.

"Beautiful, yes?"

"Yes," Francine said. "And magical, and wonderful, and musical, and—"

"Dangerous," Uncle Rene added.

Francine shook her head, though she didn't say anything.

The potential for danger was there—she wouldn't deny

that. But she hadn't seen anything threatening. Just a feeling of peril.

"Papa was so mad," Francine told Uncle Rene, without bothering to tell him she'd been playing for the court.

"Do you blame him?" Uncle Rene asked gently. "He doesn't want to lose you."

"I...I don't know," Francine replied. "He saw me. Under the moonlight. He didn't like what he saw."

It hurt to admit it out loud.

"Darling, your papa just doesn't like to see you all grown up. He still wants to see you as just his little girl."

"No, that wasn't it," Francine said. "The moonlight, it changed them. So I could see they weren't really human. Changed me as well."

Francine found her voice growing smaller and smaller. She traced the lines of stitching on the quilt under her, not taking any comfort in the familiar patterns.

"Your Papa loves you. All of you."

No, he doesn't.

"Then how come he won't let me make music? Or gets so mad when I talk about the music college?" she asked instead.

"He just wants what's best for you."

"He wants what he *thinks* is best for me," Francine pointed out.

"And what do you think is best for you?" Uncle Rene asked. He sounded as if he really wanted to know.

Francine's searching fingers tapped the edges of her violin case, then splayed possessively across the top of it.

"To make music," she said. It really was all she ever wanted to do.

"Then go make music," Uncle Rene replied.

Francine paused a moment, feeling as though Uncle Rene had just given her his blessing.

"Thank you," she said softly.

"Anytime, darling," Uncle Rene said. "And I'll have a talk with your papa the next time he comes over, all right?"

"Okay," Francine said. "Bye."

"Love you. Bye."

Francine hung up and continued to stare at the ceiling.

She knew Uncle Rene hadn't meant that it was okay for her to run away to the fairy court. But still—it seemed like he might understand if she did.

* * *

Two girls Francine didn't know took one look at her when she walked into school the next day, then started giggling, turning away. Their laughter haunted her. Everyone stared. She knew she didn't have anything painted, drawn, or spilled on her, but she still went to the bathroom to double check.

Francine made her way to her first period, stonily refusing to even look at the boys who made grunting sounds at her as she passed.

When Mrs. Beaumont, the principal's secretary, pulled her out of class, Francine felt both relief and dread. At least Papa wasn't waiting for her in the principal's office.

Principal Martin sat behind his desk, looking more nervous than usual. He didn't meet her eye, but kept watching his twitching fingers.

"Were you aware of this site?" he asked, turning his computer monitor toward her.

Someone had done a Photoshop job on a video, pasting her head on the body of a porn star's.

Francine felt all the color drain from her face. She shook her head mutely. This was Billy's final revenge.

"We became aware of this when we realized someone had hacked your school email account. The link to this video was sent to everyone in your contact list."

"Everyone?" Francine squeaked. That included the

director of the Louisiana Music College, Papa, all her cousins—everyone.

Francine threw herself out of the chair but only made it to the outer office before losing her breakfast in the closest wastebasket.

When Francine finished, Mrs. Delacroix handed her a tissue and a glass of water. Mrs. Beaumont and Principal Martin stood back, both looking unsettled.

"I know that was a shock. Now, if we can find the perpetrators—" Principal Martin started.

"You know who did it," Francine hissed.

"We can't prove it," Mrs. Beaumont said flatly. "It was very cleverly done. For today—"

"I want to go home," Francine interrupted. "Now."

"I'll call your father," Mrs. Delacroix assured her.

Mrs. Beaumont and Principal Martin didn't look happy, but they nodded in agreement.

Francine walked back into the office to collect her books. She shivered as the moans from the fake website washed over her.

God, what was she going to say to her relatives?

Francine followed Mrs. Delacroix down the hallway to her office. Around the corner, Laura and Karyn stood. Karyn rocked her hips suggestively when she saw Francine, and Laura just laughed.

If Francine had anything left to lose in her stomach, she might have had to make another run. As it was, she felt numbness overtake her. She made it safely to Mrs. Delacroix's beige office and sat with her back to the door, looking out the window, ignoring the students in the hallway as well as Mrs. Delacroix's offer to talk.

Francine had told Papa once that she was never coming back to this school. This time, she wasn't going to bother fighting with him. She was never coming back.

She was running away to the realm of *Féerie* instead.

* * *

It wasn't hard playing sick the last couple of days of the semester. Francine's body hurt as if she'd been hit, and she couldn't keep any food down. The stillness of the house suited her. She spent hours in the living room on the sad old couch, looking out over the road. It grew quiet enough that she could hear the clock ticking away the time in the kitchen. The sunlight came briefly in the afternoons, but it didn't warm her.

Francine practiced her fiddle when she could, in between napping and anticipating.

What would it be like? Uncle Rene had said they didn't cook, but what did they eat? Would she be able to see her change more after she went with them, becoming less human looking, more animal, or something else? What kind of magical powers did they have, could she have?

What would Francine do if they didn't want her to come with them the next time she played?

Francine spent time secretly saying goodbye. She walked in the woods behind the house, leaves crunching under her feet, certain the trees would be different on the other side, in *Féerie*. The old creek where she'd loved to play as a child, catching crawfish for her Papa, nearly made her cry with its babbling water and cool, still pools. She sat in the fern house, but the rustling of the leaves made her restless.

Midwinter's Night finally arrived. Francine made a small bundle to carry with her—just the things she could wrap in an old scarf of Mama's: her best earrings; the music from her favorite symphony; an extra shirt and a second pair of boots. Francine snuck out the window from her room. Papa hadn't shown up that night for dinner. She didn't know when he'd be home or when he'd notice she was gone. She imagined it might be a few days, which made her both angry and sad beyond reckoning.

The first person Francine saw when she stepped into

Slim's was her Aunt Lavine. Grimacing, Francine stepped forward, prepared to fight for her right to play that night.

"Hi, honey!" Aunt Lavine said, turning her face up for kisses. She wore one of the shirts she sold at her boutique, which proudly proclaimed *American by birth. Southern by the Grace of God*. Large gold hoop earrings and a matching necklace bedecked her. She was too dressed up for a casual night at the bar. Francine wondered what her aunt was up to, but she didn't look guilty.

When Aunt Lavine saw Francine's fiddle case, she loudly exclaimed, "I didn't know you were playing tonight! Why didn't you let us know?"

"Don't tell anyone," Francine said, reaching out to close Aunt Lavine's purse when she started searching for her phone. "It's kind of a charity gig," she lied.

"I understand," Aunt Lavine said quietly. "Since you're playing, though, the music won't be too bad, right?"

Francine winked at her aunt. "Promise. It'll be good enough to dance to."

"That's all I'm looking for," Aunt Lavine promised. She winked back. "And maybe someone to dance with. Uncle Gilroy won't set foot in this place. Not since last time."

"It wasn't that much of a fight," Francine scoffed. Uncle Gilroy had been banned from the bar only for a month, not a whole year, unlike her cousin Walter.

"See, that's what I told him," Aunt Lavine said. "I said, 'Gilroy—'"

"I'm sorry," Francine said, interrupting the latest version of a story she'd heard too many times before. "I have to go set up." Muriel stood on the stage beckoning to her.

"All right dear. Knock our boots off," Aunt Lavine said, smiling up at her.

"I will. I promise," Francine said. She paused for a moment before swiftly giving Aunt Lavine another kiss on her cheek.

"Bye. Love you. Be good."

Then Francine wrenched herself away, making herself leave before she said something more.

* * *

Fear made Francine shake before she went onto stage. She lied, saying it was nerves, but she knew better. She didn't know if Aunt Lavine had broken her word, if Papa would be sitting, disapproving, in the front row of tables.

Francine honestly couldn't say if she'd prefer he found her or if he didn't.

However, none of Francine's other relatives waited for her.

Aunt Lavine sat with a man Francine had never seen before.

No wonder her aunt hadn't called anyone.

The first set went quickly, the notes whirling away. Francine danced on the stage with Muriel, tossing the melody back and forth with Layton on the guitar. It was a shame, really. This band was the best human band Francine had ever played with. She told herself that she could change her mind before the end of the evening.

Pierre showed up midway through the second set. The lights hid his differences well, though Francine could see them better now that she knew what to look for. She didn't see any of the others, though. Pierre danced once with Aunt Lavine, whirling her around the floor, winking at Francine as they passed.

"Is that your young man?" Aunt Lavine asked during the break, fanning herself and pointing toward Pierre with her chin.

"No, we...we just met," Francine said truthfully.

"Charity gig, hmm?"

Francine looked down at her feet.

"Don't worry about me telling anyone, sugar," Aunt

Lavine assured Francine. "Long as you're careful. He looks like a wild one."

"Might be that," Francine admitted to her aunt before going over to Pierre's table.

"Enjoying the music?" she asked, trying for casual but failing, sounding breathless instead.

"I love listening to you play," Pierre said, smiling up at her.

"Just you tonight?"

"Yes. But we're meeting later." Pierre paused, then added, "Beyond the crossroads."

"I understand," Francine said. Beyond the human roads and in the realm of *Féerie*.

"Would you like to come with me?"

Francine barely heard the question she'd been anticipating for more than a week. The moment rushed up to her, the final choice upon her. She looked at Aunt Lavine, laughing with the man Francine had never met, her bright lips flashing. Her aunt had a life, a vitality, like Mama had.

But Mama was gone.

All that Francine had left was her cold and angry Papa, a school full of bullies, a life without music.

"Yes," Francine said.

Though she whispered the word, she felt it take wings and fly out of the bar, straight into the woods.

"I'll be waiting outside, after you finish," Pierre said. "Take your time."

"Thank you," Francine said, appreciating his consideration and patience.

The rest of the evening passed faster than a turn around the dance floor. Francine played her heart out, wanting people to remember her last performance. Everyone stood up and applauded when they finished. Their tip bucket was full. More than one person asked for a CD, assuming the band had been together for a long time.

Muriel agreed to play more gigs at Slim's before Francine could tell her not to. She felt bad leaving her friend in a lurch. She couldn't stay any longer, though. The night called to her.

After a last set of goodbyes, wishing everyone Merry Christmas, Francine slipped out the door. A mere sliver of the moon shone down, making the night dark and the shadows thicker. She felt, rather than heard, Pierre arrive beside her.

"Are you ready?"

Francine nodded, not trusting her voice. Papa would be ashamed of her, leaving as she did, not finishing school, not trying for a different life.

But she couldn't live her life for Papa anymore.

"This way." Pierre walked them back toward the crossroads.

The shadows seemed heavier, thicker, making it more difficult to walk through them. The trees were strangely still, not talking to themselves or Francine.

In the center of the joined roads, Pierre stopped. He used both hands to sketch out a door, like a mime Francine had once seen on TV.

Only instead of a wooden door or a frame, a curtain of ivy sprung up. The leaves shone silver and green, lush against the dirt of the road.

"This isn't the only entrance," Pierre murmured in Francine's ear. "But it's the fastest, for us, tonight."

Francine shivered at the warmth of his breath.

The way the leaves moved reminded Francine of the kudzu in Uncle Rene's backyard. Was that a way into *Féerie* as well?

"After you," Pierre said, bowing slightly.

Francine squared her shoulders. She told herself she could come back anytime, that she wouldn't get lost in *Féerie*, like the stories of the other travelers there. This was what she wanted.

With a deep breath, Francine took a step forward, lifting her hands to push the leaves apart. They felt cool against her hands and moved easily out of the way.

Darkness lay before Francine. Without another word, she stepped into it.

Suddenly, Francine stood on a crossroads of small, dirt trails instead of roads. The woods crowded up close to the edges, and the clean smell of pine and juniper washed over her. Like in the human realm, only a sliver of the moon shone down on her, but its light was as bright as when the moon was full.

Francine took another deep breath. Her shoulders relaxed, though she hadn't realized they'd been tight. It felt so *right* to be here, like a home she'd never seen before. She would have sworn she heard the trees whisper, "Welcome." Cool breezes tickled her cheeks and hands.

Pierre appeared beside Francine. He'd grown taller, thin and twiggy. His hands took on a sheen like oak saplings. The extra joints in his fingers looked like knots of wood.

Francine looked at her own hands, but she didn't see any difference.

"It's mainly your face that changes," Pierre told her with an amused smile. "Your eyes glow now, with your spirit. Golden and bright. And your face is longer, thinner, and more pale. I don't see wings, but maybe your legs are longer, too. Like a crane's."

Francine wished for a mirror that would let her see the changes more than anything else in the world.

Pierre indicated the path they should go down, letting Francine go first, into the forest. She'd been right—the trees were different here. They grew closer together, supporting each other's limbs. Taller, too, looking like they reached high enough to scrape the moon. They seemed both more friendly and more distant. Francine didn't see a way to pass between the trunks, except on the path: The undergrowth sprouted too thick, and thorns the length of her palm dotted the branches.

Still, they didn't frighten her. If the trees wanted her to pass, they'd make a path for her.

Even though everything was new, it was all familiar as well. Francine knew the woods around her house well enough to recognize the fern house, though here, it towered over her head, looking like an empty mansion instead of a shack. Despite its size, it still seemed warm and inviting to her, a place she could escape into.

When they came to the little creek, Pierre crossed first, then turned back, holding out his hands to Francine. She firmly beat down on the foolish tripping of her heart as he warmly gripped her and helped her across.

Finally, they walked over a rise that Francine didn't remember. From the ridge, they looked down onto a clearing. Music rose to greet them. Soft lights twinkled along the edges. Many figures gathered in the space between the trees. It took Francine a moment to notice that the clearing was higher than the ground around it.

If the area flooded, the clearing might be high enough ground to keep people dry.

"Would you like to meet the court?" Pierre asked. His voice had grown deeper the longer they'd been there.

"Yes," Francine said, smiling up at him. "Please."

Pierre offered his arm. Francine took it, marveling at how warm he felt, as well as at the smoothness of his skin. She tried not to be nervous, pushing down hard on the butterflies that had captured her stomach.

What if they didn't like her? Would they kick her out, even though she was their blood?

As they approached, Francine got the impression that it wasn't merely a clearing. Tall trees formed both pillars and walls, as if lining a great hall. Kudzu covered the branches, creeping down to mingle with the soft moss, steeping everything in green. Twisted bushes squatted here and there, with sparkling flowers twined through their branches, adding light to the moon shining down on them. Music streamed through the air, as thick and heavy as morning fog.

Pierre climbed the stairs to the wide, clear space, then paused beneath the arch of two trees, waiting for the music to slow and the dancers to take a break.

Francine squeezed his arm in gratitude. She needed a minute to get her bearings.

The creatures—her relatives, Francine reminded herself sternly—wore gowns stretched out with hoops and coats with long tails, like an old-fashioned royal court. Gloved hands carried fans used for flirting. Top hats extended flourished bows. Gems and glitter adorned skin, fur, and clothes, giving them an extra glow.

Francine had never felt so out of place, not even the day she'd worn a sleeveless shirt and Karyn had called her birthmark a swamp stamp.

"It's okay, *ma chérie*," Pierre whispered, covering her hand with his. "They do not expect musicians to follow the same style as they do."

Francine bit her lip. Pierre wasn't dressed like the rest of the court, either. His clothes still resembled what he'd worn earlier that night. Though his jeans had transformed into fitted black pants, and his sneakers into boots, his T-shirt remained the same.

Finally, she straightened her back and nodded. She did have other gifts.

Pierre smiled at Francine. At the next break in the music, he started walking forward. The moss covering the ground felt as springy as Uncle Leroy's new shag carpeting. Dancers moved to the edges, giving them a corridor to walk through. The music started up again, but softer this time; not a dance, but a quiet conversation.

Francine could finally see the throne at the end of the hall, carved out of the stump of a tree. The back arched up on either side like giant butterfly wings, trimmed with red flowers and strings of silver beads. Braided branches made up the arms, covered in moss.

A dark African American woman dressed in all white and shining like new frost rose to greet them. Francine recognized her from her golden gator eyes.

"Queen Yvette," Pierre said, bowing low.

Queen Yvette? Francine curtsied, very low, bowing her head to hide her shock.

"Welcome, cousin," Queen Yvette said.

"Welcome to my realm."

Chapter Five

When Francine looked up from the ground, Queen Yvette gave her a predatory smile, her teeth shining as whitely as her gown. All of the warnings about how perilous the *Fée* were came rushing back at Francine.

The creature before her was not human; none of them were.

But then again, neither was Francine, not completely.

She pulled herself up to her full height and smiled back at the queen. She'd called Francine *cousin*. Did that mean Francine, and her papa, were some type of royalty? Did Francine have some sort of position of power here?

Queen Yvette seemed pleased with Francine's reaction.

"Pierre. You will make the introductions," she instructed.

"Thank you, my lady," Pierre said. He took Francine's elbow and turned her, leading her to the side, toward the column of trees that made up the long edge of the court.

"Just follow my lead," he whispered. "The queen has called you *cousin*, and put you in the care of the Master Fiddler for the court. This means you have enough potential position to matter to the court. Everyone will want to meet you."

Pierre directed Francine to stand under the bow of a tree.

People immediately began to drift from the dance floor and form a line to the right of them.

Francine wondered at the jostling as ladies and gentlemen laughed and tried to cut in, stealing each other's place.

Pierre just rolled his eyes.

"They're all trying to pull rank, to see who gets introduced to you first."

A spur of embarrassment went through Francine. These gorgeous ladies and gentlemen were fighting to see who talked with her? Nothing like that had ever happened to her. She'd dreamed about it: forming a famous band, writing killer songs, and starring in videos. But that would have been based on skill, talent, and hard work. Not on who she was or who her relations were.

Finally, the first lady stepped forward. She wore a gown of the brightest robin's-egg blue. Intricate silver lacework decorated the sleeves and hem. The plunging neckline showed off her ample breasts, while the dress clung tightly to her womanly curves. She appeared mostly human, except when the light caught her skin just right, making it appear a curious gray color.

"Lady Melisandra, this is Francine Adelaide Giscard, daughter of Charles Guiscard."

"Charmed," Lady Melisandra said, holding out her hand.

Francine took the lady's hand, surprised at how hotly it burned. The lady caught her eye. Something gleamed there, ancient, powerful, and alien.

Pierre nudged Francine subtly, then cast his eyes toward the ground.

Francine gave a low curtsy.

"Absolutely charmed," Lady Melisandra repeated, smiling at Pierre.

"I will be inviting ya'll for some sweet tea later."

Pierre smiled. "It would be an honor to attend your table, ma'am."

After she moved on, Pierre leaned over to speak in Francine's ear. "That went exactly as planned," he murmured. "Stay on her good side."

Francine bit back her sigh. Had Papa been right? About the politics and the cliques? Only this would be worse than high school, because she had no cousins or family to escape to.

Pierre gave Francine clues for how to treat everyone who came up. Some received a curtsy, while others got only a brief nod.

Francine would never remember who'd received what treatment. Of course, if this were anything like high school, she wouldn't have to—they'd remember her greeting and would snub her accordingly.

At least everyone had their human face on, with only a hint here or there as to their mixed parts: maybe twig-like hands, or horned-owl tufts for ears, or even a dog's snout.

A commotion toward the end of the line cut short Francine's greeting of an older man with cat eyes. A young man with the head of a donkey came barging up to Francine.

"Cousin!" he exclaimed, throwing his arms wide.

More than one person in the line sniggered softly.

Francine froze. Was this really a relation?

Pierre scowled. "Jacque. Come to make an ass of yourself again, I see."

Jacque shook his head and the glamor of the donkey head disappeared, replaced with a sly, mostly human face. His white skin was covered with orange freckles, and his hair curled tightly up around his scalp. His eyes seemed extra wide and sparkled with an unnatural green.

"Couldn't possibly do that as well as you," he said,

turning his attention to Pierre.

Before Pierre could reply, another young man came running up, holding his hands out to Francine.

"I just heard!" he said. "I'm Brooks. We're cousins!"

While everyone Francine had met was beautiful, Brooks outshone them all. His hair was black and perfectly cut around his face, his dark skin looked smoother than polished obsidian, and his brown eyes held specks of gold and green, like brilliant stones.

Jacque threw his arm over Brooks' shoulder. "Me and Brooks thought we'd come back when we heard news a relation had shown up."

Francine looked carefully between the two, startled to see that though their eyes were different colors, they still looked similar.

"Brooks," Queen Yvette said, coming up. "How nice to see you."

All the light faded from Brooks.

"Mother," he said formally bowing his head. Jacque did the same.

"I don't suppose you'll be staying," Yvette said.

Francine found it difficult to read the queen's expression—her gator eyes made her face too alien. She still thought Queen Yvette wanted them to stay, at least for a while.

"I'll be playing later," Francine offered.

"Will you now?" Jacque said, looking intrigued. His features had shifted as he'd stood there, looking less human and more rabbit, with a dark nose, whiskers, and floppy ears, what Francine guessed was his true nature. He and Brooks exchanged a look.

"Yes, of course. She must win her place in the court," the queen said. "Prove her worth."

Shock made Francine take a step back. She wasn't accepted yet? She had to show them she could play? Then why had she been introduced to everyone? And hadn't they heard her play the other night? Hadn't that been enough?

"Merely a formality," Pierre murmured.

"A formality," Brooks said, crossing his arms over his chest. "For a cousin."

Queen Yvette shrugged.

"Then maybe I shouldn't waste any more of the court's time with introductions," Francine said, fuming.

Who were they to turn her away? She'd show them.

Brooks turned to Francine.

"As much as I might love to see you show them all up," he said, "Jacque and I really must be going."

"When you get tired of playing at tea parties, let us know," Jacque added with a wink. "We know where the real hootenanny is."

"Boys," Yvette said, a warning edge in her tone.

"Goodbye, mother," Brooks said with a bow.

Jacque repeated the words and they sauntered across the grand hall, arm in arm, before disappearing into the trees on the far side.

"So you want to play for us," Yvette said.

Francine looked at her, confused.

Wasn't that why she was here? Because she could play? Wasn't that what drew them to her initially?

"Yes, ma'am," Francine replied finally, still wary.

"Pierre, you'll be playing against her."

Pierre grew stiff beside Francine.

"But, my lady—"

"You were her champion. Surely you don't think she'll take your spot."

"Take your spot?" Francine asked.

"As Master Fiddler for the court," the queen explained.

"How about just for the evening?" Pierre proposed. "Master Fiddler for a day?"

"No," Queen Yvette said. "I don't want you throwing this

competition. You will play for your position. And you will beat him, or else," she added, turning to Francine.

"Or else?"

"We'll drag you back to the crossroads at dawn," Yvette said, smiling sweetly at both of them before she walked away.

"Pierre—" Francine started.

"I can't lose my place," Pierre interrupted her. "I'll lose my standing at court."

Francine stared at him. How did that compare to her not being allowed to live here at all?

"You're kidding me, right?"

"Maybe she'll decide it's only for a day," Pierre murmured, not paying attention to Francine.

Brooks suddenly reappeared behind them.

"No, she won't," he said. "You know how much she likes these games."

"What am I going to do?" Pierre asked, looking lost.

Francine bit her tongue to keep herself from telling him to grow up.

"You're going to play your heart out," Jacque said, coming out of nowhere. "That's what she's going to do." He paused, then added in an over-solicitous tone, "You do still have a heart, don't you? Haven't sold off that body part yet?"

Pierre scowled at Jacque. Then he looked at Francine, and the lost expression filled his face again.

"What about..." he said, waving vaguely in her direction.

"What about me?" Francine asked, crossing her arms over her chest. If Pierre thought she might have any regrets beating him in this contest, he was sorely mistaken. She'd been so attracted to him before. Now, she wasn't sure if that attraction had been a mistake.

"We'll take care of her," Brooks told him solemnly.

"She'll be in good hands," Jacque added.

"She better not actually end up in anyone's hands," Pierre growled, glaring at both of them.

"She's a virgin, and she should still be one by the end of the night."

"I think I can make my own judgments about that," Francine said hotly, stung by how freely he shared this information.

How had he known? How was it anyone's business?

Pierre said softly to Francine, "Just make sure that you do." He paused, then added, "I really hadn't expected this. I don't want to hurt you."

"I know," Francine said.

Pierre's standing in the court seemed to be too important to him for him to knowingly jeopardize it. But his assumption that he would win also added fuel to her already burning anger.

"She'll be safe with us," Brooks promised.

Pierre merely nodded, then walked away.

"Come, cousin, let's get you dressed for battle," Brooks said, extending his elbow to her.

Francine didn't want to go with this man. She didn't want to have to prove herself again.

She also didn't want to be judged as inadequate and thrown out of the fairy realm. She couldn't go back.

Gingerly, Francine took Brooks' arm.

"No gowns," she said firmly. Dressing up like some court mannequin was the last thing she needed.

Brooks laughed.

"Oh cousin, I have something much better than that planned for you."

* * *

Francine slid the ivory silk shirt over her shoulders, buttoning it quickly. She believed Brooks and Jacque when they said they wouldn't peek through the vast shrubs of the grove where she changed her clothes. Yet, it wouldn't do to tempt them by moving slowly.

The shirt felt cool against her skin and didn't seem to warm like normal clothes. On top of the shirt, she added a black vest that fastened tightly just under her breasts, emphasizing them. Even without a mirror she knew she looked good in them. She quickly changed into the black jeans that Mama always fussed about, saying they were too grown-up for her. They fit her legs tightly and made them go on forever. After trying on the fairy boots, she put back on her own; the new ones didn't have the weight she was used to.

With a final sigh and a wish for a mirror, Francine walked out of the grove.

Jacque gave her a low wolf whistle.

Francine found herself smiling at him.

"You look like a proper warrior," Brooks added.

"You just need one more thing."

He brought his hands forward from behind his back with a flourish. He held a beautiful fiddle made out of smooth white wood. Gold lined the scrolls of the head and around the openings in the middle of the body. The silver metal strings gleamed.

Francine took it from Brooks reverently, feeling its weight. She plucked one note, then another, then shook her head and handed it back to him.

"Thank you," she said. "It's a beautiful instrument. But I need to play my own fiddle, the one I know."

While Francine suspected this new instrument could easily become an extension of her soul, it would take time—time she didn't have. Better she stayed with something familiar for now.

However, based on the matching grins Jacque and Brooks gave Francine, she knew she'd made the right decision. The boys weren't trying to trick her or put her at a disadvantage—she didn't know what they had against Pierre, but they really wanted her to win.

"Any advice?" she asked as they walked back toward where the court was gathered.

Brooks shrugged. "The queen always changes the parameters to these sorts of challenges, so you never know what's expected. Just—play your heart out."

Francine nodded.

She wouldn't try anything too fancy, just pour everything she had into her music, as always.

The atmosphere in the grand hall under the trees and kudzu sparked now, not sparkled. Ladies and gentlemen lined the walls, clustered in tight groups, whispering urgently to one another. Francine thought she saw money being passed between them.

Were they betting for her, or against her? It didn't matter. She was determined to win.

Pierre already stood at the front of the hall beside the queen. His outfit was similar to hers, except in different colors: a blood-red shirt covered by a green vest so dark it seemed black. His instrument would have matched the one the boys had tried to give her, only instead of white and gold, it was black and gold.

At the prompting of Brooks, Francine sank into a low curtsy as she was presented.

"I approve," Queen Yvette said, her golden gator eyes sparkling.

"Thank you, your majesty," Jacque said woodenly. "You know I live for your approval."

"None of your cheek," Pierre said hotly.

"Save your ire," the queen said calmly.

"What are the terms of the battle?" Francine asked. She really wanted to know what was expected of her.

"A duet," Queen Yvette said, looking between the pair of them. "Followed by each of you playing alone."

It seemed strange to Francine that they'd play together first—maybe the queen wanted to make sure that she wasn't a hot head, unable to play with anyone, though she'd shown that already at the crossroads.

Pierre picked up his fiddle, cradling it gently against his chin.

Francine followed suit, bow raised. Anticipation and relaxation ran through Francine. Nothing felt better than playing, even in these circumstances.

When the notes spilled out, Francine cursed. She'd let Pierre pick the tune, without insisting he play something she know. It put her at a disadvantage, forcing her to play second fiddle.

Pierre smirked as he speeded up, Francine's fingers tripping.

Francine refused to give up. She picked up the melody by the second time Pierre looped around to it, adding her own flourishes and arpeggios. She couldn't steal the lead from Pierre, not when he went into the bridge. She skipped up and down it as best she could, adding sweet harmonies and a syncopated beat. They ended with a prolonged improv at the end, both trying to outplay each other and get the last note in.

The court applauded politely. Francine grimaced. Though the queen awarded that round to Pierre, she felt they'd both lost.

No one had gotten up to dance.

Now, it was Francine's turn to do her solo. Without a second thought, she started in on "Zydeco Queen," the song she'd written. It moved fast and hard.

Francine felt like a wind that had finally been set free. She whirled in place, unable to stop herself from moving, stomping her boots and letting her fingers fly.

She poured all her anger into her song. She'd lost both Mama and Papa. Not even those who called her kin accepted her. She hated being called young and inexperienced, which Pierre had done with his comments about her being a virgin.

But mainly, Francine wanted those creatures to move. Proper zydeco was music that you *had* to dance to.

Done right, even the dead would rise and twirl to her tune.

When those in front started swaying, Francine knew she'd won.

Before the second verse, the power of Francine's heritage washed over her and the thrill of magic coursed through her. She couldn't control it—she didn't really even know what to do with it. She felt like she'd finally come home. This was what she'd been born to do: to bring this music to life, to make it solid and real.

By the time Francine reached the final chorus, the court wasn't merely swaying.

More than one had started dancing.

Francine had expected them to do a type of courtly dance, partnered and refined, though speeded up for her zydeco.

Instead they stomped in time, like how old people did when they could no longer swing their hips. They'd also lost some of their human countenance: The man closest to her now had the head and claws of a wolf, while the woman he danced with shimmered with the sleek black skin of a rat snake.

Queen Yvette frowned at Francine, but she didn't care. It didn't matter to her if she lost to Pierre. Tonight she'd played better than ever before.

Tonight she'd finally tasted real magic.

Francine threw in an extra chorus. All the court moved now. They formed lines and stomped back and forth. Animal howls echoed through the great hall. At first they startled Francine, then she used them, incorporated them into the song, casting it higher.

The queen had said only that Francine would play alone. She hadn't specified the number of songs she could play. So Francine slid into another tune without stopping, "Run, Gator, Run." She didn't speed up the melody—it was normally played triple time—but she did hit the bass notes hard, sometimes slipping down into a lower octave, to drive the tune forcefully.

Cool moonlight joined Francine's tune, curling around it and casting the notes far and wide. Even the trees limbs started swinging in time. Kudzu shivered in invisible winds, twitching with the steady beat.

Francine laughed as the court danced. This was the power she remembered from her few gigs, only amplified ten thousand times. *She* controlled the court, directing them from the sidelines. They might be fairies, inhuman and alien, but she held their hearts and minds.

Something coolly whispered to Francine that she could make them tear each other apart if she wished. It would be easy to cause them pain and make them hurt like she'd been hurt.

The magic inside her welled as she made her notes brighter, sharper.

The court responded with a swelling growl. All the hairs on the back of Francine's neck stood up. She remembered Uncle Rene's backyard suddenly, the trees there.

Beautiful and perilous.

Quite possibly deadly, if under her command.

"Stop!" Queen Yvette commanded.

Francine kept playing but she turned her attention to the queen. The intensity of the music faded and just the notes continued.

"You will stop. Now."

Slowly, Francine let the melody die away, the tune left unresolved.

The court growled again, sounding frustrated.

"That music isn't appropriate for the court," Queen Yvette declared.

"I don't care," Francine told her hotly. "That's the music I want to play."

"Then play it on your own," the queen told her.

Pierre spoke up. "What you played—it's the music of war. The court needs a different kind of music. Something lighter, more playful."

Francine grit her teeth. Damn them all for letting her think she might have a better life here.

"So I should leave, then?"

Queen Yvette blinked at her. "Heavens, no, child. What gave you that impression?"

With a snap, Francine closed her mouth. What kind of game was the queen playing? She'd just been told to stop playing, which meant she'd lost, right?

"Ya'll are powerful, but undisciplined," Queen Yvette continued. "You can stay, and learn, under Pierre's guidance. You're too untamed to be the Master Fiddler, even for a day. Later, though, she still may take your place," she warned.

"Thank you, my queen," Pierre said, stumbling forward, bowing low.

At Pierre's nudging, Francine also said, "Thank you, Queen Yvette." She gave a curtsy, but not as low as before. Anger still shimmered through her blood.

Though Francine had no doubt she'd won the contest, she still felt as though she'd lost, too.

* * *

Pierre insisted on playing the next piece alone: A slow lullaby that calmed Francine's shimmering rage. The fairies were more affected by it, quickly dropping their claws and fangs, becoming more human, their heads nodding. The lights in the trees dimmed, and the branches inched higher, as if giving one last good stretch for the night.

Francine gathered her things together and stood awkwardly to one side, shifting from one foot to the other, while Pierre played the last few notes. She wished Pierre would at least play a waltz, but he seemed determined to keep the fairies from dancing.

When Pierre finished, the court drifted away, flitting off into the woods, disappearing up the dirt trails. After he put his fiddle away, he turned to Francine and told her, "There's a place set up for you. This way."

They walked straight east, along a twisting path. The woods seemed more welcoming to Francine now; she could see several opening through the thick undergrowth. The moon had set, but leaves and branches shifted out of the way, making it easy for her walk and not stumble.

The trees opened up to a small clearing. At least half of it was taken up by a flattop hill. A steep ladder lay against the side of it.

"You're kidding, right?" Francine asked. She wondered if she was supposed to camp out.

"You'll see," Pierre told her, inviting her to climb the ladder first.

Francine put her foot on the first rung. The ladder looked as though it was made out of bamboo—skinny and green—but it easily took her weight. The wood felt smooth under her hands and smelled newly cut.

At the top lay a collection of stumps covered in kudzu. Between two trees at the back hung a living curtain of purple flowers. Though it was pretty, Francine still didn't see where she was supposed to live. She supposed that two of the stumps that kind of grew together might have served as a couch, but there was no bed, no place private.

Pierre stood expectantly at the top of the ladder, looked at her. "Well?"

"This is where I'm supposed to live?"

Pierre pressed his lips together and kept his expression bland for a few moments, before he grinned at her.

"No. Not here. Come."

He walked across the hill and pulled aside the flowers. Warm light spilled out.

Francine shook her head and walked into the space. It didn't belong there: the hill should have ended at the curtain. A tiny thrill went through her that her even her house was magic.

The first room didn't remind Francine of any place she'd ever been. It felt like a nest. Small woven branches made up the walls, with wide openings that looked out over more woods. Overstuffed pillows, brightly colored in gold and red, lay scattered across the grass floor. The kitchen had a wooden table and chairs on one side. On the other wall hung a single shelf. Half a dozen fluted glasses stood in front of three golden tubes that ran floor to ceiling.

The bedroom contained a mattress heaped with pillows, furs, and soft blankets, as well as a cupboard built into the wall. It smelled like fresh-cut pine. For a moment, Francine missed the cedar-lined wardrobe that Uncle Leroy had built her.

Then she saw the clothes.

"Are those for me?"

Rich silk shirts and jackets, mainly in whites and blacks, hung there. Only two gowns were included; one in a dark brown, the other, a light blue.

Pierre smiled at her.

"Consider them payment for your playing earlier."

"What do you mean?" Francine bristled.

"You surprised the queen with the power of your music and passion. I don't know why she was surprised—your father was that good. You shook up the court. Gave them a new experience. They value those."

Francine bit her lip, but finally asked, "What happened,

exactly, when I played? And what was that challenge all about?"

Pierre looked at the ground.

"I'm sorry about what happened," he said. "Let's..let's talk."

He led her back into the kitchen and showed her how to open one of the tubes and pour out some of the moon wine contained there, then led her out the back door of the kitchen into an intimate yard.

The space immediately reminded her of Uncle Rene's backyard. A fountain in the center splashed water against a fluted white bowl. The scent of mint filled the air.

Pierre gracefully sank to the ground, sitting cross-legged.

Francine followed suit. They toasted each other and Francine took a sip. The moon wine was cool like the best lemonade, tart and sweet, and it filled her up completely, more so than any drink she'd ever had. Just a mouthful and she was satiated.

No wonder the fairies didn't cook.

Francine put the glass to the side, determined not to drink too much, not yet, while she waited for Pierre to start explaining.

"I don't have any noble blood," Pierre said softly. "My mother isn't recognized by the court. I was born and raised in the fairy realms, on the outskirts, though my father was human. I had to earn my way into the court. Without my position, I'm nothing. It took me years to get any status. Just losing the one battle meant I would have lost everything."

Francine tried to understand.

"Wouldn't your friends have stuck with you?"

"*Ma chérie*, still so human," Pierre said, shaking his head.

"We don't have friends, not like that. The only family that counts are the royals. No, I would have lost it all, and had to fight for years to gain it back again. Or be forced back into the woods, no civilized place to call home."

So Papa was right. But she didn't say anything about that. Instead, she asked, "What happened while I was playing?"

"Fairies go to war sometimes. Amongst ourselves, mainly," Pierre said. "The battles are driven by the music, by the fiddlers and drummers. A good general is nothing compared to a good war tune."

"I didn't mean to play war music," Francine said, frowning.

Pierre shook his head.

"It didn't matter what you played, what tune. Your passion, and your anger, changed the music." He looked directly at her.

"You gotta learn to control yourself. Or you're going to get yourself, and others, hurt."

"What do you mean?" Francine asked, stung.

"As the queen said, you're very powerful. Undirected, your music could make someone attack, without knowing what they were doing."

Francine nodded, remembering those few moments at the end when she'd twisted the music, turning it sharp and bitter.

"Teach me," she said after a moment. "Teach me how to use what's in me."

She'd always wanted magic, power, and control. This was her chance.

"I will," Pierre said. "Not just the war tunes, but the joy as well. The laughter and fun."

He smiled at Francine and she remembered how attractive he'd been when she first met him. The attraction was still there. He was as beautiful as all the fairies, a great fiddler, and she could learn a lot from him.

"All right," Francine said slowly. She was willing to learn it all.

But she really wanted to learn how to fight, too.

* * *

After Pierre left, Francine went back out into her backyard. The trees sang quietly to her. She got out her fiddle and played to them, creating soft lullabies. Flowers growing up the walls blossomed, their stamen glowing. The sweet smell of midnight jasmine crept through the air.

When Francine laid down on the ground in the middle of the yard and looked up, she saw millions of stars.

The trees understood where she looked and slid their branches out of the way so she could see more. The moon had set long ago, but the sun seemed reluctant to come out and start the day.

Francine didn't recognize any of the constellations. Either she was now someplace completely different, or there were too many stars for to recognize the Earth-poor configurations.

The first time Francine thought she heard someone calling her name, she wondered if she'd fallen asleep and it was part of a dream. The voice came in under her usual hearing, she felt, pinging bone and not ear.

Finally, Francine realized someone was just beyond the gate in the back, calling to be let in. Francine roused herself and threw it open.

Brooks stepped across the threshold.

"This area is private," Francine hissed.

"Sorry," Brooks said, not looking repentant at all. "I wanted to see you, and it's better if no one else sees me."

Francine nodded, though she still wasn't happy.

"Why don't you come in for a minute?" she asked, indicating the kitchen. "I have some moon wine," she said.

Brooks ducked his head, then nodded.

"Thank you," he said quietly, preceding her into the house.

Francine got out two fluted glasses and coaxed a tube to drip into them, filling them with the golden, sweet liquid.

"Cheers," she said, handing one to Brooks. They clinked glasses, Brooks catching her eye. The way he smiled at her made her heart beat faster. She told herself not to be stupid. This wasn't just her cousin: He was a wild, unknown character, as well.

"We're only related through marriage, you know," Brooks said, as if he'd read her mind.

Francine's cheeks grew warm and the flush moved through her body.

"No, I didn't," she said, glad that she kept her voice steady.

"I don't know how I'm related to anyone, here."

"The queen—my mother—is a lot older than she looks," Brooks warned. "Centuries old."

That surprised Francine. The trees gave a feeling of great age, not the people she'd met.

"She's outlived more than one husband. Rumor is that she killed some she grew bored with." Brooks grimaced.

"She killed your papa?" Francine asked, horrified.

Brooks laughed.

"No, mine merely died. Jacque's father—he was banished. We're half-brothers."

"You don't live with the court, do you?"

"No. We live out on the edges, near the swamps, in the bayou."

"Why?" Francine really wanted to know what had driven him away. Were these the outskirts that Pierre dreaded so much? She wasn't sure she wanted to stay in the court, but these woods were more home than anywhere she'd ever been. She didn't want to leave them.

"Mother has certain ideas of what is fun...." Brooks

paused and sighed. "Let's just say tonight's entertainment, forcing a man to chose between his protégé and his position, was tame. Though you certainly surprised them." He raised his glass and clinked it with hers again.

"You were part of the 'entertainment' once, weren't you?" Francine asked, sickly certain.

Brooks nodded.

"That's why I'm here. If you ever decide you want to stay in *Féerie* but not in the court, you'll always be welcome with us. Jacque and Josephine and the others. We'd make you a house—as good as this. Maybe better."

Francine had the feeling Brooks wasn't telling her everything.

"Why?"

While it was nice her cousin wanted to help her, it wasn't just because she was kin.

Laughing softly, Brooks shook his head and studied the glass in his hands.

"I told Jacque you were smart enough to ask." He sighed, then looked up. "The lands of the court—they're real. Or real enough. Where we are is only as real as we make it. Your music, though, could make it much more real."

"I don't understand."

Brooks waved his hands around. "This all feels solid, smells and tastes like life. Is it?"

Francine blinked, remembering stories of fairies paying travelers with gold coins that turned into acorns and leaves, beautiful palaces dissolving into hovels at dawn. She looked around carefully, but it all seemed real to her.

"At the heart of all of this is fairy magic. And that doesn't exist in the human world," Brooks said softly.

"So it isn't real."

Brooks shrugged.

"It's real here. Where we live is less so. You'd make it stronger."

He handed her what looked like a glass lily with obscenely red petals and a sprinkling of orange pollen at the center of it.

"Break this in your hand. The door to the wilds will appear."

"Thank you," Francine said.

After Brooks left, Francine spent a long time looking at the glass flower, wondering how real his offer was as well.

Chapter Six

Francine waited, as directed by Pierre, bow poised above her fiddle and toe tapping, until Pierre reached the point where she joined in. They played in a cozy meadow covered with brown winter grass. Twisted, leafless tree branches reached down to form a canopy over their heads, twigs clacking in time with the music. Tart breezes tugged at Francine's shirt, sending unexpected shivers down her back.

The weeks had flown by, time in the *Féerie* realm more fluid, harder to count and hold onto. They'd been practicing almost every day.

Francine ached with holding herself in all the time, afraid she'd burst at just the wrong time. At least she had her house, and her backyard, where she could play how she longed to.

When Pierre nodded, Francine picked up the melody, keeping it light and airy as any dancing lady. She wanted to skip ahead, to move the tune faster, but she didn't. She kept the original beat, following Pierre's lead. She was used to doing it in school, with the band. There, it felt normal. Here, it felt like she was always playing at half speed.

When they reached the chorus, Francine took the lead

for a bit. She played with the melody, sliding it up half an octave.

Pierre frowned at her.

She knew it wasn't one of the classical forms, but he needed to trust her. She knew what she was doing.

When Francine slid back down into the traditional melody at the appropriate place, Pierre picked back up the lead. Francine followed, but she pushed at him now, trying to get him to speed up.

Pierre finished without any type of flair, bringing the tune to an abrupt end.

"You have to learn the proper forms," he fumed, glaring at Francine.

Glaring right back, Francine said, "I know most of those. When are you going to learn about loosening up?" She knew they'd gelled well, playing together on the crossroads. What had happened, that he played so differently here? Had that all been a dream of magic and moonlight?

"Really?" Pierre challenged. "Follow this, then."

He started a piece by Paganini, playing it at a brutal pace. It was the first time Francine had heard him play something classical. She joined in the counterpoint. Fortunately, she'd learned this piece at her school; otherwise she would have been lost.

Pierre didn't glare when they finished this time. Instead, he replayed a couple of bars, making Francine repeat them, showing her a new bowing technique. Then they played the piece together again. They seemed to gel for the first time since that night on the crossroads, tossing the melody back and forth, smiling at each other. Magic glittered all around them, and even the winter trees started bobbing their branches in time.

When the music died, Pierre seemed to remember himself again.

"Back to the other piece."

Francine swallowed her sigh. She knew she had to learn the court music. It just didn't suit her. Still, she nodded. She waited while Pierre played, until he came to the place where she could come in again, banking her fire, promising herself a real kick-up later.

* * *

Francine followed Pierre through the woods, along the winding path back to her house. Her fingers hurt after hours of playing and her back and knees ached from having to stand still, not moving to the music. The evening wind carried the sweet scent of rain. Francine was looking forward to sitting in the peace of her backyard, listening to the trees.

"Tomorrow we won't have practice."

It took Francine a few moments to process Pierre's statement.

"Okay," she said when she realized she had a day to goof off. Though she couldn't count the days she'd been here, it felt as though it had been a while since she'd had a good lazy day.

"Though you'll still have to go to Lady Melisandra's party."

"What?" Francine said. "When? Why?"

"She's having a tea party, and you must go."

Pierre stopped and looked back at Francine.

Francine realized they were in front of her house; she could hear the trees in the back calling for her. She itched to escape to there.

"One of her tea parties?" she asked, scowling. At Pierre's nod, she continued.

"You've said it won't be any fun. *You* won't go because you'd be bored stiff. Why do I have to go?"

Pierre sighed.

"It's Lady Melisandra. She knows everyone. She'll

introduce you to the ladies of the court at the right level."

"I thought that's what you did the first night."

Pierre shook his head.

"Not as well as Lady Melisandra will. Her tea parties are legend. Some people would do just about anything to be invited."

"But—"

"You need to go. To prove to the queen and everyone that you can be a member of this court."

"Fine."

Francine would go, then she'd leave as soon as she could. She started up the path to her house.

"You did well, today."

Pierre's halting words made Francine pause. When Pierre said nothing more, she said, "Thanks." Then she escaped up the ladder, running across the hilltop and throwing aside the living curtain of flowers. She didn't know what had happened to Pierre, why he changed so from minute to minute.

Why couldn't they find that magic together again?

Francine knew she that while she respected him, she never wanted to be like him.

She'd been bullied in school, but she'd never given up like he had: living with one eye over his shoulder, always awaiting an attack, while a vice held him still.

* * *

Francine woke to soft winds sliding through the branches, inviting her to come outside. She took a sip of moon wine and went into the backyard, fiddle already in hand. She spent the morning playing her own music, tunes that were a mixture of the court music she'd been learning and the zydeco she loved. The fountain bubbled sparkling water higher during the fast bits, the flowers decorating the base of the walls opened wider, and the trees bent in closer, as if saying hello.

That afternoon, Francine got ready to go to Lady Melisandra's tea party. She put on her new clothes, savoring the hunter green, knee-length leather coat, the white silk shirt, and the black leggings. She stubbornly stuck to her human boots, though they weren't as rich or fine as her other clothes. The fairy ones just never felt right.

Just as Francine was about to leave, she heard someone calling her from the back. Fuming, she went out, intending to rip Brooks to shreds for breaking his promise.

Jacque stood in the middle of Francine's garden instead.

"What do you want?" Francine hissed, keeping her voice down in case someone was listening

"Cousin, is that any way to be?" Jacque asked unrepentantly, but also keeping his voice low. "I'm here to invite you to a picnic."

"Sorry. I have other plans," Francine said primly.

"Our party will be much more fun," Jacque promised. "Moon wine. Magic. Laughter. Not the stuffiness of the court."

Francine paused, tempted. However, Pierre had assured her it would ease her life if she went to Lady Melisandra's party.

"I kind of promised."

"Then let me make a promise," Jacque said, his eyes twinkling.

"We'll do this the right way, and step through the gate sideways. That way, time will slide too. You'll spend hours there but it will only be minutes here. You'll be back in time to attend your other party. You'll just be stylishly late."

Both Mama and Uncle Rene had told stories about how time moved differently in the *Féerie* kingdom. Francine had wondered how much time had passed for Papa out there, though she didn't really know how many days she'd spent here, either. She nodded, eagerly.

It was the perfect compromise.

"Just step this way," Jacque said, leaning over and turning his hand, as if opening a door.

"Now remember, step through sideways!"

Francine nodded and did as he'd instructed, stepping through with her right side first.

The air on the other side of the door struck Francine's skin differently, much more humid and soft. She smelled familiar sweet rushes and mud. Her family hadn't set up camps on the bayou every year, but she'd visited relatives there often enough over the summer to recognize the general feel of the place. The court was closer to where she'd lived in the human realm, while this world was close to the coast.

Spanish moss hung from the trees like lace shawls. Raucous birds sang out of tune like rowdy drunks at a show. The brush here was less dense, though the same palm-length thorns grew along the branches.

Francine hummed at the trees, saying hello. The rush of wind and leaves in response surprised her. While the trees in the court danced to Francine's faster tunes, their first response was always gentle. The trees here wanted to shout as loudly as drunken tourists at Mardi Gras parades.

And yet, for all their bluster, something felt off pitch. Francine whistled a quick tune, then listened carefully for the echoing wind. It came back high-pitched and hollow. Though all Francine could see were trees, their song was thin. Francine bet if she walked too far in any direction, she'd run into some kind of border.

Brooks was wrong. The land here felt real enough. The problem was that it didn't have deep roots.

Jacque grinned at Francine as he stepped out of nowhere. "See, you're getting along just fine," he said.

"Just fine," Francine confirmed, though she was glad that he'd appeared when he did. This place made her uncomfortable. Though the trees were welcoming, they weren't quite right. Everything felt a bit off kilter.

The trail through the trees wasn't as smooth as the trails in the fairy court. Roots and fallen twigs reached out to trip Francine if she wasn't careful. The path curved unexpectedly, sending anyone not paying attention into the bush and thorns. Francine wondered if it was possible to learn the tricks of this trail, or if it was wild like everything else here and would change when the mood struck it.

Jacque led them out of the trees and into a fair meadow. The winter grass here was more golden than brown, as if it still held summer sunsets in its veins. White fluffy motes—like cottonwood seeds—drifted lazily through the air.

"Over here!" Brooks called, sitting up, his head popping up above the grass. He had a beautiful, rich, red-and-blue tapestry rug laid out and a few feet of cleared space around it. A picnic basket sat in the center of it, with a bottle made of iridescent fairy glass filled with moon wine next to it.

"I'm glad you made it," Brooks said, handing them both flutes.

Francine wrinkled her nose as she lifted the glass to her lips. This wine bubbled. It tasted like liquid gold, but with more kick, warming her throat and her belly as it slid down.

"I can't stay for long," Francine warned as she sat down, setting the glass to the side. Much more of that would affect her senses, she could tell. Just the one sip had made the day more honeyed.

"We're still glad you came. If only for a little while," Brooks said. He opened the basket and got out fall-colored leaves that had been frozen with magic, curled into small bowls. Tiny nuts and colorful berries sat piled in the center of each.

"Try these," Brooks said, handing Francine one of the bright yellow berries.

An explosion of spring danced across Francine's tongue,

like the first honeysuckle and daffodils.

"Wow," she said, taking another sip of wine to chase it down, to bring her tongue back to herself.

"Those are amazing."

"I know, right?" Brooks said. "The queen forbids them in her lands."

"Why?" Francine asked.

Brooks shrugged. "Says they're too powerful."

Francine nodded. Her fingers were starting to tingle. The berries were potent, like the wine.

"I probably shouldn't have any more of these," she said mournfully, pushing them away.

Jacque promptly scooped them up, eating three.

"Probably best left to those with a tolerance," he said, sounding mockingly wise.

"Try these," Brooks suggested, handing Francine a leaf of fuchsia-colored berries, each as big as her thumb.

Francine tentatively bit into one. It tasted as cool and refreshing as lemonade on a hot day. She grinned at Brooks, who smiled back at her, raising his glass.

"Welcome to the other side. At least for a picnic," he added hastily.

Ducking her head, Francine clinked glasses with him, then with Jacque. These were her cousins, she told herself sternly. He didn't mean anything by what he said.

"Let's play a game," Jacque suggested. "Here." He dove into the basket and pulled out another leaf.

Francine wasn't sure what it held. They looked like flat coins made out of translucent glass, all pale blues and greens.

"Let me show you," Brooks said, sitting up. He took one, held it in his palms while he rubbed them together, then he blew between his thumbs.

Something forced Brooks' palms apart, growing slowly with each breath.

When Brooks took his hands away, a soft bubble sat there instead of the flat coin. He bounced his hands once, twice, then a little harder, casting the bubble into the air. It floated across the meadow, reflecting the colors of the sun.

"Pretty!" Francine exclaimed. Then she put her hands over her mouth. She'd had too much to drink. Or eat. Or something. It wasn't the same feeling as when she and her cousin Vida had snuck some of the grownup punch from Aunt Redina's wedding: She could still feel her cheeks and her toes. But something inside her had loosened and it wasn't just this place or the company.

"You try."

Francine took the flat coin and looked at it curiously. On the one side she spotted a tiny hole, probably where she would blow into it. She warmed it in her hands, feeling it grow less stiff and solid between her palms.

On her first try, Francine managed to blow a small bubble, a little bigger than her fist. It wasn't as big as Brooks', and it didn't float away as far, but she considered it a success since it was the first time she'd tried. Especially since Jacque's barely grew bigger than his thumb.

The afternoon passed quickly. They raced their bubbles, stalking beside them and creating wind with their hands as they went across the field. Jacque tried to juggle them without touching them, just through blowing on them, one after another in the air. Brooks and Francine both rolled on the ground laughing at his antics.

Only when the first shadow reached the blanket did Francine remember the other party.

"I have to go!" she said, jumping up.

Brooks and Jacque looked at each other.

"You know you'll be late," Brooks warned.

"Not too late. We went through the gate sideways, remember?"

Brooks glared at Jacque, who looked down at his shoes.

"Yeah, about that—"

"You lied," Francine accused. The golden sheen of the afternoon started fading.

Brooks smacked Jacque on the back of the head.

"I told you not to lie."

"She wouldn't have come if I hadn't."

Francine had to nod when Brooks looked at her for confirmation.

"I was supposed to go to Lady Melisandra's tea party."

"You'll get to the next one," Brooks said. "Pierre will make sure of it."

Francine didn't understand what these two had against the master fiddler, but she didn't care.

"You've made me look bad," she said quietly. "To the court."

"I'm sorry," Brooks said.

"It isn't your sincerity I doubt," Francine said. "But your intentions."

The wine must have still been bubbling in her blood for her to say something like that out loud.

Brooks looked at Francine, his lips pressed into a thin line.

"I don't want to hurt you," he assured her.

"Just use me."

Brooks opened his mouth and shut it again before he started denying it.

"No. I don't. Not really. It's just—"

"Send me home." Francine said, hurt and suddenly very tired. She needed to get back to her house where the trees were soothing and would sing to her all night. She had to get away from golden afternoons filled with laughing men who had honeyed tongues and sparkling eyes that saw too much into her soul.

Brooks opened the doorway right there.

"Be careful," he said quietly. "I also want you to be

happy. And the others—who also want to use you, by the way—don't."

Francine walked through the doorway without another word. She stood again in her backyard, the light already dim. She would have to explain to Pierre tomorrow what had happened.

The trees overhead started swaying to a wind Francine didn't feel. She didn't know if they were scolding her, cautioning her, or just singing welcome.

* * *

Francine listened again to the clean creek running at her feet. It sang of a light dance, flowing and constant. Dappled sunlight shifted beside her as the wind caressed the trees, tossing the remnants of their leaves. The afternoon felt open to so many possibilities, like Francine could do anything.

"Try it again," Pierre coaxed from his place on the far side of the water.

Nodding, Francine brought her fiddle back to her chin. She steadily refused to use the white-and-gold fairy instrument, though she knew it would be easier. The few times Pierre had coaxed her into trying it, she felt as though it channeled the magic better.

However, she stubbornly stuck with her regular, human fiddle. She knew the magic was here, in this land, and if she went back to the human lands, she wouldn't have any power.

Still. All that magic flowing through her fiddle might have some effect, right?

Francine tapped out a beat, timed to the song of the brook, then caught one of the notes and threw it back up into the air, like a fish leaping out of the water. She kept the tune nimble and light, reflecting the shadows in the water as well as the cool depths. She drew on her classical training, keeping the beat precise.

"Good," Pierre said. "Now build the bridge."

Francine directed her tune to the water, building a solid passage. For a moment she thought she saw what Pierre had shown her—a transparent bridge rising from the center of the creek, as frilly as the arpeggios she ran up and down.

However, before it fully rose, it splashed back into the depths, casting water all over Francine's boots.

"Dang it!" Francine said, wiping drops off her face as well as her violin. "How do you keep it above the water?"

"Patience," Pierre said.

When Francine glared at him, he said, "Seriously, my dear. Patience. You can't leap into these things like you do everything else. You need to build a phrase at a time. Don't try to do it all at once. Connect the phrases, one at a time."

"I don't much see the point," Francine said stubbornly. "I could step over that creek without stretching my legs."

"What if you were going from one island to the next, or between groves in the bayou?" Pierre said. "Water bridges are important here."

Suddenly, Francine understood what Pierre meant. She could see the type of bridge he talked about, shallow and long, a mere walkway between places. Then she glared at him again.

"The water there is still. Quiet. Not babbling and running like this. Why are you having me practice here?"

She didn't know how she knew, but the structures were different.

"You need to learn to do both," Pierre said stubbornly.

Francine merely continued to glare at him.

"What if there's a storm and you need to get away?" he said. "The water even on coast will be dancing. And you need to be able to tame it."

Francine didn't want to admit that Pierre might be right.

"What else can you build with music?" she asked instead.

"Want me to show you?" Pierre asked, grinning at her.

Francine's heart did that funny beat again. She shushed herself. No need getting all excited. Pierre wasn't really her type, she kept telling herself.

"Sure," she said. "If you want."

Pierre hopped over the creek.

Francine rolled her eyes at him.

He walked a bit under the trees, pulled out his fiddle, and started a quiet tune. "A Place to Rest," he said, naming the song.

Slowly, thin branches in the underbrush wove themselves together. Moss bloomed along dead limbs, covering the dark brown in green. The smell of fresh-cut grass tumbled over Francine. The earth split and a seat unearthed itself under the back provided by the brush. Greenish bark chased away the earth and newly budded leaves stuck to the legs.

"Did you find the bench first? Under the earth?" Francine asked, curious, as she walked over to it, running the tips of her fingers across the springy moss covering its arms.

"Or did you create it?"

"Both." Pierre said.

Francine frowned at him.

"That's not helpful."

"But it's true," Pierre said, gesturing for her to sit.

"It won't up and disappear, will it?" Francine asked, pausing, remembering how the bridge wouldn't stay above the water.

"It won't," Pierre said, sitting first. "Trust me."

Francine sat, staying on the edge of the seat, not relaxing.

"You don't trust anyone easily, do you?" Pierre asked quietly.

"So what?" Francine said, her voice hard.

"You're not still angry about the first battle, are you?"

"Angry?" Francine asked, puzzling it out for herself. "No."

Disappointed, more likely.

"Good," Pierre said. "I was thinking about the ball coming up—"

"What ball?"

Pierre narrowed his eyes.

"You did go to Lady Melisandra's tea party yesterday, didn't you?"

"I forgot," Francine said, looking away to hide the lie.

"I'll get you another invitation," Pierre said smoothly. "But we should do a mock battle at the ball, a skirmish that doesn't end in war-cries, to show how far you've come."

Francine bit her lip and nodded. This was when she didn't have to remind herself that Pierre wasn't her type. She'd been learning technique under his tutoring, as well as the music that pleased the court. They never gelled, not like they had, when they did those gentle tunes.

It wasn't the type of music that pleased Francine.

Zydeco danced in Francine's blood, and not just the slower waltzes. She wondered if it was because she'd been born in human lands. She loved the fast, driving beat of songs that suited cars barreling down dirt roads and trains howling into the night.

"We should go practice," Pierre said.

"I want to try that bridge again," Francine said stubbornly.

"After you, *ma chérie*."

Francine led the way back to the creek, determined to find the path that lived under the water, between the earth and the land, if only because she couldn't follow Pierre much longer.

* * *

Ice-cold sweet tea trickled down Francine's throat,

sweeter than the homemade eggnog Aunt Lavine served at Christmas. It tasted of flowers and tea, as well as honey and summer sunlight.

"You're right, that's good," Francine told the assembled ladies. They all sat in Lady Melisandra's front room, lounging on overstuffed pillows and squat chairs. The air was just warming and cicadas sang in the grass. No one wore gowns, just regular clothes—skirts, pants and shirts—mostly gauzy, though, iridescent and shimmering. Francine had tried to match, wearing a bright, white shirt. She still felt out of place with her jeans and her boots.

"I'm so glad you like it," Lady Melisandra told Francine. Her complexion was darker than the other fairies; smoother, too, as if age had burned away all her wrinkles. She wore a shawl that Francine's mama would have been proud to own, made up of delicate white lacework, over a green gauze top and matching skirt.

"I do, ma'am," Francine assured her. It was delicious.

But it wasn't like Mama's. Or Uncle Rene's. And there were no biscuits. Though the moon wine, the sweet tea, even the water filled Francine up, she still found that her mouth wanted to chew something sometimes.

"Is it true that Brooks helped you? The first night?"

Francine finally realized someone was talking to her. "Yes. Him and Jacque."

"Some champion." Lady Ezora sniffed, wrinkling her long nose.

"You don't think I'd let anyone fight my battles for me, do you?" Francine asked, outraged. "I had to defend my place. No one else."

"Child, no one doubted your talent." Lady Melisandra shivered. "Or your power. That dance...that dance...was some dance."

The other ladies in the circle all nodded, a couple of them fanning themselves. Francine bit back her smile.

Though they might say otherwise, the court had *liked* what she played.

"But showing your power isn't about being strong. Sometimes it's about being soft. Or finding that middle ground."

Francine held back her snort. That wasn't how things were done anymore. Lady Melisandra was obviously too old-fashioned.

"So did you hear what Buford said last night to Ezora?" one finally asked the others.

Francine tried to make herself listen, tried to be interested in the missteps of people she didn't know. She bit back more than one yawn.

Lady Melisandra leaned over and patted her knee.

"Don't worry. You'll sort them all out," she said softly.

"Yes, ma'am," Francine replied, just as quietly. She didn't think she would.

"Tell me about Charles," Lady Melisandra asked. "How is he doing?"

"When Mama died, he…he…got mean," Francine said, the hurt still deep, making her heart ache.

"Your papa did have a temper," Lady Melisandra said, nodding. "One time in court, when one of the young bucks challenged him, he cut him to shreds. Cast hard notes that tore his clothing apart. Left the man near naked. Apologized afterward, of course. Tried to make amends. However, no one challenged your papa again for a long time."

Francine nodded.

"That sounds like him."

She would have liked to see that, see her papa take on someone.

She didn't wonder if she could beat him at a battle like that, though; she knew she could.

* * *

After the others had left, Francine stayed with Lady Melisandra. There wasn't really anything to clean up: The cups returns to being flowers when Francine placed them on the nearby branches. There hadn't been any biscuits or cookies, so no plates or crumbs. She watched as Lady Melisandra held her hand over the pillows and shrank them back down to normal size.

Finally, Francine got up the courage to ask, "You knew my papa?"

"I did," Lady Melisandra said. "He was a good man. Too wild for the court. Like Brooks."

The way Lady Melisandra looked at Francine made her wonder if possibly she, too, was too wild.

"But how did...I mean...why did he go to the human world?" Francine asked, confused. There was so much more she could do here. The power and the music thrummed in her blood. She would never turn her back on it like he had.

"He found your mama," Lady Melisandra said quietly. "And we all just faded away on gossamer breezes after that. She was the most real thing to him."

Francine nodded, though she didn't really understand. Mama had been the force that kept them together, and at peace, not tearing each other apart. She didn't seem as real or heavy as Uncle Rene, to Francine, though. While the queen and the court, the moon wine and songs, floated through her consciousness as lightly as the bubbles she'd blown with Brooks and Jacque, the trees grounded her. More than anything else, they were her home.

Lady Melisandra nodded, as if she'd been reading Francine's mind.

"Yes, your place is here, in this realm, in these woods. But," she paused, considering. "Possibly not with the court."

Francine froze. Had she made a bad impression? Pierre hadn't told her, but he'd certainly implied that she needed to win Lady Melisandra's approval.

"I don't want to go back to the human lands," Francine said.

She didn't like how hoarse her voice sounded—almost raw.

"Oh no, no, you don't belong there, either," Lady Melisandra said, shaking her head and laughing. "No, I think you need some time in the wilds, to take the edge off. Or to find your place there."

"Like Brooks and Jacque?" Francine asked warily.

Lady Melisandra shook her head.

"They aren't all the way in the wilds, though you wouldn't know it to listen to them, how they think they're 'roughing it' away from the court. The place they made is actually very tame."

She gave an unladylike snort.

"No, the true wilds might be where you need to go, not their world or the outskirts. Away from the courts and their creations. Give yourself some time with just the trees and the wind." She looked speculatively at Francine.

"Time to heal."

Francine didn't dare nod, though a part of her was already longing for what Lady Melisandra described.

"Come to me when you decide," the lady said. "I'll help you."

"But won't that get you into trouble? If you help me leave?"

"Yes, but I'm too old and important for the court to do much about it, other than give Lady Ezora something to talk about for a month or more." Lady Melisandra looked amused.

"I might tell her that I did it anyway, even if I have no hand in it. Just to get her riled up."

"Thank you," Francine said. She was suddenly sorry that she hadn't made it to the first tea party.

"You're welcome. Stop by anytime. I mean that."

Francine gave the lady a deep curtsy, as low as what she'd given to the queen the first night. She didn't know how else to thank her, for giving her friendship, as well as a different way out.

Chapter Seven

Francine puttered around her bedroom and spent at least a minute—maybe two—debating about the outfit she'd wear to that night's ball.

Pierre had sent over a gown that was both elegant and deceptively simple.

Francine had loved it when she'd tried it on. The pearlescent colors shimmered when she walked. It accentuated what little bust she had as well as her thin waist. The sleeves fell only to the middle of her forearms so she could easily play.

It was gorgeous.

It was also safe, and not her.

Another gown had appeared on Francine's front porch late that afternoon.

The fiery red made her pale skin glow. Rich gold laces strapped around her torso and her waist, then hung down the front and sides of the skirt like parade streamers. The material didn't glitter like most of her fairy clothes; instead, the color subtly shifted from red to burgundy to almost black. It felt heavier than it looked, and that weight made Francine more comfortable. Though it covered her more demurely, it gave the impression of being more daring.

Francine didn't know who had left it for her. Brooks? Lady Melisandra? Or someone else? She didn't care either. It fit her perfectly, both her spirit and her body.

The mask that came with the dress was made out of nice-smelling leather and painted red and gold. It swirled up above her right eye and down along her left cheek. The way the mask curved reminded Francine of the cutout in the body of her fiddle.

After Francine put the dress on, she went into her backyard and played a smooth tune on her fiddle, turning the water in her fountain glass-still so she could see herself.

For the first time Francine saw some of the differences Pierre had mentioned.

Large golden eyes stared back at Francine through the mask. They weren't gator shaped, though the color was the same. She thought they looked more like a bird's. Her dark hair had blue highlights in it, deeper and richer than any her aunts would have been able to give her. The dress made her look taller and thinner, more willowy. She realized with a start that she looked like Pierre. She wondered if they were closer kin than she'd realized, or if she merely looked like a fiddler. She checked carefully for wings, but only saw her human arms and hands, her skin pale as white feathers.

Stepping out of her house and heading toward the grand hall, Francine could taste the excitement in the air. It might not be a stomping party or a *fais do do*, but it was still a party. Everyone wanted to have a good time.

The fairies wore splendid costumes that night. Francine was glad she'd chosen the gown she had. While some wore paler colors, most of the outfits had richer, darker hues.

For the first time, she looked as though she fit in.

Francine didn't know the court well enough to recognize any of the masked ladies and gentlemen. She passed fairies wearing cat, butterfly, pelican, and bat masks. Some had simple dominos with feathers floating three feet up above them. One group of four fairies Francine passed she would have called elemental: The ends of the one in the red mask flickered upward like flames; the gray mask swirled like water; the blue and green one looked like the planet Earth; and the silver gauze one floated in midair, never still, like wind.

Other musicians had already started playing by the time Francine got there. She nodded to the few she knew, then got out her fiddle and joined in. She played support, not the lead, in the music they made together. She wasn't bored—the musicians were too good for her to be uninterested.

It still wasn't music that stirred her soul.

Suddenly, the soft waltz they were playing changed into a stirring march.

Francine frowned, but followed along. She saw Queen Yvette walking from one end of the hall to the other and finally understood: Though the queen didn't have an anthem, the musicians were expected to still announce her.

When Pierre arrived, Francine had second thoughts about her dress.

Pierre wore a long gauzy jacket that would have matched the gown he'd sent her.

She decided when she went to stand next to him that they complimented each other anyway: While he was light, she was dark, while he was air and floated, she was earth and grounded.

The edges of his white mask rose at least a foot in the air and looked like snow-covered branches.

Of course, Pierre didn't see it that way.

"What are you wearing?" he asked, dismayed.

"A gown," Francine said simply, smiling at him.

"Yes, but whose?" Pierre asked. At Francine's shrug, he continued. "You know that wearing a person's gift shows you favor them. It isn't an innocent expression of thanks."

Francine glared at Pierre, angry with him as well as herself. She should have thought through the consequences. She didn't want to care about the court alliances, but Pierre kept telling her that she must.

At Francine's continued mute treatment, Pierre finally sighed.

"I hope you know what you're doing. The outfit you were supposed to wear came from the queen."

"Why didn't you tell me?" Francine asked, even more angry now.

"You let me think it came from you."

"Would that have mattered?"

Francine bit her lip. She honestly didn't know.

Pierre led the next dance, a beautiful waltz that had everyone dancing, the women swirling in their beautiful gowns. Francine watched and listened carefully; she knew she could still learn a lot from Pierre.

Then it was Francine's turn. She picked a faster two-step. The beat wasn't as quick as she would have liked, but it was fast enough that the fairies twirled and leapt.

Pierre and Francine played together on the next few songs, finding a sweet rhythm between Francine's need for faster music and Pierre's preference for slower waltzes. The queen walked the hall while they played, stopping to talk with small groups of people. When she reached the stand where the musicians played, she asked a gentleman in a bright red fox mask to dance.

"She approves," Pierre murmured.

Francine knew that should make her happy. Instead, she merely shrugged.

More important than the queen's approval, Francine needed to be happy as well.

When the song ended, Queen Yvette clapped her hands. Instantly, everyone's attention was on her.

"Tonight we will watch a different type of battle," she said.

"Pierre and Francine will play for favors."

The crowd grew more still. Francine's back stiffened. What did that mean?

"All I would ask for is a single kiss," Pierre said with a sweeping bow.

Francine's cheeks grew red. She still didn't know if she liked Pierre or not. Or rather, she liked him, but only sometimes.

"And the lady—being too demure to ask for herself—shall get a day of service," Queen Yvette announced.

Francine glanced at Pierre.

He grinned at her and nodded, happy with the proposed prizes.

Francine gave him a shy smile, pleased that this time, the stakes weren't so high.

That didn't mean Francine didn't intend on winning.

They each played two sets.

Francine kept her rhythms modest, well in keeping with the preferences of the queen.

Then Pierre played a different piece by Paganini. Fast, full-throttle.

It wasn't the same as Francine's beloved zydeco. Pierre kept the music classic and traditional. It had tremendous zing, though. More than one of the court swayed, twitched, or otherwise looked like they wanted to move with the driving music.

Francine hung her head. After Pierre finished, it was obvious to her who had won. She'd have to give up a kiss, and maybe that was okay.

Queen Yvette stepped forward.

"Thank you, Pierre, for such an exhilarating experience."

"I live to serve," Pierre said grandly with yet another sweeping bow.

The queen looked between the pair of them.

"In the opinion of the court, Francine is the victor here."

"I beg your pardon?" Pierre asked before Francine could ask the queen what game she played.

"I liked her music better."

Francine didn't need to tell Pierre the queen lied. He could see it. She mouthed, "I'm sorry," as she moved forward, taking the queen's hand as requested. She curtsied low to the court.

"You've been promised a day of service, haven't you, my dear?" Queen Yvette purred.

The hairs on the back of Francine's neck stood up. Fear gripped her sides, forcing her to breathe shallowly.

"Yes."

"And you love the trees here, don't you?"

Francine couldn't stop herself from looking up. The branches moved; maybe there was a high wind she didn't feel, or maybe they were waving.

"Yes."

"Then Pierre shall serve you best as a tree."

"No!" Pierre screamed.

The force of the magic hit Pierre like a gale. He threw his hands up to cover his face, but they kept going, up and up, as his arms elongated.

Francine shook in horror as loud *cracks* filled the air: Pierre's bones breaking as the magic took hold.

His white mask branched into more tree limbs and his body took on the mask's white sheen, looking cold and alien in the warmly lit hall. A large, black knot formed over Pierre's open mouth, effectively stopping his screams but not Francine's shudders. Roots grew out from his feet, rippling across the stage.

The queen laughed and merrily skipped out of the way as they tried to trip her.

The roots made a wide path around Francine. She didn't

know if it was because Pierre pitied or despised her.

"Shall I transport him to your backyard?" the queen asked sweetly. "Or leave him here?"

Francine wondered if Pierre could hear them, if he had an opinion. She didn't know if tearing up Pierre's roots, making him grow them again would be more painful than making him stay here, in full view of the others.

However, it would be more painful for Francine if Pierre were forced into her private space, particularly like this.

"Leave him here."

"So we shall. Let's dance! Play something cheerful for us," Queen Yvette said, twirling away.

Francine glanced at the other musicians, then out at the court. No one else seemed to be horrified at what the queen had done. Francine swallowed down the bile in her throat and stopped herself from frowning.

She couldn't make herself smile.

She could make herself play. She lifted her fiddle to her chin, counted the beat of three, then started to play a song of spring that Pierre had taught her.

The pale tree above Francine swayed.

She wanted to believe he was happy, or that maybe he was dancing to the music, but she knew he wasn't.

* * *

Much, much later, after the stars had gone to bed and the sun was almost rising, Francine finally escaped back to her sanctuary. Exhausted as she was, she didn't rest. She walked directly into the backyard then stopped, looking up. The trees crowded close to her, dropping their limbs so she could reach up and touch their branches.

"How many of you were people?" Francine asked softly, stroking leaves and bark. "How many of you want to move again?"

The trees didn't reply, just sighed and whispered.

Francine could learn to live with the politics and games of the court. She'd been able to ignore the queen, her pettiness, and her mean games. But the queen had just torn the heart out of Francine's home, disturbed her peace, given her more doubts than even Francine could walk away from.

With regret, Francine pet as many of the tree limbs that she could reach before she left the backyard and walked into the kitchen.

On the table, the red glass flower waited. It was one path of escape. She remembered the golden laughing Brooks, the lost afternoon with him and Jacque, the sweet berries and strangely thin trees.

Francine picked the flower up. The intense color belied the cool weight resting against her palm. She wanted to throw it. She wanted to scream. She wanted to tear apart all the branches of her cozy nest so it looked as destroyed as she felt.

Instead, Francine changed back into all human clothes, wrapped up her small scarf of things, wrapped herself in a cloak, picked up the flower, her fiddle, and walked out the door for the last time.

* * *

"I was expecting you," Lady Melisandra said. She sat on a moss-covered stump on her front porch, sipping a flute of moon wine. The early morning birds were just waking up, calling softly to each other.

Francine was suddenly glad that the trees had grown silent; she'd been afraid she'd hear Pierre's screams in their shuffling branches.

"You upset the queen by wearing an unknown person's favor."

Francine frowned.

"I thought she approved of my outfit."

Lady Melisandra shrugged.

"She liked the dress. She didn't like not knowing who it was from."

"How did the queen know that I didn't know who'd given it to me?"

Lady Melisandra blinked. "Not that you didn't know. That no one knew. I thought you knew."

Francine shook her head.

"It came from me, my dear," Lady Melisandra said, standing.

"Why would you give me something that you knew would upset the queen?"

Lady Melisandra shrugged.

"I was only thinking of currying your favor. Not of what effect it would have on *her*." At Francine's puzzled look, she continued. "I wanted to become your patron. Steal you away from the queen and the court. Have you attend only me. It was the only way I could think of to protect you."

The tears that Francine had been expecting all night suddenly welled in her eyes.

"You were trying to save me, to keep me here," she whispered.

"And a mess I've made of that. Come." Lady Melisandra led the way into her home.

Francine took one last look at the lands of the fairy court—the beautiful trees, the graceful paths, and the cruel shrubs with their palm-length thorns.

The front half of Lady Melisandra's home was decorated in rich reds and browns, giving it a homey feel. Shelves covered the walls, covered with beautiful leaves, unusually curved branches, and odd-shaped stones. A round mantel stood on one side, and for the first time, a cheery fire burned in the hearth. It startled Francine—she hadn't seen a fire the entire time she'd been there, she realized. She drew closer to examine it, then leaned back, disappointed. The fire was magic: It burned with a blue hue, but gave out no smoke, no heat, and was strangely silent.

Lady Melisandra waited for Francine in the kitchen.

This felt more fey to Francine.

Gauze streamers of blue and red hung from the ceiling, hiding the solid walls they were tacked to. The colors changed as the fabric slid across itself, making the room fluid and airy, the boundaries unknowable.

Lady Melisandra turned ancient eyes to Francine, eyes that had seen plagues kill babies and long winters madden strong men. Her eyes didn't remind Francine of an animal, plant, or even stone. She was just *other*.

"Ask what you want of me," Lady Melisandra intoned.

"Send me to the wilds of *Féerie*," Francine asked formally.

"What have you brought to ease the passage?"

From under her cloak, Francine produced the glass flower.

"Clever, very clever," Lady Melisandra crooned. Her hair had turned white and her back had bent, as if her age could no longer be denied.

"This would have made you obligated to them, if you had used it."

Francine nodded. She hadn't known; however, she wasn't surprised to learn the truth.

Lady Melisandra curled over the flower, her head bending further down until it was even with Francine's waist. She held the brilliant glass in one hand while she bobbed her other hand over it, fingers drooping, as if dripping unseen magic onto it. She spoke in a language Francine didn't know but still felt in her bones. It stripped skin and moved blood, saying only the truth of things.

The obscene red of the flower dripped out between Lady Melisandra's now-wrinkled fingers, leaving the petals a hazy purple—the color of smoke in bars.

"That's more like it," Lady Melisandra rasped. She

grinned at Francine with a toothless mouth, her skin all wrinkled and covered in age spots. "This is what you need."

When Lady Melisandra placed the flower in Francine's hand it had a pulse, like a triple-time waltz. Her heart speeded up to match the beat, and she couldn't stop her head from nodding in time to it.

Lady Melisandra chuckled.

"Exactly what you need."

Francine expected being able to say goodbye, or at least thank you. But Lady Melisandra grasped Francine's wrist, turned her hand quickly, and smashed the flower against the table. Glass shards pierced Francine's skin, making her cry out.

"Blood given for blood received," Lady Melisandra crooned.

Smoke rose up from Francine's hurt hand, mingling with the gauzy streamers. Francine blinked surprised tears away, drawing her hand up and cradling it against her chest, examining it carefully. The glass shards sank under her skin, drawing the blood with them. She shivered and felt nauseated.

What had Lady Melisandra done to her?

When Francine looked up, she stood in a very different woods with her knotted scarf and the white fiddle at her feet.

Her human fiddle was gone.

* * *

The trees—leaner, darker, more sinister here than in the fairy court—swayed with the syncopated beat Francine generated from snapping her fingers and stomping her boots as she danced across the winter meadow. At the edge she swayed as well, bending almost in two, dancing like the trees around her did, before picking up the white fiddle and carrying on with the tune.

Golden drops of honeyed liquor bobbed in the air, clustered together like a small cloud. Without missing a note Francine leapt up and sucked one into her mouth. It exploded against her tongue: sweet with a dark warmth, spiced with nutmeg and chicory. Francine laughed and twirled, hazy ropes of smoke spiraling out from her fiddle.

If any of her cousins saw Francine like this, human or otherwise, they'd think she was insane, dancing like a wild woman with no one around.

She stubbornly didn't care what they thought, what anyone thought.

She was finally able to make the music she wanted, the music she loved. She felt more complete than ever before.

Francine lived off the music, the trees, and the meadow. She coaxed sweet dew from the grass to quench her thirst and cool her off when she got too sweaty. Branches easily formed into a nest for her, rocking her gently to sleep. Honeysuckle, moon wine, and sweet berries fell into her hand when she wanted to eat.

Time seemed irrelevant to Francine. She ate when she was hungry, slept when she was tired, and danced and played music the rest of the time. Though the fairy court had felt right, it had only fit one side of her.

Here, she could be gentle and harsh, fast and slow, ride the delight she felt up into clouds of ecstasy or slide down into the depths of mourning.

She'd never given such free reign to her emotions before, though she'd always felt deeply.

The trees challenged Francine sometimes, acting indifferent to her music. Then she'd whip them into a frenzy, causing rain to lash down while thunder and lightening tore the sky apart. She suspected it was what they wanted, why they'd ignore her, to get her riled up.

Today, Francine played with rhythm as opposed to notes, knocking with her knuckles on her fiddle, finding new patterns. She'd play a melody off and on, incorporating all the parts of the song together, then focusing on just one bit or another.

When Francine reached the end and turned, she saw a figure step out from under the tree on the far side.

Francine didn't stop playing. It was her best protection.

The figure approached slowly, using a dancing step, then paused and looked around before coming forward again. It seemed as if he was the one who might spook and run away, not Francine.

She did but didn't care if he made it all the way across the meadow. She'd missed her cousins sometimes, and mourned the loss of her parents, but the trees and the wilds made up for so much.

Only when the figure drew closer did Francine realize he was a faun. From his waist down, he had the furry legs of a goat. His cloven hooves shone black against the brown winter grass. Perched on his forehead rose two small horns, starkly white against his thick curls. His eyes had that same golden gator glint that Queen Yvette's had, making Francine wary. She played to the trees, waking them to the possible threat, knowing they'd protect her if she couldn't defend herself with her music.

The faun nodded to Francine, then started to dance nimbly, bolder now that he was closer.

Trees whispered at Francine, urging her to challenge him.

Francine picked up the pace, changing the tune. The wind swirled around her, making little dust demons of fallen leaves dance with her.

The faun grinned and kicked up his heels, happy to move to her beat.

So Francine added more. A storm brewed up fast, reflecting Francine's emotions.

Why hadn't the other court accepted her like this

stranger appeared to? Why hadn't they liked the music of her heart? Why hadn't her papa?

Thunder rolled across the land.

Francine howled as she played, stomping down the grass with her heavy human boots, throwing not just smoke but blue fairy fire from her fiddle. Sparks cascaded around her, falling silently to the ground.

Without hesitation, the faun kept up, losing himself in Francine's power and song. He sweated freely, drops thrown from his body to the ground by the fierceness of his dance. He gladly went where she directed, laughing as his legs and arms moved faster, his body contorting in its attempt to manifest the music. He clapped his hands and seemed to feed the energy Francine spewed back to her, like an appreciative audience did, though he was a single person.

Francine could have gone on for days, fed by the trees and the dancer, but her curiosity eventually got the better of her. She rounded up the chorus, playing a frenzied closing before halting with three grand, drawn-out notes.

"Whew!" the faun said. He bent over, placing his hands on his knees and breathing heavily.

"That was sure something. Mmm mmm."

"It was," Francine said, finding herself grinning. She felt good and loose, like all her stored-up tension had just been flung into the creek. The storm clouds started peeling away, leaving gray skies of indecision behind.

"I'm Erastus," the faun said, extending his hand.

"You can call me Francine," she replied, taking it.

His hand was surprisingly dry given how much the rest of him was sweating. It was also smooth and overly warm, like Lady Melisandra's had been the first time she'd touched it.

Erastus brought the back of Francine's hand to his mouth for a kiss.

It wasn't like when Pierre had kissed her hand—this kiss

chased fire into her blood, quickly spreading up her arm.

Flustered, Francine drew back. She raised her fiddle again, ready to drive this strange being away.

"Aw, sweet girl, didn't mean nothing," Erastus said, ducking his head.

"Can't help it. Just in my being."

Francine viewed the faun suspiciously but lowered her instrument.

"What do you want?" she asked, deliberately being rude and not asking if he was hungry.

Her mama would be ashamed of her, but Francine didn't trust this stranger.

"Come play for me. At my court."

Francine's spine stiffened at the mention of a court. She took another step backwards.

The faun chuckled.

"I see you've had dealings with Yvette."

Then his eyes narrowed.

"No one told you there was a second court, did they?"

"No," Francine said, anger spiking through her. Of course they hadn't.

"They think they're the most special fairies of all," Erastus said, shaking his head and grimacing.

"Please, darling. Let me show you a real court. One that isn't all tied up in tea parties and fancy dresses. You can play whatever you like for us."

The offer tempted Francine.

Fairies who let her play her own music? Dancers that moved like the faun had, letting Francine direct them however she chose?

"I give you my solemn word that you can leave and come back here anytime. No tricks." Erastus stood with his hand over his heart.

Francine brought her fiddle up and played a quick tune, weaving the three notes of Erastus' name into a melody, then breaking them apart.

Erastus cringed, his back bowing as if he'd been hit.

"If you break your vow, I'll hurt you," Francine promised.

"That you will," Erastus said, straightening slowly.

Francine turned her back on the faun and walked over to the closest trees. They shifted branches down for her to take and hold.

"I'll come back," she promised.

She'd never leave these trees forever.

* * *

Erastus made a doorway that Francine easily stepped through. She almost stepped through sideways, still wanting the myth of lost time to stay true. Instead, she walked through head-on, willing to face whatever was ahead of her.

The trees on the far side were darker than even the trees that Francine had left behind. Their bare limbs didn't sway to meet her as much as try to scratch her. One large oak reached down with a branch and tried to push her into the thorny underbrush. She saw faces in their bark: mean, scarred fairies who hadn't become trees for punishment, but because they would always be around to pick on others.

Francine wasn't scared of bullies.

She brought up her fiddle and played a stilling song, the one she'd used to turn the water in the fountain in her backyard into glass, the one that she often played to settle her own trees before going to sleep.

The trees here mocked Francine, their branches shaking with laughter as they continued to try to knock her around. They started shifting their roots under the path, trying to unsettle her feet.

Glaring, Francine changed her melody to a whirling song. This caught the trees' attention. First one, then another, stopped trying to push Francine or pull her hair.

Their boughs raised and they swayed together, then apart, knocking into each other in a rough dance. The wind hooted around them, loud and obnoxious. Even the underbrush drew back in on itself, the bushes crackling and rustling in a syncopated beat.

"I knew you were something," Erastus said from behind her.

The woods settled down at the sound of his voice.

Francine finished off the tune quickly, lowering her fiddle but keeping it in her hand.

"Was that a test?" she asked, still angry.

"Good heavens, girl, no. That was just me taking my sweet, idiot time. I'm sorry I left you alone with these hoodlums."

Francine shrugged.

"I took care of them."

She reached out and stroked the rough bark of the nearest tree, unsurprised when it pricked her finger.

"They just want a taste, to get to know you," Erastus assured her.

It was more than that, Francine knew. They'd been testing her, wanting to see if she was easily cowed. She knew they'd try again. They would tease her, and try to trip her still, but they also now respected her enough to let her be when she asked.

The dirt path smoothed out under Erastus' cloven hooves until it reminded Francine of the trails in the other court. She ran her hands over the top of the encroaching branches, fingering the dead leaves, wondering what they'd look like come spring. Fog circled the bases of the trees, hiding their roots. The scent of dried winter grass filled the air, spiced with juniper, crisp and clean.

Francine was surprised when they passed what she had called the fern house. Here it was smaller, more rundown, the moss grown black and the bushes twisted.

Like in the land of the other fairy court, they climbed a ridge, then paused to look down.

Kudzu also covered this grand hall, a long raised rectangle where many were gathered. But the rough trees didn't merely stand at the sidelines: Twisted limbs reached right into the center, dancing with those gathered there. These fairies wore jeans and boots, not gowns or finery. The musicians played on a stage to the right, casting out music with a driving beat.

Francine grinned at Erastus. The lights shone with a neon glow, strange and familiar at the same time, casting double-shadows on the fairies gathered there, as if they were dancing, too.

This looked like her kind of party.

Erastus skipped ahead, as if he were unable to hold himself back, joining a group of dancers at the center.

Francine made her way to the musicians. She caught the eye of the stork-like man playing the guitar, then held up her fiddle, questioning if she could join them.

He nodded at her.

Francine listened to the other musicians for a few minutes, finding her place in the tune before stepping in, adding a frenzied descant above the main melody. The other musicians followed quickly, as did the dancers. Their hoots and hollers rang loudly through the trees, echoed back by the night creatures drawn to their light. The band gelled quickly, each anticipating the other's rhythm and tune, supporting and showcasing one after another.

When it was Francine's turn, she stepped forward and played her heart out. The entire court moved to her music. She gave them everything she had and they gave it back, loud and distorted, better than any rock band concert. She felt as though she could dance on air, the energy a solid force all around her.

Francine knew she could get used to this.

Chapter Eight

Francine danced around the stage with the other musicians. The stork-like man with the guitar leapt into the air, easily going above Francine's head. A woman with a pointed face and buckteeth like a beaver played a blood-red accordion and wove in and out with Francine. At first Francine thought the rub board man wore fancy picks on his fingers, but eventually she realized they were claws.

Though Francine was new here, had only just arrived and asked to join in, these fairies all smiling at Francine, invited her to play the lead, and happily followed her wild bridges and driving beat. They encouraged her to go faster, almost daring her, like the trees had. They'd only played a few songs together, but Francine already felt more welcome here than she had after weeks and months at the other fairy court.

When Erastus came to dance in front of the stage, the stork-like man nudged Francine, then deliberately slowed the pace a little.

Francine swallowed down her spike of anger and followed, letting him lead them to the closing chords of their current song and bring them crashing down.

The court howled their approval, clicking their claws and stomping their feet. Erastus hopped up onto the stage and addressed the crowd.

"Francine!" he called out, drawing her forward.

"Our Zydeco Queen!"

Francine had to swallow against a large lump in her throat. She lifted her chin high, then curtsied, deeply touched. She couldn't believe her luck. She'd finally found a place where she could do what she loved: Make people dance to the music of her choosing.

"Want to meet 'em?" Erastus yelled the question so everyone in the clearing heard.

The crowd cheered in response.

"I'd love to," Francine said.

Erastus looked over his shoulder, and the stork-like man started up a quick two-step.

Puzzled, Francine followed Erastus into the clearing. She was even more puzzled when he made it clear they were going to dance together.

Smiling, Francine danced with Erastus. His palms remained overly warm but not sweaty. He made it easy for her to follow, showing Francine where to go with strong hand gestures and footwork.

At the end of the song, Erastus handed Francine off to another partner. He had the snout of a pig and hooves for hands, with the body of a man. He wore a beautiful gray suit, complete with a white shirt and red silk tie.

Francine tried not to hesitate but to accept her new dance partner and flow into position. She took his warm hoof and tentatively placed one of her hands on his shoulder, sliding on the silk of his jacket.

"Julius," the pig-man said smoothly.

"So pleased you're here."

He moved with an unmistakable grace. Erastus had been a snappy dancer. Julius was more sedate and moved with an enviable grace.

"Let me know if you need anything, anything at all. I have a nose for finding things," he said with a wink.

Despite Julius' frightful appearance and beady, hard eyes, Francine relaxed. He seemed charming and she appreciated the offer of help.

Francine's next partner had tan skin and two large diamonds in variegated colors on her cheeks. Only after Francine took her hands did she realize the pattern was that of a copperhead.

The woman blinked lazy snake eyes at her and smiled with thin lips. Her hands were cool against Francine's, her skin smooth and scaled.

"Eula."

She moved more stiffly than Francine expected, but quickly, leaving Francine breathless as she was handed off to the next person.

Francine couldn't remember everyone's name, though she did try. It was exhilarating to move around the clearing like this, constantly dancing, trying to match a new partner's style. The court laughed and joked with each other, not trying to outdo each other or cut each other off. Their behavior helped Francine relax more. They all understood when she took a misstep or when they bumped into each other.

Though this court looked more frightening, they acted more like regular people and less like high school teenagers.

Finally, Francine escaped back to the stage. The musicians took turns introducing themselves: Amos, the stork-like man; Claire on the accordion; and Harley played the washboard.

Francine happily joined them, making music until dawn. She took a few more turns on the dance floor, dancing again with both Erastus and Julius, learning new steps.

It was obvious to Francine when the party started

winding down. A few hardcore dancers remained on the floor, but many had already flitted away, up the winding paths.

Amos announced that the next song would be their last. It was a quaint lullaby, a classical piece that Francine didn't know but loved instantly.

When they finished playing, Julius made his way to the stage.

"I'll show you where to sleep when you're ready," he assured her.

Francine nodded, grateful that someone had offered to look after her.

"Have fun?" Julius asked as he led Francine away from the clearing.

"More than you can imagine," Francine assured him. She took a deep breath, savoring the spicy scents of the woods. She'd expected to be still riled up, the excitement of playing still surging in her blood, but as they walked she did find herself crashing. She plodded along the path, pleased that Julius seemed to sense her mood and didn't try talking to her.

"Here," Julius said, finally stopping on the edge of a clearing.

A quiet brook ran through the trees just ahead. The wind barely rustled the grass and leaves.

Francine looked at him, puzzled, her whole body sagging with exhaustion.

Julius chuckled softly.

"Just coax some limbs down to make a nest."

"Ah," Francine said, nodding. She'd done this in her meadow, in the wild lands. She walked up to the closest tree and petted it softly. The bark didn't try to prick her this time. Instead, the tree made a sighing sound and bent over, easily arranging its limbs into a nest for her. Francine eagerly crawled in, already mostly asleep.

"Good night," Julius softly called.

"Good night. Thank you," Francine said as she curled up.

She had a brief moment of worry before sleep claimed her: Was this all too good to be true? Would the fairies revert to being petty and nasty the next day?

Then she couldn't worry about it anymore.

She could always go back to the wilds if she discovered that she hadn't found a home here.

* * *

Francine woke to bright sunlight and blue sky above her, the earth far below. She stretched and thought about what she was going to do, whether she'd try to find the other musicians for a jam, if she could find something to eat. Finally, she reached over and tickled the tree. With alarming speed it bent over and Francine scrambled to find her feet before being tossed out.

When Francine looked around, she spied Julius standing a short ways under the trees. He wore another suit, this time a more somber black, with a dark blue shirt and no tie. A solid gold chain hung around his neck, thick and rich.

"Let's find some grub," he said, his eyes twinkling.

Francine fell in beside Julius easily, walking to a clearing filled with clumps of bushes. The leaves were budding on many of them, bright green against rich brown stems.

It was the first sign of spring that Francine had witnessed.

It made her pause: Her first spring without Mama. Then she shook her head and banished those thoughts.

"Allow me," Julius said, walking over to a bush and humming at it, then placing one of the twigs between the split of the hoof on one hand and stroking it gently with his other.

Bright yellow berries formed following the passing of his hoof. They looked like candy.

Still, Francine was wary, remembering the lost afternoon with Brooks and Jacque. She took one cautiously, then nearly spit it out, surprised at its sour taste.

Julius laughed at her face.

"Let me guess. The Seelie only fed you sweet things, yes?"

"Seelie?" Francine asked. She cautiously took another berry. The sour taste remained, but more like lemon, less like grapefruit. She didn't feel any warning warmth of liquor, so she took another one.

"Child, they told you nothing. Here."

Julius led Francine out to the center of the field, trampling down some of the grass before sitting with a grunt. Francine sat next to him, nibbling on the berries he'd carried with him.

"Two courts make up the *Féerie*," Julius explained.

"The Seelie have been called the light court. I think it's because they like wearing gauze," he confided.

Francine giggled. Even the queen had wanted Francine to dress lightly, not approving of her boots.

"The Seelie are supposed to help travelers, polish shoes, and make you oatmeal when you're sick. Except that court would lead a traveler off a cliff, use acid so your shoes fell apart, and put sneezing powder in your soup."

"What happened to them?" Francine asked. She remembered the stories that Mama and Uncle Rene had told her about kindness returned for kindness given.

Julius shrugged his shoulders expressively.

"Maybe it was coming here. Maybe it's the queen. But they're not as kind-hearted as they once were."

Francine nodded, thinking. She couldn't deny that the Seelie court had a dark edge to it that made her uncomfortable. Papa had been right.

Then she shoved that thought away and asked, "So if

they're the Seelie, what are you called?"

"They call us the Unseelie. Just because we wear black instead of gauzy things, and don't hide our true nature, we're labeled *unblessed*." Julius snorted. "King Erastus is a good king. You'll find more goodness here, mark my words."

Francine nodded. She'd certainly found more passion in the Unseelie court. Some of the court had been kinder, too, at least so far. She wasn't surprised to discover that Erastus was the king. It fit him, somehow.

"How long have you been here?" Francine asked, feeling bold.

Julius grinned at Francine, showing sharp teeth. "Was born here. Grew up in these trees, near the bayou. Danced at the blood moon and celebrated every solstice. I know these byways and trees better than the back of my hoof. Never gone to the human lands."

His eyes changed as he spoke, from dark to solid black. He seemed to grow larger and his skin grew more mottled.

"Welcomed the change of the moon and the coming of the sun."

He shook himself, shrinking back down, his eyes going beady and dark again.

"Well, only when I stayed up all night. Otherwise I generally slept through the sunrise."

Francine laughed. Julius reminded her in some ways of her Uncle Rene, steady and strong, but always calling his own tune.

He'd also reminded Francine that regardless of how friendly this court was, they were still fairies, still *other*.

* * *

Francine wandered back to the fern house after Julius left, wiggling under the fallen tree branches to get in.

The burned moss felt stiff under her fingers, and she missed the smell of the sweet bushes that bloomed along side the human version.

Homesickness engulfed Francine. She missed *everyone*: Mama, Uncle Rene, Papa, her cousins, even her teachers. She wanted to eat one of Uncle Rene's hush puppies, or even some of Aunt Lavine's crawfish stew.

When she'd felt this way before, in her meadow, she'd played wild songs, either sad enough to make the trees weep, or crazy enough that everything around her danced and whirled.

That was where Francine really wanted to go. But how? No one had ever taught her how to create an arch.

Francine made her way back to the grand hall. Erastus wasn't there, but Eula was. She sat on the far side of the hall, hissing up at a tree. Francine wasn't quite sure what Eula was doing with it—making it grow, or perhaps giving it fangs.

Eula looked up as Francine approached, the diamonds on her cheeks bright red, her eyes yellow and staring.

"Hey, how you doing?" she asked, her voice more friendly than her alien demeanor.

"I was looking for Erastus," Francine said.

"No idea, hon," Eula said, shaking her head.

"Anything I can help with?"

Francine remembered that Eula was the second in line, after Julius, to dance with her. She assumed that meant something in the Unseelie court.

"I wanted to go visit my old woods," Francine admitted.

"And no one's showed you how? I swear, those men are worse than useless. Here." Eula stood and turned Francine around, so her back was to Eula's front. Eula wrapped her left arm around Francine's waist, then lifted her right hand by the wrist.

"Now cut the air. Like this."

Eula moved Francine's hand in the rough shape of a doorway.

Nothing happened.

"Ya'll know where you want to go?" Eula asked.

"You got to think of it, now, hard. It's important to know where you're going."

Francine nodded, flushed and unsure. They tried the gesture again, but still no doorway formed.

"Okay, sugar, let's try this." Eula let go of Francine and she stepped away.

Francine tried not to shiver. The snake-woman had been so warm against her back, the regular air suddenly felt chilled.

Eula looked critically at Francine for a moment.

"So, you know, air's always moving."

Francine nodded, not sure how that made any difference.

"You got to make it solid, hard enough to cut. Like weaving tree branches together."

"But how do I do that?"

Eula opened her mouth, then closed it again.

"You're a musician, right? So how would you make a note solid? I've seen you flinging sparks. This is the same thing. You can do it."

Though she smiled at Francine, her eyes stayed cold.

Francine turned away and frowned at the blank space in front of her.

How did she make her notes solid?

With passion and belief.

Francine closed her eyes for a moment, letting her longing return. She heard the notes she'd play as soon as she was in her woods again, watched them weave together into a thick braid, made up of long, silver fiddle-strings. When she opened her eyes, she made a C with her hand, imagining the braid pressed against the webbing of her thumb, then pulled the braid along. Once she got going, she could actually see it forming, solid and thick, outlining a round opening.

The air inside the outline of the rope shimmered.

Francine couldn't see anything on the other side. She knew where she wanted to go, where she'd imagined.

"See?" Eula asked. "Now don't just stand there admiring your handiwork. Get going."

"Thank you," Francine told her. She took a deep breath, then pushed her way through.

Suddenly, Francine stood in her meadow. She looked around, not quite believing that she'd managed this all on her own. She laughed. She could go anywhere now.

Why hadn't anyone in the Seelie court showed her this? Francine's ready anger came up. They'd wanted her to be dependent on them. Why had she needed the flower and the pain? Why hadn't Lady Melisandra merely shown her how to make an arch? She flexed her hand. Tiny white scars still dotted her palm. Such a waste.

Would Francine be able to get back? She turned and saw the vague outline of her doorway still standing there. Plus, even if it collapsed, she knew where she was going. She could form another doorway if she needed to.

With a grin, Francine pulled her fiddle from her back and raced to the edge of the meadow. She stood under her trees and played a welcoming trill at them.

No response.

"Aw, don't be sore at me. I'm sorry," Francine said, still smiling. She played a longer piece, a little faster.

The trees stirred slightly, but that could have been from the wind as much as anything.

Worried, Francine played a full song, driving the notes up into the air, into the limbs of the trees. One by one they began to sway, but slowly, sluggish and old.

Maybe they'd been asleep. Francine reached out to pet them, worried. She examined their trunks. She didn't see any bugs or disease.

However, more than one had silver spiderweb thread

encircling them, something she'd never seen before.

Puzzled, Francine played more. The trees just ignored her fast-driving tunes, and didn't respond at all to anything quiet, so she had to find a medium rhythm that they'd follow. She played for hours, until her fingers cramped and her legs shook, but she still felt like they'd never fully woken.

Though it broke her heart, Francine couldn't stay there that night. The trees weren't aware enough to make a nest or protect her. With regret, she told them farewell and went back to the Unseelie court.

It was dark there as well when Francine stepped through. She easily made it through the woods to the meadow Julius had shown her, and coaxed a tree into scooping her up for the night.

The next day, Julius waited under the trees when Francine rose, inviting her for food and conversation again. They ended up sitting at the base of the black walnut trees next to the meadow.

When Francine told him how her trees wouldn't wake up, Julius sighed heavily. He looked over his shoulder, as if making sure they were alone. Then he said, "It was them. Her. I bet."

"What do you mean? Who?" Francine said, hairs standing up along the back of her neck and her anger already rising.

"Yvette."

Julius spit after saying the name.

"She probably came to see you. When she couldn't find you, she punished those who had helped you. They've been put to sleep, their will stripped from them so they could tell her about you."

Francine didn't know what to say. She believed Julius, though. Maybe the spiderwebs had been the leftover residue of the magic. After a few moments of silence, while Francine clenched and flexed her fists, she finally spit as well.

"Damn her."

It was like high school all over again: When Billy couldn't attack Francine, he and his buddies attacked her locker and her things.

Julius looked around again.

"Did you hear what else she did?"

"No." Francine already felt her gut rolling.

"She tried to push her court's boundaries out. Again."

"What?"

"She's trying to increase her territory. Take over our woods."

"She can't do that!" Francine said, outraged. "These are our trees," she said, reaching out and stroking the rough bark. The bare winter branches rubbed against each other, a tinny protest.

"But what can we do?" Julius asked, giving that expressive shrug of his.

"Fight her off, sure, but we can't patrol all our territory, all the time."

"We have to stop her," Francine said. Though it might be as unfair as high school, this time, Francine had more power.

"Don't you worry, darling, I'm sure Erastus will come up with something."

"Let me know if I can help," Francine said seriously.

"They can't get away with it."

"Thank you," Julius said sincerely. "If it comes to that, I'm sure we'll find a use for your talents."

Francine continued to think about their conversation that afternoon. She made a doorway and went back to her meadow, then spent the evening coaxing all her trees awake again, one by one, getting them to dance for her in the pale moonlight.

Once they seemed back to normal, Francine spent the rest of the night practicing throwing shards of magic, thorns, and smoke from her fiddle. With a complicated, woven melody, she found she could make ropes as well.

Among the *Féerie*, fiddlers were also warriors.

Francine was going to be prepared.

* * *

"Come on, Julius. Please," Francine pleaded, not caring if she sounded like she was whining. They sat on the empty stage in the great hall. Braids of rope lay scattered next to them; Francine had shown Julius her latest trick. The trees moaned to themselves, like they carried bad news. Storm clouds covered the sky, the filtered light turning the kudzu into a pale shroud.

"No, I will not take you to the borderlands," Julius said firmly.

"It's too dangerous. Erastus will answer Yvette's challenge."

"But I could help! Wake the trees, make sure they're ready," Francine said stubbornly.

Julius shook his head.

"No. The trees can take care of themselves. You shouldn't go waking them unnecessarily. They'll just get into mischief."

One of the oaks next to the stage reached down and caught Julius' hat, carrying it far above.

"Hey!" he complained, surging up.

Francine couldn't help but laugh.

"See? They agree with me."

Julius walked over to the tree.

"Give that back." He glared up at his hat still perched on a branch far above his head, then back at the trunk.

"Now."

The tree didn't move.

Julius knocked on the trunk, first with one hoof, then the other, a complicated rhythm. The tree shimmied, then his hat fell onto the stage.

"What was that?"

"Tickling," Julius assured her.

Francine suspected Julius lied to her. Though the knocks hadn't been delivered with physical force, they'd resonated with power through the trunk of the tree.

She wasn't going to ask him to show her that.

Julius looked over at Francine. With a sigh, he finally said, "Let me go talk with Erastus. See if he'll take you to the borders."

"Thank you," Francine said.

After Julius left, Francine stayed in the great hall, playing first one quiet melody, then another.

She didn't want to wait. She didn't see why she had to. She knew she could do this. Oaks made the perfect guards. She knew that from the wilds. The pines were too mean, and the Cyprus trees were too hard to keep awake.

The problem was that Francine didn't know how to get to the borderlands. She'd never been there. She remembered what the other fairy court had been like: gentle hills, wide easy trails, and oaks that murmured and sang. She knew what this fairy court felt like, with its wild brush that always snagged her clothing, trees that grew bitter and teased too much, trails that hid and changed.

Francine imagined a place where the two types of tree met, maybe intermingled. She thought about an open meadow with sharp-edged winter grass blending into the shorter, more easily trampled grass of the other court, where cooler, crisper air met the soft, felted breezes.

The doorway formed strongly under Francine's hand, more easily than any other she'd tried. The space enclosed by the silver rope wavered and darkened, as if storm clouds lay ahead.

Magic pulsed on the other side.

Francine shivered, all the hairs on the back of her neck standing up. After just a moment's hesitation, Francine picked up her fiddle and walked forward.

Chaos reigned on the other side.

Crazy clouds darted across the sky, torn apart by scornful winds. Thunder shook the meadow, out of place and time. The trees stood shoulder to shoulder in the distance, menacing and dangerous. Smells of smoke and decay overwhelmed everything else. Insects howled.

A creature of living dust crashed across the meadow, heading straight for Francine. It was three feet high, its shape always shifting and changing. It reminded Francine of a collection of cells, dividing and dying off at the same time. Tentacles formed from the body, each moving like a snake's tongue, touching and tasting everything in its path.

Francine couldn't jump back quick enough. The thing touched her as it made its way past. Cold and wet, the dust marked Francine's cheek. Grit stayed on her face, drying and making her skin itch.

The creature turned in place, then started coming back toward Francine. In its center gaped a huge black maw. It didn't need teeth—the darkness inside it sucked in in all light.

Frantic, Francine turned around.

Her gate no longer stood behind her.

How could that be? She swung around, searching, trying to find her gate. Across the meadow, she saw a glimmer of light. She covered her ears and ran, the roaring of the dust creature behind her.

Then the glimmer moved, shifting to the right. Her gate had jumped from one place to another.

Without pausing, Francine put her fiddle under her chin and started a song of homecoming, hoping to get the doorway to stop moving. She glanced over her shoulder. The dust creature stood, unmoving, directly behind her. Then it took off to the right.

When Francine turned back, she saw her doorway had also moved much further to the right.

The dust creature ran directly toward it.

Frantic, Francine changed her tune to an old song her mother had sung to her, "Come Home to Me, Irene." She teased out the melody, trying to draw the doorway to her as she continued running straight.

At the very last moment, the doorway shifted again, away from the dust creature and toward Francine.

Francine ran faster than she ever had before. She held her fiddle in one hand, the bow in the other, and she pumped her legs to make it to the gate first.

Glancing to her left, Francine saw that the dust creature had gained speed. It growled and made a deep grinding sound, as if chewing gravel. The smell of rotten eggs and burnt sand rolled before it.

Francine flung herself through the doorway head first. She slid across the kudzu of the grand hallway, scraping her chin and her belly. She would have scraped her hands but she held them up, out of the way, trying to protect her fiddle.

"You went anyway."

Panting, Francine turned over. Every muscle ached. Her cheeks felt as if stinging sand had abraded them. She had to blink her eyes more than once to clear the grit from them.

Julius stood above Francine, glaring down at her.

"I tried," Francine said. She coughed, surprised at how rough her voice sounded. Her throat ached. Had she been screaming and not even realized it?

Julius squatted down next to Francine.

"You can't go someplace you've never been," he said gently. "Or your mind makes up somewhere to go."

"That wasn't a real place?" Francine shivered. Was

something that awful all in her own head?

"I can't say." Julius gave his typical shrug.

"It might have been someplace you imagined. Or it might have been some other border. Like between night and day. Or madness and sanity."

Francine nodded.

"Won't try that again."

Now she understood why Lady Melisandra hadn't just formed a doorway for her. She'd actually created a world for her, her own place out in the wilds, then sent her there.

"Good." Julius extended one cloven hand to Francine, helping her sit up. That prompted another coughing fit. When she finished, Francine drew her knees up to her chest and leaned her forehead against them.

"I think the air was bad there. There was this creature there…."

Julius grew very still. Then he said, "Come on. We need to go."

"What?"

"Let's get you to the creek." Julius tugged on Francine insistently. "You need to get cleaned up. And healed."

Slowly, Francine stood. She felt ancient.

Julius guided Francine through the woods to where, in the human world, Francine had always caught crawfish with her cousins. Here, the creek ran like a small river, wild and fast. Julius directed her to a small bay where the waters ran still.

Francine lifted her fiddle to warm the water, as she'd done in her own woods. She was so exhausted, though. It felt like too much effort.

"Don't bother," Julius said, taking her fiddle from her weak arms.

"Just walk in."

After taking off only her boots, Francine slipped into the water. The cold shocked her into wakefulness. She ducked her head under the water, rinsing her hair. The waters turned silky in her hands, cleaning better than shampoo.

Francine washed her cheek where the creature had touched her several times. The first few times her skin stung, then it began to heal. By the time she got out, Francine felt considerably better. Not completely recovered—exhaustion still darkened her vision and her lungs ached—but she'd stopped coughing. Her clothes were soaked and dripping. Julius hummed under his breath, drying them with a *whoosh* of sweet air.

"Swear you won't try something stupid like that again," Julius told Francine sternly.

"I swear," Francine said solemnly.

"You said there was some kind of creature. Was it—bloody or something?"

"Nope. Just the opposite. Dusty and dry. Multiplying and dying."

"Darling, what did you say your mama died of?" Julius asked suddenly.

"Lung cancer."

Francine stilled, suddenly making the connection.

The creature had looked like a collection of cancer cells, grown three foot high and wild.

"Don't ever go back," Julius said.

"Never."

At least now Francine knew why the other fairies had never taught her how to make a doorway. It was too easy to get lost in a nightmare.

"Why didn't Eula tell me the dangers?"

She had said it was important to know where you were going, but not why.

Julius nodded, thinking.

"Could be she thought you already knew. Plus, most fairies land in the swamp or get soaked in brackish water. We don't have as much imagination as your kind, you know.

Or maybe she meant it as a prank, thinking you'd sometime fall into the bayou, not realizing where you'd get to."

Francine swallowed around the lump in her throat. Of course the Unseelie would play tricks, like the Seelie. Eula probably hadn't meant anything by it.

She hadn't meant for Francine to almost be killed by her own nightmares.

Or at least Francine told herself that.

* * *

Francine woke slowly, shivering in the cool spring air. She was going to have to find more moss for her nest, or weave the branches tighter, or something to keep the winds away at night. Maybe after breakfast she could take a snooze in the sunlight, let it soak all the way through her skin and into her bones.

Both Erastus and Julius waited under the tree when Francine finally made her way to the forest floor. Erastus was bare-chested, his skin naturally tanned, his curly hair gleaming as brightly as his polished black hooves and white horns. Julius wore a more casual suit today, pale blue, with a rich golden tie, looking chic as always.

"Morning—afternoon?" Francine asked, uncertain if she should bow or not. Was this a formal visit? Though she often saw Erastus with the rest of the court, at night when they'd all dance together, he'd never sought her out again, not since she'd come to the court.

"You hungry?" Erastus asked with an easy grin.

It was as good a greeting as any.

"Sure," Francine said, falling easily into step behind the two men as they led the way down a path Francine hadn't seen before. It made her smile more, thinking how the forest responded to all of them, putting up barriers when it was teasing or wanted to play, or making things easier as well.

This path led straight to the marshes, turning into a high

trail of packed dirt as they got closer to the water. Good thing Erastus was with them: Francine knew the land might disappear and leave her in stinking swamp water the first time she came here on her own.

They reached a wide grassy harbor, where sweet moss had overgrown the roots of a gnarled tree. Twisted, dark green bushes with bright pink berries grew on all sides, their thin leaves twitching in the slight breeze.

Erastus handed Francine a handful of the berries.

She hesitated before she took any, not knowing how strong they'd be. But she still took a few. He was the king, and she'd been raised right by Mama.

The slightly smoky taste surprised Francine; she'd expected something sweeter from the bright color. They tasted like lettuce roasted on the grill with butter. She ate only one more before her fingers started tingling.

"I know you're wondering why I asked you to come with me today," Erastus said.

Francine nodded, putting the rest of the berries to the side, not willing to float away.

"I'm going to ask you to play tonight," Erastus said seriously.

Francine sat up taller. She'd never seen the king look so stern.

"I want you to give it everything you've got. And I mean everything, Francine. I want you to play, and play *hard*. Then I trust you to pull it back when give the signal."

"Yes, sir," Francine said, pleased that the king had such faith in her.

"Tonight, well, tonight's gonna be a special night. And I won't lie to you—you're a big part of why it's gonna be so."

Francine didn't understand what Erastus meant, but that was okay. She would find out. She trusted him as well.

* * *

Francine twirled like a madwoman, sending sparks flying from her fiddle. She didn't care who they struck. The court danced like never before, puppets on her strings. Francine made them leap and grovel, howl and sing.

Power filled Francine, causing her to strut as she played. Even the king followed her tune. She could crush them all with a simple melody, or raise them higher. Anger mingled with her giddiness—she'd never been allowed to use her full strength before.

She understood why the Seelie had been frightened of it.

Her music could cause madness.

Yet, she still resented their fear, their ties.

If only Francine could bring this ability with her to the human world. She'd have her revenge on Billy and the others from high school.

The courtiers had lost their human appearance. Creatures from daydreams and nightmares filled the space: men and women with the heads and claws of wolves, bears, snakes, foxes, pigs, panthers, and goats. A few had lost mobility, turning into oaks, willows, Cyprus, and reeds. Shambling mounds of rocks and moss circled the floor.

Finally, Erastus gave Francine the signal. She took the song to the end, played a rousing, flourished finish, then held the band back from leaping directly into another tune.

A deafening roar rose from the court.

Francine's skin tingled from the magic racing through the air. She beamed at them.

She'd done this. Affected everyone so they could only hear her music, their hearts still pounding with her beat.

Erastus leapt onto the stage. He shouted over the continued howls.

"They've taken our woods! Stolen our trees! Diverted our streams, diluted our magic! Are we going to let them get away with that?"

The force of the shouted "NO!" forced Francine to take a step back. It felt like a solid wall of sound crashing into her. She hadn't been aware of all the other court had done. It made her more angry. She added a trill of her fiddle, high-pitched and frenetic.

"What are we going to do?" Erastus asked.

"Fight! War! Kill them all!" came the shouted replies.

"Now, hush," Erastus demanded. He glanced at Francine, who played a quick, calming melody. The court grew quieter, though they were far from motionless, shifting in place as if they couldn't contain themselves.

"I am asking the court to declare war on the Seelie," Erastus said, suddenly formal.

A sigh sounded through the hall, like the spring wind that came from the gulf, open and free at last.

"What say you?"

"Aye," Julius said, stepping forward.

"I say we war."

His mottled skin shone with power, and his eyes had turned black. His beautiful suit jacket hung in tatters, torn to pieces with his frenzied dance and magic.

"Yes," hissed Eula, also stepping forward.

"Yes, yes, yes, yes," said one after another of the court.

"War?" Erastus asked one last time.

"War!" they shouted back as one.

At Erastus' nod, Francine started a battle march.

"War!" the court chanted in time. This time they stomped their feet and snapped their claws and teeth in time, precise and angry.

Joy filled Francine, though still tinged with bitterness.

She couldn't confront those who'd caused her pain most of her life.

However, she'd still get her revenge on the others.

Chapter Nine

After they finished breakfast the next morning, Julius asked Francine, "So, darling, you want to learn to fight?"

Though Francine still felt tired from all the playing the night before, she still nodded eagerly.

"Yes."

"Then let's go to the borderlands. Not to wake the trees—that's Erastus' job. But the air is more full of something there. Just stay near me," Julius directed her.

"And if I tell you to run, run."

"But—"

Francine could defend herself with her fiddle. She already knew how to do some things with it.

Julius turned to face Francine.

"Darling, if I say run, that means there's something comin' that I can't handle, not by myself, not even with you. I ain't scared of the Seelie, and neither should you be. But I value my skin. We wouldn't be running less it was really bad. A few Seelie warriors?" he snorted. "We can take them on our own. A slew of them, though?"

Julius shook his head.

"I understand," Francine said, nodding. She needed to

trust Julius, trust that he could judge a threat.

Francine just wasn't used to trusting anyone but herself.

Julius went through the arch first.

Francine followed right after, but still arrived a few minutes later. She eagerly looked around, trying to find a landmark or two so she could come back here herself later if she wanted.

It was easy to see the actual border: the trees changed abruptly, the Unseelie side darker and more twisted, the Seelie side more fair and willowy. The trees from both sides loomed at each other, as if jealously guarding their realms, their branches not touching. A line of stumps ran behind the line of trees on the Unseelie side, sickly and gray.

How dare the Seelie take over the Unseelie woods that way? Francine's blood boiled. She pulled out her fiddle and sent a mournful tune to the stumps, hoping to soothe their pain.

The music bounced back at her, oddly disjointed.

Puzzled, Francine tossed another melody out, a smooth jazz piece that her trees in her woods liked, but that the Unseelie trees didn't. The Unseelie trees growled and shivered, but the stumps settled down, soaking in the tune.

"If you're finished saying hello?" Julius asked, a sly smile on his face.

Francine swallowed nervously and looked around again. She nodded but didn't say anything, coming over to stand next to Julius, moving away from the stumps.

The stumps weren't Unseelie trees. They were from the Seelie woods.

It was the Unseelie trees that had killed them, the Unseelie that had expanded their border.

It didn't matter, Francine told herself. They were probably just doing a counter attack, to balance out trees they'd lost in a different place along the border, where the Seelie had attacked first.

"Such a shame, no?"

Francine made herself nod.

Julius didn't realize she could tell the difference, and she wasn't about to tell him.

"So what should I play?"

"Don't you have a favorite ass-kicking song?" Julius asked with a grin.

Francine nodded, and started in with "Wild Nights," one of her favorite zydeco songs. It had a beat that reminded her of going down the highway in her cousin's truck in the middle of the night, way too fast, the wind blowing her hair like crazy.

When Francine got to the chorus, she started flinging the bass notes out. They flew like black darts, scattering in front of her.

"Sharper," Julius commanded.

Francine nodded, and played shorter, staccato notes, pounding down on them with all her strength. The notes grew spiked heads, like wicked arrow tips, the ends glowing red-hot.

"Those are good," Julius said. "Now what else can you do?"

Francine looked at Julius, puzzled. Wasn't he supposed to be teaching her?

Well, maybe he needed to know what she already knew.

So Francine showed him the sparks she could throw, as well as the rough winds she could make circle. Julius gave her a few suggestions, but nothing that Francine couldn't have figured out herself.

When Francine finished the next piece, she lowered her fiddle and looked at Julius expectantly.

"Don't you have any specific music I should play?"

Julius shrugged.

"I'm not a musician. I'm a warrior. I just know it needs to be hard and fast."

Francine swallowed down her disappointment, remembering how much she'd learned from her time with Pierre. She really needed to study with another fiddler.

"Now, just because I don't know your tunes don't mean I don't know how to fight. The general attacks you have are good, but let's make 'em more personal. All right? And later we'll work on defense too."

"Okay," Francine said, raising her bow and fiddle again, waiting.

"Imagine someone who's wronged you," Julius instructed.

That was easy. Billy's smarmy smile came instantly to Francine.

Julius touched her arm and gestured.

Billy suddenly stood in the clearing. Francine saw him clearly. She directed her attack at him, setting him ablaze.

"Good, good. Now others."

Laura and Karyn. The teachers who had never said anything, had never helped.

Even Papa, who'd denied Francine her heritage, forbidden her from knowing her kin.

Francine tore all of them apart with fire and rage.

When Julius finally called a stop, Francine found she trembled and panted as if she'd been sprinting. She nodded, collapsing onto the ground, sitting with her forehead resting on her drawn-up knees.

Julius sat next to Francine.

"You're doing well, darling," he said, his voice gravely.

Francine snuck a peek at Julius, slowly moving her head but not raising it. He also looked exhausted and pale from the amount of magic he'd used making her imaginings real.

"How much longer do we have to prepare?" Francine asked, worried that she might not be strong enough in time.

"Until the fall equinox."

"What?"

Francine suddenly found the strength to raise her head. "But that's months away!"

"The timing of these things is of great importance," Julius told her.

"Erastus wants more than to just win a battle or two."

Francine looked over her shoulder at the Seelie woods.

"What's he going to do?" she whispered, suddenly wary that others might hear.

"Oh, don't you worry," Julius said, with a vague motion toward the trees. "They've already negotiated the results. If we win, we hold their queen for one hundred and one days."

"What will that do?" Francine asked, puzzled.

"Strengthen us," Julius assured her. "After we hold her, we get to bind her power."

It didn't make sense to Francine. Then again, the formal declaration of war hadn't either. The two sides had met for days, negotiating, while she and the rest of the court had watched tensely from the sidelines.

"What happens if we lose?"

"Same thing. Only Erastus will have to go with them." Julius looked away, his back tense and his jaw tight. "We'd lose power and influence. It wouldn't be pretty."

Francine swallowed and nodded. She remembered what Queen Yvette had done to Pierre for the merest slight.

What would she do to Erastus?

Julius patted Francine's knee. "Don't worry. They won't win."

"You're right. They won't."

Francine would do everything in her power to make sure they didn't.

* * *

Francine slept, dreaming of honeyed wind that teased her as she played, swirling around her and carrying her floating notes away on a golden breeze. The trees danced and swayed to her tune, sensitive to every phrase, the perfect audience.

Then the wind snapped at her, dropping the notes and carrying her name.

"Francine!"

Startled, Francine sat up and looked around. The late summer afternoon had grown warm, the air wrapping around her like a soft blanket. A lazy chorus of bugs called from the underbrush. Clear blue sky winked at her from above the green ceiling of leaves.

"Who is it?" Francine called out, stretching slowly.

"It's me." Pierre stepped out from behind a tree.

Francine scrambled to her feet, putting her fiddle under her chin instantly.

"What do you want?" she asked, prepared to defend herself, her heart beating hard in her chest.

Pierre kept his hands wide to show they were empty, though Francine could see the head of his fiddle poking over his shoulder.

"I wanted to talk with you."

"Are you here to join us?" Francine asked. It seemed reasonable to her, given how Queen Yvette had tortured him.

"What? No."

Pierre shook his head.

"I been watching you practice the other day. With Julius. You're very good."

He paused, then added, "The best I've seen."

"Yes, I am," Francine said, pride drawing her up, making her stand taller. Both Julius and Erastus had told her that as well. She knew it was as much her anger as her technique.

"You can't fight," Pierre said.

"What the hell are you talking about? Of course I can fight."

"It'd be better if you didn't."

Francine snorted. "Better for you. Why shouldn't I?"

"The Unseelie can't win."

Francine restrained herself from bashing Pierre with a string of notes, driving him off his feet.

"Why not?"

"You don't know what all they're doing. What they're really after."

"They want more power," Francine said, shrugging.

"It isn't like we'll kill Yvette after we win."

Francine deliberately didn't use the queen's full title.

"It's more than that. If the Unseelie win, they'll have more power in the human realm. They'll make people darker, meaner, more chaotic."

Remembering Billy, Laura and Karyn, and the others who had hurt her, Francine laughed.

"People there are already like that."

She let her fiddle rest by her side.

"You don't really know what they're like. How mean and cruel. Like the Seelie were to me. And to you."

"Queen Yvette—" Pierre started, then stopped.

"She's done that to you before, hasn't she?" Francine said.

"And maybe again after I left."

"But she isn't dark and twisted like the Unseelie!"

"Just cruel and twisted."

Pierre looked to the side.

"It's one of my own powers, you know. To be a tree."

"So she's taking something you love and twisting it!"

Francine thought she couldn't be more angry with the Seelie. She'd been wrong.

"Why do you stay with them? What else have you given up?" she asked, remembering Brooks and Jacque accusing Pierre of lessening himself.

"Please," Pierre said softly. "Lower your voice."

He sighed.

"*Chérie*, there's always give and take."

"What do you get?" Francine hissed.

For the first time, Pierre gave Francine a smile that was a little wild around the edges.

"This."

He dragged his fiddle over his shoulder before Francine could stop him and started playing a soft, fast tune.

The air grew thicker and the leaves golden. A new forest shimmered into being. The trees grew tall, there, right up into the sky. The smell of rich earth and fresh mulch washed over Francine. She could taste the sweetness of this place. Francine nodded, feeling the pull on her own heart. It reminded her of the woods Lady Melisandra had created for her, with meadows and trees fit for a fiddler.

"No place else is home," Pierre said softly, letting the music die. His personal woods faded away.

Francine gave an unwilling nod. The call of her own forest filled her, the trees that she'd claimed as her own.

"We're still going to fight you. And win," she said stubbornly.

"I suppose it doesn't matter to you that the Seelie didn't attack first? That the Unseelie did? Sending their trees into our territory?"

Francine bit her lip, remembering the borderlands. She'd wondered about that. Julius had told her that Queen Yvette had raided them first. Had he lied to her?

"You're right. It doesn't matter," Francine said quietly. The fairies were still going to war.

Pierre sighed. "Doesn't blood mean anything to you?"

"What do you mean?"

"You know your papa and your uncle have joined the court, right?"

"I don't believe you," Francine said hotly.

"Your uncle is sick. He has something like what your mama had. The wasting disease."

Francine's face suddenly felt hot while her stomach hollowed out with fear.

"No," she whispered.

"He says he's lucky—they found it early. If he lives with the Seelie, well, time moves differently here. He'll live longer."

Francine nodded numbly. She'd used the healing waters of the land herself. She doubted they could cure cancer, but they might slow the process. She shivered, remembering the creature from the land she'd made up.

"Come with me. I'll show you."

Francine shook herself, then sneered at Pierre.

"If you think I'm going to walk with you into the Seelie court and be captured, you're a fool."

No matter how much she wanted to see Papa, and Uncle Rene, she couldn't just go with him.

"It isn't a trick," Pierre assured her.

"Look."

He slowly laid his fiddle on the ground.

"This is my heart," he said stepping back.

Pierre stood completely defenseless before Francine.

"I swear by my fiddle that what I'm saying is true: that the Unseelie started the war, that they'll gain more from it than you know, that your papa now lives in the Seelie court, and that I'll take you there to see him, and return you here, safely."

Sweet chords filled the air, music from Pierre's heart.

Francine recognized the truth of every word, striking like sunlight through the trees.

"Then take me there."

* * *

Pierre tried to lead the way along the trail. But the path worked against him the whole time: sending up roots to trip him, snagging his pants on thorns, making curves and twists unexpectedly.

Francine thought about suggesting she walk first, but seeing the how hard it was for Pierre, who'd always been so graceful, made her grin.

Until it finally occurred to Francine that when she got to the Seelie woods, she was likely to have as much trouble.

"Here, let me walk first," Francine offered.

"No, we're almost there." Pierre paused and looked back at Francine.

"I'm surprised the path doesn't attack you as much. You're not Unseelie."

Francine shrugged.

"They've learned to respect me," she said, indicating the trees.

They still teased her sometimes, but she also teased them right back, with tunes that whipped them into frenzied dancing, causing them to tear up their roots and some of the younger saplings to fall over.

"Will I have the same problems when I get to the Seelie woods?"

"No," Pierre said, shaking his head.

"You're part Seelie. It will still recognize you."

They passed the fern house, crouched on one side of the trail, all the leaves surrounding it curled and black, as if burned from the inside out. Like in the Seelie lands, it rose far above Francine's head. Here, though, it looked haunted.

"All the lands are just layers, one on top of another, aren't they?" Francine asked quietly.

Pierre nodded.

"You could think of them that way. Or like old film, where the images from one negative bleed into the next. If the Unseelie win—they'll bleed into every other layer, more than they already do."

After they walked a bit more, Francine finally had to ask,

"So where we going?"

"Do you think I could just walk into the Unseelie lands?" Pierre asked, amused.

"Now mind, I'd been to the court before. But both Queen Yvette and King Erastus have put up barriers to stop people from coming and going as they please."

"Wait. Do you mean I can't get to my woods anymore?" Francine asked, stopping.

Erastus had promised her that she could always get back there.

Pierre turned to look at her.

"You mean the place Lady Melisandra created for you?"

At Francine's nod, he continued.

"You should be able to get there. Probably. That place—it isn't completely real. It's *your* place. The place that's formed out of you, for you."

Francine's palm suddenly tingled. The one that had been cut by the glass flower. That was why the lady had cut her hand, mingled the glass shards with her blood. So the place would be hers, and only hers.

"But I don't know if you could come back here, afterward. The barriers—they might make it impossible."

Francine pondered that as they made their way down the other side of the ridge. She may well leave sometime and not come back. She didn't want to, but it was good to know she could.

That made her ponder something else.

"Have you seen Brooks or Jacque around at all?"

"No," Pierre said.

"They haven't been around since—ah."

He stood nodding, rubbing the back of his head.

"You think they can't come home."

"Would they want to?"

Pierre gave a bitter laugh.

"As much as they might hate their mother, those boys'll

do what's right. Can you get us there?"

"Yes," Francine said, the memory of their golden afternoon still bittersweet.

"Let's get them first. Then I'll take you to see your papa."

Francine looked around, placing trees and the stream in her mind. She wanted to be able to come back here, to the Unseelie court, on her own, if necessary. If the barriers would let her through.

Pierre whistled softly at the doorway Francine drew.

"Who taught you that?"

"My friends here," Francine said hotly.

"You know the dangers, right?"

"I'm not a little girl."

"You ended up in the swamp," Pierre said.

Francine glared at him, the memory of the cancer-like creature she'd created fresh in her mind. She opened her mouth to say something, then shook her head.

"After you."

"Ah, *ma chérie,* ladies always go first."

"Fine."

Francine forced down the shiver of fear that threatened to overtake her—what if she'd judged wrong and was taking them to another awful land? But she still made herself step through.

The air was the first thing Francine noticed. Instead of merely humid, it reeked of rank mud and rotten wood. All the kudzu hanging from the trees had turned gray and tangled, mixed with the Spanish moss. No birds sang. The underbrush held no leaves, merely twisted branches.

Francine whistled to the trees, and only got a soft moan in response, brittle as deep winter ice.

The place was dying.

Francine whistled again. The trees not only sounded thin, but scarce. She wondered if the land had shrunk.

Pierre finally stepped through. He looked around, dazed.

He took a short breath, as if the air here wasn't enough for breathing.

"Come on," Francine said, more relieved that he'd shown up than she'd care to admit. She grabbed his hand and tugged him along the path.

It didn't make any effort to impede them; it didn't interact with them at all.

Before long they reached the meadow. The grass stretched out, black and burnt. It dissolved into powdery ash, like graveyard dust, when Francine brushed against it. The sky held shroud-white clouds from end to end. Francine shivered from the cold wind pushing against her.

On the far edge of the meadow, Brooks and Jacque lay side-by-side on a tattered, moth-eaten rug. They looked peacefully asleep.

Francine wondered if they were trying to dream things better.

They also looked a lot less human. Instead of clear, beautiful skin, Brooks now had scales across his face. Rough brown hair covered Jacque's, his nose had turned black, and floppy rabbit ears grew out of his head.

Gingerly, Francine reached down to shake Brooks awake. He opened eyes that held a golden gator hue, like his mama's.

She didn't see any recognition in those reptilian eyes.

Luckily, she snatched her hand away before Brooks snapped it with his sharp teeth.

"Brooks! It's me! Francine. Your cousin."

With a rumbling, deep voice, Brooks replied, "I don't see why you calling me kin. You're his kind," he said with a sweep of his paw, indicating Pierre.

"Not mine."

"They've been dreaming too close to the spirits," Pierre said quietly.

"I still got legs," Brooks said, shoving Jacque hard to

wake him. "Not too close yet."

"Come back to the Seelie court," Francine said. "We'll help you."

"Don't need no help."

Jacque sat up beside him, looking bewildered. His eyes had turned dark and liquid. He opened his mouth to say something, but all that came out was a chittering sigh.

"That's all right, Jacque, old boy." Brooks laid a heavy, clawed hand on Jacque's knee.

Jacque turned large, scared eyes to Pierre, who in turn nodded and pulled out his fiddle. He played a bright, courtly dance. Francine quickly followed, not trying to speed up the tempo for once.

Brooks shook his head once, twice. The scales faded, and the glitter in his eyes dimmed. "Not going back to that bitch," he said bitterly.

"Can't stay here," Francine pointed out.

"Could if you'd stay," Brooks said, sighing as he shrugged back into his coat, his strong shoulders no longer pressing at the seams.

"Can't stay."

Jacque cuffed Brooks on the back of the head. "We're going."

His face still held patches of fur.

Brooks hummed and a streak of sunlight broke through the clouds. For a moment, the air turned golden again. But he couldn't spread the light out, couldn't maintain it. Clouds quickly recaptured the day, turning everything gray.

"Fine. We'll go."

It took three tries for Brooks to find his way to his feet.

"Don't blame us for fighting against you, though," he said, pointing at Francine.

"You won't win."

"And don't blame us for that either," Jacque said darkly.

* * *

Pierre found them a hole to the Seelie lands, into the backwoods where the trees grew on top of each other and the air bustled with late summer insects.

Francine walked easily along the smooth dirt paths, sometimes reaching out to drag her fingers across the rough bark trunks of the familiar trees. Her heart ached for the gentle breezes and whispered winds.

These woods were much closer to her dreams.

Brooks walked more upright with each step, and Jacque regained his teasing voice. It seemed to Francine that they didn't remember what had happened after a short while. Julius had said they didn't have much imagination. Did that mean they didn't have much memory, either?

Francine wondered what would have happened if she'd been trapped in her world like they'd been. Would she have turned into a tree, like Pierre? Stretched her arms up tall over her head and grown roots? Arranged her branches so the wind would make music when it blew against them? Or grown white wings and turned into a stork, content to forever dance under the trees that stayed?

Pierre pulled Francine to the side at the top of the ridge, looking down on the great hall.

"Let them go first. Then I should go. The queen will be too excited about her sons to look around elsewhere, see who else might be in her lands."

Francine nodded and stayed to the side, hidden among the shrubs. They respected her here and didn't try to prick her or slyly snag her clothes. The trees gladly granted her shelter, puffing up their trunks and growing darker in the bright sunlight.

As soon as Brooks stepped into the grand hall, a voiceless cry rang up through the trees.

Francine didn't see where Queen Yvette came from, but she was suddenly there, hugging her boys to her. At least as much as they suffered her to.

The rest of the court gathered quickly. Francine didn't understand why their graceful steps as they came running up made her sad, as if she'd lost some grace herself, but they did.

A laughing voice made Francine's heart catch in her throat. She'd recognize that laugh anywhere.

She searched the edges, finally finding Uncle Rene walking into the hall. He moved like a solid mountain through the fluttering *Fée*. Francine found herself drawn to him, standing without realizing it. She wanted to go to him so badly, to hold his big hands in hers, to listen to his stories.

Papa stood beside him.

Francine recognized the crane in him now, with his proud head and white, tufted hair. She'd thought of him as a bear before, growling with anger. Now, he had black eyes and a pointed stare, cutting through those around him.

It hadn't just been anger, but stubbornness.

Together, they laughed with the fairies, clapping Brooks on the shoulder as if he'd been the one who had freed himself.

When Papa stepped on the stage, touting a black fiddle, playing alongside Pierre with ease, Francine felt torn in two. Uncle Rene stepped up as well, playing a beautiful golden tenor saxophone that she'd never seen before, the notes deep and low. They laughed and joked with each other, tossing the melody back and forth.

Francine wanted to be on stage with them. Wanted to make music with them in this wild place, to have them follow her tune and to maybe play with theirs.

They both looked young, younger than she remembered, without a care weighing them down.

They skipped around each other, dancing lightly on their feet.

Francine could listen to them for hours, pouring out music as easy as breathing.

Everything was easy with them.

And that was the problem.

Francine's fingers tingled and her breathing grew short as her rage rose.

How dare they forget Mama so fast?

Francine remembered her every day. She played her heart out and her rage for Mama being taken so young. How could they play such lighthearted songs? How could they make such easy music?

Even in her lighthearted tunes, Francine still layered an undercurrent of hurt and anger.

Had Mama been just a dream for Papa, and was this now the only place that was real?

Francine left before she did something stupid, like pull out her own fiddle and start a fight. She marched back to the edge of the woods, the trees pulling back from her, no longer a comfort.

It was easy to draw the doorway back to the Unseelie, to the dark woods and twisted paths. They matched Francine's heart, the hatred she felt.

No barriers withstood her rage.

Only when Francine was back under the familiar trees did she pick up her fiddle. Her first song tore up roots and bushes, as well as cast fire in spiraling circles around her.

Francine swore to never forget Mama. Never.

And when the battle came, Francine also swore she'd make Papa and Uncle Rene remember as well.

Chapter Ten

Francine waited with the rest of the Unseelie court in the raised hall. Excitement buzzed over her skin like electrified ants. Even the trees swayed anxiously, their twigs quivering.

The first battle would start soon, very soon.

Francine stood with the musicians. They looked practically dowdy compared to the other groups, as their attire was closest to human, with sensible shirts, pants and vests. Their instruments were the flashiest bit about them.

Francine had her bone-white fiddle, ready to rain fire down on the Seelie, while Amos' guitar looked like he'd grown it out of a black crystal. Claire's accordion was all pearl and ivory, sleek looking despite its bulk. Harley's washboard had red designs painted on it for the battle, sharp-edged, spiky patterns.

The warriors were the other ones who didn't look like much. They wore black cloaks darker than a root cellar at midnight, and had bright red paint striped along their arms, faces, and legs.

Francine wondered if the paint was magic or something, because it didn't look like much, not like armor or really like it'd provide much protection at all.

The dancers who stood beside the warriors looked ethereal, as if they'd float away on a strong wind. They wore majestic purple and blue, wrapped in thin gauzy strips around their bodies and legs. The ends of the strips swirled as the dancers moved their arms, or fluttered when they lifted up a leg to stretch.

Amazing gold and silver ropes, strung with gems and pearls, hung around the necks of the priests and priestesses, hiding their plain blue smocks. Francine wondered if they represented the richness of the kingdom or, if when the sun struck, they were merely supposed to be blinding.

Finally Erastus arrived. He wore a powdered wig that curled around his neck. Francine had seen a TV show with old-fashioned British royalty wearing something similar. Fine white fur edged his great cloak, while blood-red silk lined it. Brilliant gold- and silver-embroidered brocade made up the rest of it.

Erastus shone brighter than all of them combined.

"Friends!" Erastus said, clapping his hands and stomping his feet to get the court's attention.

"The day has finally come! To avenge ourselves on our enemy, and to finally have the influence that is rightfully ours!"

The court hooted and cheered, Francine joining in. Her heart beat hard in her chest. Finally, she would have some of her revenge.

"Now, I know ya'll are as eager as I am, but this has to be done right, if we're gonna do this at all."

The words quieted the crowd effectively.

Francine focused all her attention on the king, pushing down on her excitement.

"The priests must go first, set the pace," Erastus said, nodding in their direction.

They bowed and curtsied in response, their heavy ropes clanking as they moved.

Francine had never seen the Unseelie court show so much respect toward one another. It made the butterflies in her stomach gain weight as the seriousness of this was impressed upon her again.

"Dancers, I've know you've got some great moves. Show 'em everything you got."

The dancers twitched and shimmered, giving aerial bows.

Francine wasn't sure how they'd fight—they looked the lightest armed of all the groups. Most of the fairies who made up the dancers didn't even have long claws or fangs.

"Now, you musicians. I don't have any worries about you."

Francine grinned. Her excitement rose again, making her shiver.

"Just don't hold back, and you'll be fine."

Francine curtsied with the others, her head held high.

"Warriors, my brothers, as always, the cleanup is left to you."

They shared a knowing chuckle.

Despite the heat, Francine shivered. She'd never heard a laugh sound so menacing.

"Today, I want you to clean up *everything*. Lick their bones dry. Understood?"

The warriors roared their acceptance, and kept roaring, the howl building through the top of the clearing and out through the woods.

The sound struck Francine in the center of her chest. She shivered again, glad she fought with them, not against them.

Erastus caught Francine's eye and nodded.

Francine fought down the prideful smile that threatened to take over as she brought up her fiddle, trying to hide how pleased she was that Erastus had asked her to play again.

She listened to the cadence of the swelling growl, then added to it, shaping it, giving it focus.

The warriors easily followed Francine, breaking off their continuous roar into a recognizable beat. They started stomping their feet and clicking their claws in counterpart.

Francine nodded to the other musicians. They picked up the melody easily.

The rest of the court joined in with their own shrieks and growls. The priests clanged their metal ropes together, while the dancers flew higher, tumbling through the air, doing impossible leaps and flips.

Julius waved at Francine from his place in the middle of the warriors. Francine almost didn't recognize him without his suit. His skin was a mottled brown and white, his chest solid and barrel-like. He looked like he could power a mountain. He lifted his hoof in a bouncing motion, raising it higher and higher.

Francine nodded and backed down from the war chorus slowly, subtly adding higher notes and making the music lighter. Amos on the guitar joined her as did Clair on the accordion. Soon they played a straight march, but still with a bouncing tune. It sounded like Mardi Gras music.

"This way!" Erastus said. He'd sketched a huge opening, strung up between the arch of two trees. The court danced through as if at a parade, following the order Erastus had laid out.

Francine had no fear stepping through the gate. Though it was inconceivable that they'd lose, she knew how to get back.

She would not lose this home, too.

* * *

The sun shone brightly on the other side of the arch, bringing more warmth to their fervor. Tall grass with knife-like blades separated the two armies. Water encircled them, kept them crowded close in their camps. Rows of trees marked each end of the field, providing comfort and shade.

At first, Francine thought they stood on an island, until she saw the shore beyond them shift. It wasn't an island: They went to war on a floating mass of marshland.

No wonder the land was so green. It had been freshly raised from the water. Francine had heard stories about the marsh turning this vibrant after storms had flooded the swamps.

Though Francine longed to see the other army, to get a glimpse of Papa, Uncle Rene, or even Pierre, she made herself stay under the trees, away from them. She'd see them soon enough, when they battled and she won.

The Seelie priests came out from under their trees first, coming toward the Unseelie camp. They looked like they were on their way to a party, dancing to an unheard beat as they took the field. Like the Unseelie, they wore plain blue smocks underneath an amazing number of ropes of jewels. Mixed in were colorful Mardi Gras beads. Many of them wore masks as well, made of leather and feathers, making them more fantastical.

Then the Unseelie priests went out, also dancing, but to a song full of smoke and a sultry beat.

Both sets of priests stopped when they reached the center, a few feet apart.

They puzzled Francine. She didn't see either group carrying any weapons.

Francine took a step back with the rest of the court when a priest of the Seelie court let loose with a brilliant bolt of pure light.

An Unseelie priestess caught it easily, laughing. She shaped it into a long spear and tossed it back.

Suddenly the air filled with volley after volley of light coming from both sides. The air sizzled with the brilliance.

Francine looked anxiously from one side to the other, trying to see who was throwing what, when.

She finally had to hold up her hand and cover her eyes

when it grew too bright.

At the first curdling scream, Francine automatically reached for her fiddle.

Amos grabbed her wrist, hissing, "No. We'll get our turn."

Francine nodded and pushed down on her sudden fear.

Her ready anger rose, but this time, it was toward herself for being so naïve.

Neither the king nor queen would be killed during this battle—but no one had told her that others wouldn't be.

The scent of burnt hair filled the clearing.

Francine had to swallow down bile when she realized it wasn't just hair, but skin as well.

The air thundered as the Unseelie and the Seelie unleashed more power. Tremors shook the ground, but it wasn't like it was dancing. Dust and smoke rose, making it even more difficult to see.

All the hair on Francine's arms and along the back of her neck stood up. She thought uneasily of the firework displays at New Year's, brilliant silver stars flashing higher and brighter. But this wasn't anywhere near as friendly as that.

Before Francine could really get a sense of the battle, the brilliant lights stopped. Ash and dying embers drifted down.

The Unseelie bowed and backed away as the Seelie stood their ground. The outcome was obvious.

Bitter defeat made Francine stand up straighter.

The priests may have lost, but she was damned if the musicians would.

* * *

Francine talked with Amos, Claire, Harley, and the other musicians for a while, making battle plans now that they'd seen the field, talking about the order they'd stand in, the songs they'd play.

All the while, out of the corner of her eye, Francine could

see covered bodies being carried away. The Seelie had lost some people, but the Unseelie had lost more.

The sickening scent of burnt flesh and the tang of ozone still tinged the air.

The Seelie dancers strode out once the field had been cleared. Francine recognized Brooks in the front of the line. He looked fully recovered, his skin clear again and his eyes bright. His outfit barely covered him; really, it was just a couple of golden straps across his chest, and a few fluttering ends that covered the other important bits.

If they'd been meeting under different circumstances, Francine might have enjoyed the view.

Then the Unseelie dancers went out, skipping lightly, almost floating through the air.

Francine bit her lip with worry. The Seelie dancers all looked more muscular.

However, Erastus had come closer to the front line of the trees, looking out over the field, and he now stood grinning.

All the dancers together stamped their feet, raising a strong, steady rhythm. Without warning, the Unseelie took to the air, spinning and leaping.

It took Francine a moment to realize that some of the dancers had moved *past* the Seelie, and now they were surrounded.

The Unseelie danced over each other, throwing their partners at the Seelie, bowling them over. Dancers kicked, scratched, and clawed each other, a grotesque parody of a dance.

It was obvious the Seelie dancers had only trained with each other, blocking and dodging the heavy blows they tried to give. They were completely unprepared for the Unseelie using a punch as a starting point to climb over the Seelie, kicking them in the head on the way back down.

When a Seelie dancer did land a punch, it could be devastating. Blood flew, as did teeth.

Bones shattered with a brittle sound.

But they kept dancing.

Francine didn't see Brooks fall. However, at the end of the battle, he was carried away.

Though the officials declared the dance a tie, Francine knew the Unseelie had won a slight advantage.

She told herself that was good.

* * *

Pre-stage jitters walked up and down Francine's spine, but she refused to shiver again. The pit of her stomach rested uneasy, as if she'd had too much coffee and not enough food. At least the air was finally clean again.

The other musicians showed the same strain, tapping fingers and toes, bouncing up and down, playing small riffs and bursts of melody.

Erastus and Julius came up as they assembled.

"Make us proud," Erastus told them.

Papa had always told Francine the same thing.

Finally, the signal to approach the field came. Francine walked to the point at the edge of the woods, standing proud and tall. The other musicians lined up behind her. Harley started a steady beat on the washboard. They marched out to the field in a V formation with Francine in the apex.

The Seelie came out from their trees, but they played parade music, bopping as they marched, rolling out into a loose line.

Pierre stood at the center of their group. Papa was to his right. They all wore clean white shirts, shining with fairy light, and vests in every color Francine had ever imagined.

Papa looked—grim, Francine decided. His eyes still held a twinkle, though, as if he was enjoying this. His vest was as white as his shirt, lined with black piping, just a little bit of decoration to make him stand out. But it was all he needed.

Francine finally picked out Uncle Rene. He stood a few

lines back, wearing a powder-blue vest. He'd lost weight, Francine saw. A lot of weight. But he looked healthy enough now.

When Pierre lifted his fiddle, he glanced at Francine, as if he were going to lead.

Francine had to laugh.

"Glad you haven't lost your place in the court, Master Fiddler," she called out bitterly.

Before Pierre could get off a single note, Francine and her band attacked. No scales or easing in, just a full-on rush of war music.

The sound slammed into the Seelie, and they scrambled to keep up.

Francine almost felt sorry for them.

The Seelie stayed in their loose line, playing together well. Francine once looked beyond them to the court that stood just under the trees, bobbing their heads.

But they didn't have Francine's anger, or her training.

Francine began sending volleys, strings of notes with blunted heads whizzing into the other musicians, making them drop the beat, lose their rhythm. They valiantly tried to play through, so Francine aimed a little closer, searing through clothes and singeing hair.

At the same time, Claire and Harley kept up the beat, a defensive curtain that protected them all.

The Seelie line took a step back.

Then they rallied, as Francine knew they would. They'd talked about it before the battle.

She let them get two steps closer before she floored at least half the Seelie musicians with the first concentrated thrust, all the music from the band focused *through* her.

And Francine was just getting warmed up.

The Seelie got off a few rounds, easily deflected by Harley on the washboard, the unyielding beat blunting and turning them.

Then Francine attacked again, a solid wedge of music, forcing the Seelie back, step by step, across the field.

Papa tried to rally the Seelie as they faltered, moving in front of Pierre to face Francine directly. His eyes were no longer soft. Sweat gleamed along his forehead.

Power pushed into Francine as the music swelled behind her. She remembered destroying the false images Julius had shown her.

A cool voice inside Francine told her she could do this. *Set him on fire.*

Francine focused all her music on Papa, all her anger and frustration, throwing out sizzling notes.

Papa's clothes burned, as did his hair.

But Papa wouldn't stop.

He kept playing against her, fiddling like mad, protecting himself and trying to attack.

Finally, Francine sent a volley at Papa's hands. It wove in and under his defenses. He let go of his fiddle, surprised. Francine kept playing, turning her attention to Pierre, ignoring the fact that Papa had suddenly grinned at her.

Francine didn't want to admit it, but Papa was proud of her.

* * *

Without question, the musical round had gone to the Unseelie. They had a few injuries—nothing bad, a few scorched fingers—while half the Seelie had to be carried from the field.

Francine stayed in the center of the field, watching, working to keep all emotion off her face. The air still buzzed with the notes they'd played.

At least all the musicians she'd attacked were still alive.

When the last were gone, she turned and marched away, head held high, leading the rest of the Unseelie off the field.

Only when Francine reached the camp off the battlefield

did she realize just how exhausted she was. Clammy sweat stuck to her back. Her fingers cramped and ached. At the same time, she was filled with nervous energy, unable to sit down and rest. She wandered through the groups, the dancers stretching to keep their muscles from cramping up, the priests and priestesses polishing their soot-covered ropes of jewels.

The other musicians were either passed out on the grass or as wired as she was, tapping foot or fingers, still rocking with that unheard beat.

Francine sat down next to Amos, who handed her a smooth twig. The pair of them sat and beat out complicated rhythms. It was oddly soothing, and Francine felt herself start to relax.

The roar of the warriors drew Francine back up to her feet. She swayed, but made herself stand up straight. She couldn't crash. Not yet. She had to watch the warriors take the field.

Unseelie warriors covered a third of the field. Francine hadn't realized they had that many warriors. The Seelie warriors covered just as much. If she had to guess, she'd say at least one hundred in each army.

She wondered if they weren't all from the court—if others, from the outskirts and wilds, had joined them. If this was a way for them to gain power and rank.

The Seelie warriors looked small in comparison to the Unseelie.

Francine hoped it wasn't a trick, like the Unseelie dancers.

All the warriors wore the same types of outfits, though the Seelie wore both red and black paint with their cloaks and claws.

The war cry of the Unseelie made all the hair on the back of Francine's neck stand up and sent cascades of goose pimples across her shoulders.

She couldn't help but take a few steps back.

A stomping beat began in the back ranks, making its way forward.

Francine recognized the song, just from the rhythm: It was the same beat as the war music Erastus had her play for the court, when they'd declared war.

The Unseelie lost even more of their human appearance, turning fey and deadly.

Francine knew the Seelie went through the same transformation. She made herself stay and watch.

Growls, howls, and clicking claws drove the beat. Francine's fingers itched to play her fiddle. She knew it was strictly forbidden. She still found herself stomping the ground in time, quietly snapping her fingers, unable to stop herself from joining in.

Francine cheered when the warriors surged forward, thrust by the swelling sound.

Her joy died quickly.

Though the dancers had physically attacked each other, their battle still had a form, a context, a dance.

This was pure war, not violence refined.

Pierre had warned her. So had Papa.

The *Fée* were not human.

Even showing more of their animal form, they were too beautiful to look away from. They tore into each other, not holding back. Snarling growls and pained yelps rang out from the field.

More than one death keen set Francine's hackles up.

No one on the sidelines could tell who was winning. The figures were too intertwined to be distinguishable, and the warriors all dressed alike. The battle shifted toward one camp, then the other.

Francine caught sight of a huge boar. The smooth power of his muscles and his mottled skin told her it must be Julius. He grappled with a large tree-man. Julius caught hold of his opponent's arm, put up one foot, and *pulled*.

Julius fell back, surprised, when the arm came off in his hoof. The heat of battle still on him, he hit his enemy again with his feet, causing the tree man to topple over.

With a hard swallow, Francine sternly told herself not to vomit.

When the boar brought the arm up and tore off a piece of muscle to eat, all the blood drained from Francine's head. She swayed where she stood.

Brooks had joked about the Unseelie eating their young.

Maybe he hadn't been teasing.

The spell finally broke and Francine could turn away. She wandered, not seeing where she was going, getting as far from the field as she could.

A complex beat attracted her, and Francine found herself standing near the other musicians. Some now slept on the sides. She threw herself on the ground and tried to force the images from the battle out of her mind.

Cries, screams, and growls from the battle still waved through the air. Francine curled herself into a small ball as if trying to protect herself.

The Unseelie had been good to Francine. They'd trained her well—she couldn't help but remember Papa's proud smile.

Francine shivered again.

You didn't eat your own kind.

* * *

When a rousing cry went up from the battleground, Francine uncurled herself and made herself stand up and join the rest of the Unseelie at the edge of the field. She still felt exhausted, and her stomach hurt as if she'd been beaten. Her mouth tasted of soot. She held herself stiffly, knowing that tears were waiting to ambush her.

Four of the Unseelie warriors carried Queen Yvette in a

crude cage of bamboo. The cage swayed as they danced—it wasn't very well constructed, just loosely bound with strips of palm leaves. The queen could have escaped at any time.

But Queen Yvette stayed seated, right where she was. She was bound by honor to be the prisoner of the Unseelie for the next one hundred and one days.

The queen held her head high despite the jostling. She looked right through Francine as if she didn't recognize her.

"So high and mighty," Julius said quietly. "We're going to show her what's what."

Francine jumped. She hadn't seen him approach. She glanced at him. His red body paint had been smeared, and added to, with blood. His face was mostly human, but his teeth were still too long; his eyes, too wild.

"We will," Francine said, making herself agree. However, she also made a promise to herself to visit the queen in her prison when she could. Maybe even sneak her something to make her stay more comfortable.

It wouldn't be too hard.

Julius gave Francine a toothy grin, then moved on.

Francine held herself very still, keeping a smile on her face.

Julius moved like a panther.

She couldn't afford for him to turn against her. She shivered despite herself, remembering the tree-man and his blood.

As the warriors left the field, Francine looked over at the Seelie camp. Pierre, Papa, and Uncle Rene stood with the other musicians in a knot, staring at the queen.

Francine didn't wave goodbye. She couldn't. All that blood the fairies had spilled stood between them.

Papa did catch Francine's eye. He nodded.

Francine nodded back.

Anger and grief fought inside her.

The grief won and she turned away, eyes stinging,

following the fairies she'd chosen back through the portal, to the dark woods and wild lands.

Chapter Eleven

A party had already started in the Grand Hall by the time Francine stepped through the gate. Amos, Harley, Claire, and the other musicians stood on the raised stage, playing a fast, rocking song. The dancers stayed in a tight group at the foot of the stage, leaping into the air and twirling each other as if they'd never suffered a defeat.

The rest of the court mingled and chatted, growling and cheering. Flutes of golden wine passed from hand to hand, as well as berries of all colors, bright and potent.

Francine didn't feel like playing, dancing, or talking. Despite the driving music, her feet felt leaden. Even the cool evening air couldn't revive her. She was happy the Unseelie had won, but too much had happened for that joy to be pure.

Slowly, Francine made her way to the edge of the platform, saying hello to a few members of court before stepping onto the forest trail.

Before Francine took three steps, Julius appeared in front of her.

"Good evening," he said gravely. He'd wiped most of the paint and blood from his torso, though he hadn't dressed again in one of his suits.

His face and teeth were mostly human, but his eyes remained *Fée*—black and wild.

Francine stopped herself from jumping when he reached out to touch her elbow.

"You did well today, *ma chérie*."

"Thanks. So did...so did the warriors," Francine made herself say.

"We just cleaned up, as Erastus asked us to." Julius smiled with obvious pride.

Francine felt her stomach churn and swallowed quickly. She was *not* about to be sick in front of him.

"Not gonna join the party?" Julius asked, pointing to the raised platform with his chin.

"I just—I can't. I'm exhausted," Francine said, which was the truth.

"I understand," Julius said nodding.

"But you do need to get here early tomorrow. The king wants you to attend Yvette's imprisonment."

Francine slowly nodded.

"Of course."

"The king wants you to help fetter her," Julius further explained.

"Why me?" Francine asked. For all her power, she was still a new comer to the court.

"You'll see," Julius said with a soft smile—the softest Francine had seen in a while.

"Go. Sleep. Talk with the trees. Be back here tomorrow before noon, yes?"

"Okay."

As Francine turned to go, Julius stopped her, one tentative hoof on her shoulder.

"You made me proud today, darling."

"Thank you."

Francine knew she needed to say something more. She

was so tired. The words came slowly.

"It was your teaching."

"Thank you," Julius said. "But it was still your first battle."

Francine suddenly swayed, remembering the stench of burnt flesh, the bodies carried from the field, an Unseelie fox licking the blood off his hands.

"Yes. Go," Julius said, pushing Francine's shoulder, setting her to move again.

"See you tomorrow."

Francine nodded and left. She didn't run—she didn't dare—the paths were never that forgiving. Still, she made her way as quickly as she could to the grove she called her own.

Before Francine had called out, the trees bent over, letting her catch at their branches and pulling her near.

It wasn't a soft embrace, or remotely human.

Francine stayed with her face pressed to the unyielding tree trunk, leaking quiet tears until the whispering of the leaves soothed her enough to turn away. She only had to crawl a foot to reach the nest the tree had made for her.

Despite her exhaustion, racing thoughts kept Francine from sleeping.

What was she going to do?

She'd thought she hated Papa, but she really didn't. She'd thought she loved the Unseelie, but now she wasn't sure.

And what did the king want with her in the morning?

The trees had no answers for her. Neither did the wind.

The ache in Francine's heart felt as hard as if a weight pressed against her chest. She would give anything, even her precious woods, to talk with Mama one more time, to get her advice.

Instead, there was only restless sleep and unresolved dreams.

* * *

Fairies filled the floor of the Grand Hall, pressed tightly together, all turned toward the far end, waiting. They wore somber robes that dragged along the grass, brilliant gowns that swooped out around them, suits cut tight and fitted to show off broad chests and shoulders. Many of the women wore their hair piled high, with jewels, flowers, and fairy dust woven in.

Francine felt shabby in her solid human boots, jeans, and shirt. But Julius hadn't told her any different. Maybe she should have guessed though—the Unseelie were here to watch their enemy imprisoned.

Why did Erastus want her to fetter the queen? Maybe it would be a good thing. If she knew how the locks worked, maybe she'd be able to loosen them, or something, to give the queen respite.

Not to help her escape. No.

Francine awkwardly pushed herself forward, making her way to the front of the Grand Hall, where the king's throne stood. Fairies grumbled around her, but they let her pass.

Queen Yvette sat, still and poised, in her bamboo cage.

Julius had transformed himself again, as if vanquishing the warrior who'd been there the day before, wearing a peagreen silk frock coat that shimmered with fairy lights over an off-white, ruffled shirt. He gave Francine a polite smile when she caught his eye, then motioned for her to come forward. Suddenly, the press of people ended, with the ones closest to Francine stepping to the side, a path cleared for her.

Uncle Rene would look great in that outfit, even despite how much weight he'd lost.

Francine shook her head. She couldn't afford to think about her human family now.

"Good, good," Julius said, catching Francine's hand and giving the back of it a quick, formal kiss.

"You look perfect."

Francine glanced at her casual clothes, then at Julius, then at the rest of the court. "I do?"

"Trust me," Julius said.

Francine kept the smile on her face through sheer willpower.

"Of course," she managed to reply, swallowing down her shock.

Until Julius had said those words, Francine hadn't been able to put her finger on what had changed so dramatically between yesterday and today.

Francine didn't trust them. Any of them.

Not Julius, not Erastus, not even Amos and Claire.

It wasn't that Papa had been right. The Unseelie just weren't human, and Francine was only now starting to realize what that meant.

A doorway shimmered to life beside Queen Yvette.

Francine turned, startled, but Julius was nodding his head, smiling.

Erastus came through the gateway, prancing on his goat legs. Unlike the rest of the court, his chest was still bare. He did wear a magnificent black-and-gold cloak that swirled with a life of its own. A small silver circlet wreathed his dark curls, making him look like a prince. His horns glowed with fairy light, weird and startling.

Behind Erastus came four warriors, dressed in red paint and cloaks.

Francine choked down her sudden fear. She made her hands stay still by her sides instead of reaching for the fiddle strapped to her back.

The warriors scared her now.

Francine worked hard to keep her trembling to the inside, to not show it in her face or stance.

The four warriors carried a heavy wooden box, made of long planks, dirty and scratched, like it had been dug up recently. It wasn't big enough for a coffin, and it was shaped square. The ends were pegged together, like an old-fashioned jewelry box.

Francine would bet no gems lay inside.

Something about the box made Francine want to squirm, as if spiders were crawling up and down her spine.

Something was wrong with that thing, something bad that didn't belong in *Féerie*, like chainsaws come to cut down the trees.

"My friends!" Erastus called.

The court settled immediately, shushing each other. Silence wove its way up through the trees.

"It is only through you, my people, that this day is possible!"

Francine expected cheering, but the fairies remained eerily silent.

As one, the fairies in the front row, closest to the king and that box, had all stepped back.

None of them looked at the king.

They all stared at the box.

"Today, today is the start of our greatest triumph! Our influence shall grow, stronger than ever before! We will be the directing influence of all the worlds! They will all dance to our tune!"

A soft sigh went through the crowd, as if they were accepting their fate.

"Release the Seelie queen! Bring her forward!" Erastus demanded.

Grinning, the four warriors went over to the bamboo cage. They shook it, growling, as if daring Queen Yvette to shrink back from them.

The queen continued to stare into space. However, she no longer looked serene—merely blank, stone-faced. Her gator eyes didn't blink as the warriors suddenly pulled the walls of her cage apart.

Erastus went over to Yvette, offering his hand to help her rise from her knees. She took it without looking at him.

"See their queen!" Erastus said, bringing her forward, their hands held high as if part of a dance.

"See her here, in our power!"

Julius leaned over to Francine.

"Open the box," he said. "And take out the fetters."

Francine blinked. Her spine stiffened.

What kind of fetters gave off such a feeling of wrongness?

She didn't want to get anywhere near them. She looked at Julius, biting her lips together so she wouldn't just tell him no.

"Go on," he said, smiling at her.

Either he wasn't afraid of them, or he didn't feel them.

Refusing to show how scared she was, Francine made her way across the stage to the box. The lid was hinged with wood and leather, not metal. The dirt was just age, not soil. And the scratch marks looked like ordinary use, not like they'd been made with claws.

Francine touched the top of the box lightly, ready to draw her hand back if anything growled or moved.

The box felt surprisingly solid.

Too solid.

What did that mean?

Francine glanced over her shoulder.

Julius was no longer smiling.

She was taking too long.

Taking another deep breath, Francine threw back the lid, holding herself ready to jump back.

Though the box was easily three feet long, all it contained were a pair of black iron wrist cuffs with a chain between them. Instead of a ratchet, like modern handcuffs, loops on the edges of each cuff overlapped, held together with a pin.

Francine checked the corners of the box. Nothing sat there, poised with fangs, ready to attack her. Still, she only used one hand to snatch the cuffs up.

The sudden stinging in Francine's hand made her nearly drop them again.

Francine shifted the cuffs from one hand to the other, looking at her reddened palm. She didn't see an obvious mark, where she'd caught her palm on an iron burr. Plus, the other hand now stung. She examined the cuffs. The metal felt rough under her fingers and the cold of it sank quickly into her bones.

The metal never warmed in her hands.

When Francine turned to the king, he looked uneasy as well. His words continued to be brave.

"See what we have brought from the human world!"

The crowd finally roared, loud and fierce, even those closest to Francine.

"See how we will take her power!"

Suddenly, Francine understood. The box didn't belong here. It wasn't from *Féerie*. Neither were the cuffs.

In all the stories Mama and Uncle Rene had told Francine, cold iron hurt the *Fée*. But the stories had it wrong. In the human world, iron had little effect. Only here, in *Féerie,* could it bind and bleed.

Of course the king had wanted Francine to bind the queen. She was the most human, the only one who could hold the fetters without horrible pain.

Julius walked over to where Francine stood.

"You must use them," he said quietly. He wasn't looking at her, but at the dark metal in her hands.

"Now," he added, cupping her elbow and bringing her before the queen.

Francine knew she couldn't refuse. The warriors would tear her to pieces and drink her blood if she tried to walk away.

Papa wouldn't be proud of Francine for this.

"I'm sorry," Francine said, eyes downcast as she reached for the queen's left wrist.

Yvette didn't say anything, though she hissed quietly as Francine fastened the cuff.

When Francine looked up, she saw that Queen Yvette had grown ashen under her dark skin.

"I'm so sorry," Francine repeated as she put on the second cuff.

Though the queen had been cruel to her, Francine wasn't heartless. She didn't want to hurt the queen like this.

A cheer went through the court as Francine stepped away.

Queen Yvette closed her eyes and her shoulders fell forward as she hunched.

The court jeered and laughed.

Francine wanted to look away. Shame washed through her.

Revenge didn't taste very sweet.

When Queen Yvette opened her eyes again, they'd turned as white as her hair. Her stoic look returned, but lines now crossed her smooth forehead and curved around the corners of her eyes. She held her mouth in a firm line, as if to stop herself from showing more emotion and grimacing.

Francine could only guess how much pain Queen Yvette was in.

"Let the imprisonment begin!"

The giant live oak just beyond the platform groaned and the ground began to shake. Francine looked left and right, but the rest of the court stayed where they were.

A hole appeared at the base of the tree. Its sweeping branches lifted off the ground. The warriors pushed the queen back and back. She didn't look behind her, but took one step after another.

A root moved, tripping the queen. She fell backwards,

gripping the side of the hole with both her hands, fighting her captors.

Roots and limbs wrapped around the queen, then pierced her arms and torso, through her shoulder and above her hip. Bright blood marred the queen's white gown. She screamed in pain.

The Unseelie court howled louder.

The tree sucked the queen back, down into the hole.

Even out of sight, Francine heard Queen Yvette's pained cries. The tree trembled as it fought to draw the queen deeper under the earth.

Even after the hole disappeared and the trees' shuddering had died down, Francine still heard Queen Yvette's screams in the muttering of the wind.

* * *

Francine escaped the Great Hall as gracefully as she could. She couldn't escape quickly. Too many of the court came up to her, to shake her hand, wanting to touch the hand that had so bravely touched the black iron. It struck Francine again just how much they perceived her as an outsider: family, but never the same.

Their beautiful court clothing couldn't hide the fact that they were *Fée*, different.

Inhuman.

It wasn't until Francine got back to the grove she called hers that she realized she couldn't stay.

Under the constant whispering of the leaves came that single tremor from the great oak, a muted, constant scream.

Desperate, Francine shaped the gateway to *her* woods, the ones shaped out of her need and blood, that Melisandra had sent her to.

As Francine moved her hands down the edges, the center broke.

Frustrated, Francine tried again. She spread the magic a

little thicker, but it wouldn't stick.

Francine forced herself to take a deep breath. She even pulled her fiddle from her back, plucking a quick arpeggio just to calm her nerves. The wood and the strings also calmed her, the quick scent of wood and polish.

The third time was the charm. Francine formed the doorway, then hesitated. What if she'd drawn a gate to the wrong place?

Squaring her shoulders, Francine went through the doorway. She'd battled her own kin. She could get back if she had to.

Everything looked normal to Francine. She took a deep breath, then tried to take a step.

Francine's feet stuck to the ground. Deep mud lay beneath the grass of the meadow. If she stayed, it would suck her down.

Without hesitation, Francine pulled out her fiddle and played an uplifting melody, fast enough to raise the dead and maybe her little piece of land.

It took a while for the ground to dry.

Francine didn't know if it had started sinking while she'd been gone, or if her tears had soaked into it, threatening to drown the place.

As soon as Francine could dance easily along the path she did, racing to her grove of trees.

The trees swayed in greeting, sleepy but not dulled as they'd been before.

Francine played a song of greeting, then another, playing with her favorite partners. They swayed and danced with her, their leaves twirling in the talkative wind.

It didn't take too long before Francine realized she was exhausted. Her fingers trembled, skipping notes. Between the battle and Queen Yvette's imprisonment, she felt drained, emotionally and physically.

Francine reached for the nearest tree, intending to nap

in its branches.

Only when Francine had laid down in the soft nest the tree had made for her did she feel the tremor.

The echoing screams from Queen Yvette touched her trees here, as well.

Pierre had told Francine that all the worlds were just reflections of human world. If the Unseelie won, their influence would be the greatest in the human world.

Humans were already petty and mean. Francine had experienced that first hand at school.

Would the Unseelie make them even more so?

Francine climbed as high as she could. The thinner branches didn't transmit Queen Yvette's pain as much.

Though Francine didn't think she'd sleep, she eventually did, her dreams full of her own heartache and Mama dying again, her own tears mingling with the queen's.

* * *

Francine.

Her name echoed through her spine, creeping across her skin, flowing up over her shoulders and into her chest.

Francine, darling.

Still groggy, Francine blinked open her eyes. No branches blocked her view of the pale blue sky. She peered over the edge, wary. The tree she'd slept in had grown taller over night to protect her, cresting the rest of the woods, thinning the constant screams. The sky ended sharply on all sides, cut off by trees.

Nothing existed beyond what she saw.

No wonder Pierre had called it a bubble world.

Finally, Francine looked down.

Julius stood beneath the tree, one hoof resting on the trunk. He'd called her *through* the tree, not out loud.

Francine reached the ground and stood there, arms crossed, glaring at Julius.

How dare he come into *her* woods?

Julius frowned back at Francine. "What are you doing here?"

Wasn't it obvious?

"These are my woods."

"But you agreed you weren't coming back until the war was over."

"I thought—that it—there are more battles?"

The pit of Francine's stomach dropped and she suddenly felt lightheaded.

Francine couldn't watch the warriors battle again. Or the dancers. Or anyone, really.

"No, no," Julius said.

Julius put a solid hoof on Francine's shoulder, anchoring her. His palm was warm as her papa's had always been.

"Raids, only," Julius assured her.

"But darling, now is *more* dangerous to be here, away from the court, than before. You never know when a troop of Seelie warriors may blunder through."

"They couldn't just come. They'd have to know how to get here."

Francine tightened her arms over her chest, holding back her fear.

"The bubble worlds are all joined." Julius spread his hooves wide, then made one hoof pitch and swerve like a snake, approaching the other.

"And some are good at finding trails between them, traveling to ones where there's people living."

"I'm sorry," Francine said after another minute of expectant silence.

She seemed to be saying that a lot.

"I didn't mean to worry you."

Julius merely nodded.

"I knew where you'd be," he said softly.

"Now, we have to get going. We have just a bit of time

before the raid, and I'm needing your skills."

"But—" Francine paused, unwilling to step out from under her trees. They might carry the echo of Queen Yvette's screams, but they were still her home.

"What do you want me to do? What do you do in a raid?"

"The Seelie, as you know, sleep in separate houses, not sensibly in trees that would protect them. We're just going to show up at one of their 'neighborhoods.' Surprise a few. Maybe take some prisoner."

"Like the queen?" Francine asked, her voice strained. She would *not* help the Unseelie bury more of the Seelie. The trees would be untouchable.

"Child, no, not like that. We have a nice wooden cage for them. Takes too much magic to hide someone like we hid Yvette."

"Hide?" Francine asked.

"Well, you and I, my dear, and the Unseelie, we know where she's at. Everyone else just gets an echo of her. They can't find her, find the tree that binds her."

"I see." Francine said quietly.

When Julius walked away from under the trees, Francine followed him across the meadow.

Maybe he had been worried about her safety. He'd certainly sounded happy to see her.

Or maybe Francine hadn't hidden her feelings as well as they'd hidden the queen, and now Julius didn't trust her, either.

* * *

Francine had expected to step through the arch and be in the Unseelie woods.

Instead, she arrived at the borderlands. She recognized the stumps of the Seelie trees; instead of a single line, they now filled an entire field. The air held the scent of ash grown cold. Francine strained to hear the usual birdsong, but even the rustling of the trees was muted.

"Today, I want a different type of music," Julius instructed. "Slower. Gospels. Hymns. Music for picking crops."

Francine knew the types of tunes he was asking for.

"Slave music," she said flatly.

"Didn't you hear? They're now just calling us servants," Julius said blandly.

"I heard," Francine assured him. There'd been an uproar during a school trip they'd taken—a tour of an old plantation—and the guide had never once used the term 'slave'.

"Why?"

"I want to see if I can shape it," Julius said.

Francine didn't understand, but she was curious what Julius wanted. She pulled out her fiddle, starting with "The Meal Time Call."

"Slower," Julius directed.

"The Long Man in the Field," seemed to be the right tempo, just slow enough, but still rhythmic.

Smoke wriggled in front of Francine, dancing like an old fat woman, all hips and shoulders.

Julius shaped it, pushing it together, then drawing it out, like how Aunt Lavine made taffy.

"More slow."

Francine changed the tempo, and the smoke grew thicker.

Abruptly, Julius changed his movements, splitting the smoke into parts, then braiding together the strands.

"Stop."

Francine quit, mid-note.

A black rope, heavy and out of place, fell to the ground.

Without touching it, Francine knew it had some of the same qualities as the fetters she'd used to bind Queen Yvette.

"How did you get iron into it?" Francine asked.

"How do you think?" Julius asked, glaring at her with disapproval.

Magic. And slave songs. Of course.

Julius grasped the rope, then let it go. He frowned at it, then motioned for Francine to come over.

With a sigh, Francine strapped her fiddle onto her back and picked up the rope. It slid, alive in her hands.

It was going to hurt any Seelie it bound.

"Does it have to be like this?" Francine asked quietly.

"Of course," Julius said dismissively.

With a sigh, Francine coiled the rope and gathered it up on her shoulder. It lay there, a heavy weight, harder than stone, and cold.

Julius reached out and ran his hoof along one end, then left it there, as if to prove it wasn't that bad.

The set of Julius' jaw, and the red of his eyes, told a different story.

Chapter Twelve

Four warriors waited for Francine and Julius when they stepped through the portal from the borderlands into the Great Hall. They wore regular clothes but had red paint on their faces. Francine shuddered, then glanced around. No one else stood there. She'd never seen the hall so empty. The tree limbs that flowed out toward the center looked like barriers; even if she tried, she couldn't get away.

Francine started when a cold, wet finger touched her cheek.

"What are you doing?" she sputtered, though she knew. Her stomach sank and fear pressed through her as Julius put more red paint on her other cheek.

"Preparing you for the raid," Julius said.

"I'm not a warrior," Francine hissed.

"Don't matter. Everyone battles and raids."

"I don't want to," Francine pointed out through clenched teeth.

"Is your revenge such a puny thing?" Julius mocked.

"Of course not," Francine automatically replied.

However, her desire for revenge was tempered with a desire for *fair*.

What had happened—was still happening—to Queen Yvette and to all the dead Seelie...it seemed out of proportion.

Francine knew she couldn't explain that to Julius.

Fair was a human concept.

"Two groups," Julius told them after he made the arch. "Ignatius with Francine and me."

Ignatius gave a wide grin at that.

Francine thought she recognized him—a happy bear of a man. While she watched, his teeth grew longer.

Francine looked away.

"Good hunting!" the other group called as they stepped through the gate.

Francine still carried the rope. It pricked her shoulder through her shirt and made her uncomfortable. The welcome weight of her fiddle at her back couldn't counterbalance it.

The sun still sat high above the Seelie woods, making everything warm and bright. Francine felt herself relax, though she guarded against showing it. She loved the Unseelie woods, loved their passion and fire, how they'd tease her and force her to respect them.

She loved the Seelie woods, too, loved their gentle ways and talkative leaves. The paths were easy here.

Maybe it was okay for her to take an easy path for once. Not fight. Was that something Mrs. Delacroix had once said?

"Perfect," Julius said. "They're all still asleep."

"Did we just move back in time?" Francine wondered. It had been mid-afternoon in the Unseelie woods.

"What, you crazy?" Julius asked. "Where would you get that kind of notion?"

Francine pressed her lips together, not wanting to answer.

Julius snorted.

"No. Worlds just move through time different sometimes."

The leader of the second party of warriors caught Julius' attention with an tentative wave, then they went to the right, deeper into the woods.

"This way," Ignatius said, the innocence of his grin marred by his very sharp teeth.

Francine followed. What else could she do? Dread knotted her stomach. Who would she bind—and hurt—with the rope she carried?

Fear made Francine shiver and dried out her throat when she recognized where they were.

Lady Melisandra's house.

"Go knock on her door," Julius instructed.

"Don't be an idiot," Francine snapped, despair sharpening her tone.

"She knows I'm with you. She'll know something's wrong."

"Maybe ya'll decided to switch sides and came back again," Julius proposed, stroking his chin.

Francine snorted.

"She's not an idiot."

Julius looked curiously at Francine, then back at Lady Melisandra's door.

"Fine," he said after a moment.

"Then we break in. And hope we can grab her before she retaliates."

A shiver of fear ran down Francine's spine. She knew how powerful Lady Melisandra was.

"You ready?" Julius asked Ignatius.

The warrior shivered, then shook his head, like a dog shaking water from his fur. His face grew more hairy and his snout pushed out more, making him look more like a bear. He also puffed up, not growing taller so much as wider.

The hairs on Francine's arms stood up.

Ignatius crackled with power, like an electric ball. He nodded.

Julius ran for the stairs, Ignatius hot on his heels.

Francine had to follow.

Julius didn't pause when he reached the top. He bowled down the door as it were made of leaves, not wood.

Francine made herself cross the threshold. The front room had shrunk, and now looked tiny and cramped. The rich reds and browns had faded into muted colors. Very few knickknacks lined the shelves, and the leaves and stones on the far wall were dried and broken. The empty fireplace exhaled a cold waft of air, like from a tomb.

Julius and Ignatius searched the other rooms.

"Not here," Julius growled.

"Maybe she's out back," Francine said without thinking.

"Show us," Julius demanded.

With even greater dread, Francine led them through the kitchen. Gauze streamers still covered the walls, hiding sharp lines. They'd gone gray, as if faded with age.

At the back stood a solid curtain.

"Here," Francine said, drawing it to one side.

"No—don't!"

Julius' words seemed very far away.

Just beyond the curtain stood the garden Francine had expected. Brilliant spires of snapdragons, shaggy trees and trailing vines of roses, and colorful flowers—dahlias, shastas, impatiens, mums, and begonias—spread like a living carpet from corner to corner. The trees appeared as saplings, thin and flexible, but even from a distance Francine could tell they had great age. She longed to sing to them and listen to their stories.

Lady Melisandra stood at the center, emitting a soft, comforting light.

"I'm sorry," Francine said.

When she tried to walk forward, she found herself

unable to move.

"Now, what should I do with such a pretty spy?" Lady Melisandra asked.

"Not a spy," Francine whispered.

It was the loudest she could speak. The invisible bonds tightened. She could only take shallow breaths. She trembled and fought down her fear.

"This is how you reward my help," Lady Melisandra scolded. Her skin had begun to age and the light grew more yellow.

"No," Francine squeaked. She was starting to get lightheaded.

"It was the others. I—"

"Hush," Lady Melisandra said. She looked beyond Francine, her mouth set in a line of disapproval.

"Julius knows better than to come after me," Lady Melisandra said after a moment.

"They wanted you to get me to the door."

"Yes, ma'am," Francine said. She tried to nod, but wasn't able to move that much.

"You refused?"

"I told them you weren't an idiot."

Suddenly, Francine found she could take a deeper breath. Her relief was short-lived.

"The *Fée* don't have much hope. Not really."

Lady Melisandra looked past Francine, out into a distance Francine couldn't see.

"But I have faith in you."

Lady Melisandra returned her sharp gaze to Francine.

"End this," she commanded.

"What? How?" How in the world, this world, any world, could Francine end a blood-feud that had lasted for centuries?

"You can," Lady Melisandra said softly.

"You can find the bridge between the courts. Now, go."

Francine found herself hurled backwards through the kitchen, landing hard on her butt next to the door of the front room. She threw herself forward, not wanting to risk landing on her fiddle.

"Run," Julius instructed.

Francine had no problem keeping up this time. They raced for the arch, tumbling through, one after another.

The Unseelie woods greeted them with warm summer sunshine and thick air. Francine sighed as she pushed herself up. Rocks and thorns bit into her palms. The trees laughed at her.

It was hard here, harder than she'd realized.

"Thought we'd lost you," Julius said, patting Francine's shoulder and leaving his hoof there. It felt overly warm, almost hot enough to burn her skin.

"Good thing you still had the rope," Ignatius added, his grin unabated.

"What?" Francine asked, hoping to distract them. She couldn't tell them that Lady Melisandra had let her go.

"Oh, yeah, that's right. That's how I got away!"

She made herself smile at the warrior.

"She had me caught like a fly in a web. Couldn't move. Couldn't breathe."

"Next time," Julius reassured her, squeezing Francine's shoulder again.

"Just don't be going out back a fairy house," Ignatius warned Francine.

"Place of power," Julius added.

"I didn't think you knew about them. Thought you was going somewhere else."

Francine nodded. She hoped she'd never have to go on another raid. But it made sense. It was why the Seelie didn't sleep in the safety of trees. They had a place that was safe that they could get to.

Uncle Rene had had a sacred backyard as well, back in

the human world. Francine was certain of it now.

The arch flared once, as if someone had shone a light across it.

Julius pulled Francine behind him, as if to protect her from whatever was coming through the gateway.

"Let's hope the other group was more successful," he grumbled.

Francine nodded, torn between hoping the other group hadn't been, as well as touched at Julius' protectiveness. She concentrated on the gate, trying not to think about what had just happened.

Why did Lady Melisandra think Francine could help? The queen was buried beneath a tree, held by magic. And even if Francine ended the queen's pain and brought her back above the earth, would she come with Francine? She'd given her word she'd stay.

Maybe Francine could do something for the other prisoners, though.

The first warrior came through and walked straight to Francine, grabbing the magicked rope with a howl.

The other warriors quickly followed. In between them stood two additional men.

Papa and Uncle Rene.

* * *

Francine stood stock still under the trees, watching the warriors bind Papa and Uncle Rene's hands with the dark rope she'd conjured out of slave songs. The trees above her stayed strangely silent. The grunts of the warriors and the quiet hiss of pain from Papa were the only things to break the quiet.

Julius didn't bother to hide his examination of the prisoners.

Was he curious because they were the first men to shape Francine's life? Who taught her to fiddle, then lost her to the lands of *Féerie*?

It wasn't difficult for Francine to keep all expression off her face—namely because her emotions felt so contradictory, they cancelled each other out.

Francine hated seeing Papa wince in pain. Uncle Rene, too.

Yet, she felt satisfied that finally he was under her power, that she was in control.

He couldn't hurt her anymore.

Sadness came next. It broke her heart to see her proud papa bound and shivering in pain.

And anger, of course, at him, at the Unseelie, at everything that had brought them to this point.

"You know, darling," Julius drawled, "he isn't as tall as you imagined in your target practice."

"I'm sure he's imagined I'm much smaller, too," Francine said, trying to deflect everything: her embarrassment, her anger, her fear.

"I'm sure," Julius purred.

He smiled at Francine, open and possessive.

Was he glad to see that her revenge wasn't as puny as he'd feared?

Francine made herself glare at the prisoners. No honor bound them not to struggle as the warriors led them to a tree-grown cage.

The prison ceiling had been made purposefully low. Neither Papa or Uncle Rene could stand up fully. Francine wondered if they'd been put on the opposite side of the Grand Hall where the queen was on purpose.

Distance didn't matter, though. Both Papa and Uncle Rene winced when they touched the wood. They obviously heard Queen Yvette's screams. Bracketed on all sides by wood, it would be impossible to escape.

The warriors tested the cage again, though they didn't need to. The bitter old tree itself wouldn't let them go. Francine knew that type of tree: It would tease them, maybe even pretend to grow an opening, only to close it before they could escape.

Julius put a possessive hoof on Francine's shoulder, leading her away.

Francine couldn't help but start at the contact, and couldn't relax her tense shoulder muscles.

"Francine," Papa croaked out, the first word she'd heard from him in ages. "I do love you."

Francine hunched her shoulders and kept walking.

She'd been wrong.

Papa could still hurt her.

* * *

Francine stood on the bank of the water-filled bayou, carefully examining the green-and-brown island beyond. She hadn't realized how far the Unseelie woods had stretched, how long it would take her to find water. The sky above her was a surprising blue, the sun still shining after all her walking. Cold wind blew off the gray water, carrying the sour smells of mulch and marsh grass.

Finally, Francine was satisfied. No trees, not even a sapling, grew on the marsh before her.

Now, she just had to get herself over there.

Francine had never been able to raise a bridge by herself. Hell, she'd collapsed the ones that Pierre had half-raised for her to finish bringing out of the water. But she couldn't think on that now, couldn't afford to remember the half-longing, shy looks, and quiet flirtation. She concentrated instead on her music. She played a classical piece, light and airy, that skipped across the surface of the water and made the trees behind her grumble.

Not a ripple in reply.

Francine paused, considering.

Was it just the song? Did an Unseelie bridge need something different? She remembered the catch and carry song that she'd played with Pierre. Could she adapt that to a single player? Would that work?

With a nod, Francine tried a new tune—less classical, more jazzy. The only time she'd seen the Unseelie court in formal gowns was before battle. Jazz was more for everyday, here.

At least this time the water between Francine and the land lost its smooth glass surface. Something stirred below the surface, but nothing rose.

Frustrated, Francine tried some zydeco. She knew if she played with enough force even the dead would rise to dance.

However, that drew even less movement from the water. Now it was merely a slight current between the island and the land.

Francine cursed. She held her fiddle at her side, her bow in her other hand and stared. She *needed* to get away from the trees. The constant thread of pain they relayed…it was just too much.

And the Unseelie—now they had Papa.

Francine settled the smooth chin-piece against her jaw and raised her bow.

Light flicked just beyond it, a sparkle in the current, like a firefly skipping down her raised bow, making her pause.

Uncle Rene had given her that bow. It was made from white horsetail hairs plucked in the cold and the dark, without a light shining, just like every bow he'd given her.

Only now she believed his tales of how he'd made it, and why: how the dark and light needed to be balanced, like the bow, to be perfect.

And yet, he was locked in a cage with Papa.

Everything was out of balance.

Francine cursed again. She was going to get *away* from all this, damn it. She angrily sawed at her fiddle, tossing out one tune after another, some whirling, some jazzy.

The water lay still, not talking.

Something was still missing.

Maybe she should just make an arch and step through, over to the island? She could *see* where she wanted to go, could practically taste the sun-warmed air and feel the soft mud under her boots.

But—fear spiked her gut. Even if she could see it, she'd never been there. What if the island held rivers or small ponds lay beyond the grass? There was no telling where Francine would end up.

Besides, forming arches was forbidden, at least for now. No one was supposed to leave the Unseelie lands unless directly sanctioned by the king.

Which meant the only way to leave was to go raiding.

Still…it was so close. And she just wanted a little peace, away from the trees.

Francine tried one more song, a lullaby to calm the waters.

No bridge rose, but a couple of gators did, right in front of her.

One turned to look at Francine as it passed, giving her a wink with its golden eye.

Francine kept playing, not taking a deep breath or stopping until she was certain they'd gone. She could have defended herself from them; she'd learned how to fight with her fiddle.

But what if she'd done something stupid like made an arch to the island and landed on a pile of their eggs?

Francine shook her head and put down her fiddle again.

Queen Yvette had gator eyes, and her smile at the crossroads when Francine had first met her had been so warm and inviting.

With a sigh, Francine flung herself on the ground, closing her eyes and banging her head.

She knew why she couldn't play or stay focused. Papa and Uncle Rene were in a cage. The queen's screams threaded through all the trees. Fairies had died in a bloody battle. The queen had tortured Pierre and maybe, probably, others. The trees were at war, killing each other. Julius was her friend and he scared her. Mama was still gone, and the ache in Francine's chest felt heavy and old.

Both Lady Melisandra and Papa had said Mama was human, spoke of her weight.

Mama had always been the bridge between Papa and Francine, between the academy and the rest of the family.

Francine banged her head once more against the hard ground beneath her.

Of course, she couldn't raise a bridge when she herself was so divided: Seelie and Unseelie, human and *Fée*.

Cursing one last time, Francine sat up and put her fiddle away, strapping it tightly to her back.

She didn't know how to solve the puzzle of all the different strands in her blood. She didn't know where her true home or her heart lay.

She didn't need to, though. Not right away. She couldn't do everything. She just had to do the right thing.

She just had to rescue her papa.

* * *

Francine gritted her teeth and made herself wait another minute, two minutes, five.

Julius and the warriors gathered below her in the Grand Hall, about to go on another raid.

Francine hadn't been able to form her own gate, so she figured she'd use one of theirs.

The problem wasn't the waiting; it was the waiting while hidden in a tree, the cries of the queen searing through her hands where they touched the bark. Even her boots and jeans could only blunt the screams, not block them. It took all of Francine's will just to stay, to not jump out of the tree and run away.

Finally, though, Julius opened the gate and all the warriors stepped through.

Francine sneaked down to the Grand Hall, checking over her shoulder and peering through the woods to see if anyone else watched.

Just the trees stood guard.

Without looking back, Francine stepped through the portal.

In the Unseelie woods it had been dusk, the air turning dim and the trees outlined with harsh shadows.

The Seelie woods had just passed that point, where the trees had all turned black and the sky offered no relief.

Francine waited for her eyes to adjust before she struck out along an easy path, thankful that no roots tried to trip her and no branches barred her way.

This time, the arch was much closer to the Grand Hall of the Seelie. Francine wondered if Julius was just being bold, or arrogantly foolish. Seelie warriors were also good fighters.

Pierre didn't answer the door when Francine knocked, or even when she called. She listened, but she didn't hear him, either.

Where could he have gone? No one was playing in the Grand Hall. No parties that night.

Maybe he was training, though.

It didn't take long for Francine to reach that part of the woods, the meadow where they'd played. Trickling notes through the trees told her she'd guessed right. She moved quietly along the path, not wanting to interrupt.

"Come to capture me, too?"

The harsh words rang out in counterpoint to the soft melody.

"No," Francine said.

She stopped trying to move stealthily and walked directly to where Pierre stood.

Grand trees spread their limbs above his head, hiding the moon and stars. Pierre had raised a sturdy footstool and stood with one boot resting on it. His white shirt was the only light thing about him—the rest of his clothes and his face were dark and closed.

"You were right," Francine said when the music finally died away.

"Not about the battle; it wouldn't have mattered if I'd played or not. The Unseelie still would have won."

She didn't bother to keep the pride out of her voice.

"But the Unseelie influence—that isn't good."

Francine looked at her feet, ashamed to have said it out loud, but relieved as well.

"It's too late, though, isn't it?"

Pierre's voice lashed coldly along Francine's skin.

"You already have Queen Yvette. Our influence is fading. Yours is gaining."

"Their influence," Francine grated out.

"Excuse me?"

"*Their* influence," Francine repeated. "Not mine."

"So you just thought you'd change sides again?" Pierre scoffed.

"The reason King Erastus decided to fight was because of *you*. How you could rile up the warriors and the court. *Your* unbridled passion gave them the advantage. The blood of my friends is on *your* hands."

Francine held herself still, feeling herself grow as pale as the few beams of light finding their way between the trees.

"I know," she said eventually.

"I'm sorry."

"You expect that's enough?"

"No," Francine said, grimacing.

"I know it isn't. Words can be hurtful, horrible, but never enough. I want to do something. And I need your help."

"Charles," Pierre said. "He's been captured."

"Yes," Francine breathed out.

The hole in her chest where her grief about Mama lived felt extra empty and cold when she thought about Papa.

"I have to get him out."

She paused, adding, "I need your help. Please."

"Ah, *chérie*," Pierre said, shaking his head and looking to the side.

"I knew you were trouble. First moment I saw you."

Francine swallowed down any feeling of hope or want. He hadn't said yes yet.

"Darling, you're going to dance me to death, aren't you?" Pierre finally turned to face her. He still wasn't smiling, still hadn't relaxed, still stood stiff as a tree before her.

"At least it's a good night for madness."

Francine nodded and dared a small smile, the first one in days.

Pierre returned it only slightly.

Chapter Thirteen

Francine went through the gateway Pierre formed, fiddle and bow in hand. The dark woods made a muffled comment, the air humid and heavy. Clouds filled the sky, and even the birds were silent. She had watched him carefully, but she still didn't understand how he could bridge the worlds when she couldn't.

Pierre came through a moment later. He glanced around, obvious looking for others.

"It isn't a trap," Francine hissed angrily at Pierre as she put away her fiddle.

Pierre froze, then turned to Francine slowly.

"I know that," he said softly.

"I believe you, *chérie*."

"But?"

"You may have been duped, too."

Sadness washed over Francine. She no longer trusted the Unseelie. There was a good chance Pierre was right, and that they didn't trust her either.

"So we will be careful, yes?"

"*Oui, chérie*," Francine said, teasing, just to bring a smile to Pierre's face as well as her own. She tried not to let herself notice how sad his smile was.

Pierre tried to lead the way, but the roots kept tripping him, making him falter.

Francine knew it was a gentleman thing, and let him, not wanting to hurt his pride.

"Here," Francine finally said, pushing beyond Pierre as she helped him to his feet for the fourth time.

"Let me."

They made better progress now. The trees still occasionally tried to trip Francine, but it was more playful, with less intent to harm. They didn't pause again until they stood on the small rise looking down on the Great Hall.

To the left stood the tree Papa and Uncle Rene were caged by. No other Seelie had joined them, so the most recent raid had been unsuccessful. They'd unbound the rope from their wrists, and it coiled like a deadly black cloud in the corner of their cage.

Francine studied Pierre as he looked down the hill. Did he see the tree? Or was Erastus right—was the queen truly hidden?

"You didn't tell me there would be guards," Pierre hissed at Francine.

"There weren't guards there before," Francine whispered back.

She scanned the area carefully. Pierre was right. Two warriors now lazed outside Papa and Uncle Rene's cage. One sat cross-legged and leaned against the bars, while the other lay stretched out, propped up with one arm.

Cruel laughter carried up to where Francine and Pierre stood. The guard lying down tossed something into the cage.

"Not exactly guarding," Francine muttered.

The warriors probably hadn't been told to wait outside the cage and guard it. They were probably just there to have some "fun" at Papa and Uncle Rene's expense.

"We'll have to wait," Pierre said.

"No. We have to get them out now. I'll distract the guards," Francine said.

The one lying down had given her an idea.

"Not like that," Pierre said sharply, stepping in front of Francine.

"Not like what?" Francine asked, perplexed.

Pierre didn't say anything. He merely looked Francine up and down, with speculation in his eyes.

"No! Jeez, not like that," Francine said, her cheeks suddenly warm.

"Why does everything come down to sex with you?"

"It isn't sex," Pierre assured her. "It's honor."

Francine rolled her eyes. Pierre would see it that way.

"Get Papa and Uncle Rene out while I'm still playing," she said as she drew out her fiddle.

"You know this means they'll know you've turned against them."

Francine couldn't meet Pierre's eye. She knew.

The Unseelie would never understand that loyalty. If they ever caught her after this, they'd be merciless.

But she had to rescue Papa.

Francine shoved her misgivings to the side and started a bright, happy tune.

"What are you doing?" Pierre whispered.

Francine winked.

"Trust me."

Then she let the tune carry her down the hill, twisting and dancing. She didn't play a constant song, just a few notes here, a string of melody there. She also consciously stumbled, and threw out a few casual curses when she did.

Finally, Francine stumbled into the Grand Hall.

"Ooh," she said with an exaggerated whisper to the two guards, holding her hands out.

"I'm sorry, I didn't mean to wake you."

She swayed where she stood, as if she were very drunk.

"It's all right, miss," said the one lying down. He started to push himself up.

"No, no, no, no, no, don't get up, shh," Francine said. "Here. I'll help."

At first Francine continued to skip over notes, switching from one slow dance to the next.

"That's nice," said the seated warrior, swaying back and forth.

"Yeah," Francine said, keeping her own tone soft and unfocused. She changed over to a lullaby, a quiet song Mama had taught her about dolphins and the ocean.

By the time Francine had reached the second chorus, both warriors lay stretched out, sound asleep. She risked a glance at the cage; both Papa and Uncle Rene were shaking their heads, working to stay awake, yawning greatly.

She sent the next round of music up toward the tree, soothing it as well, slipping into something that more resembled a carol—the quiet winter chill needed to send a tree to sleep.

Finally, Francine looked up at the ridge and nodded. She didn't see Pierre, but hopefully he watched. She kept her playing softer now, casting a heavy blanket of sleep across the two fairies.

The gate of the cage snicked open. Francine hadn't seen Pierre approach, but he was suddenly there, urging the two men out.

Even in the dim light Francine could tell they were pale—too pale. Maybe sick. Papa stood up straight and stretched as soon as he could. Uncle Rene followed suit.

Papa's eyes never left Francine even as he rolled his shoulders and head.

Francine couldn't pay Papa that much attention. She had to stay focused on the two warriors, making them sleep and dream deeply.

Pierre shaped an archway just beyond the tree. Francine

wasn't sure how. He sent Papa and Uncle Rene through first. Then he beckoned to Francine.

"You have to go next. I have to close the gate as I go through."

Francine didn't know how to do that. There was still so much she had to learn.

And now, only the Seelie would teach her.

Francine continued to play as she walked, right up to the time she backed through the arch, bowing a little, saying goodbye to the place that had urged her to play as wildly as she could.

* * *

The notes Francine played in the arch bounced strangely through the Seelie woods, skyward and twisted. Darkness wove between the trees and pressed against Francine's skin. The air smelled right, and Francine recognized where she stood, otherwise she would have suspected they weren't in the Seelie lands. She'd never seen it so dark.

"The queen's missing," Papa said quietly as Francine looked around. "The light's...fading."

Francine stifled the urge to say she was sorry, yet again. She looked at Papa, trying to examine him in the dimness. He looked thinner than she remembered, the skin along his neck gaunt and tight. Either he'd shrunk or she'd grown—they stood eye-to-nose now, instead of eye-to chin.

"It's good to see you, darling," Uncle Rene interrupted.

Uncle Rene had lost so much weight. She remembered Pierre had said he had cancer.

The stillness holding Francine suddenly broke and she gave Uncle Rene a hug. He held her in strong arms. Francine blinked back the tears.

"I missed you so much," she said hoarsely.

"Missed you too, hon," Uncle Rene said, letting go and stepping back, dragging the backs of his now-skinny hands over his eyes.

"Same here," Papa added quietly.

"Yeah," Francine said, looking at him and nodding. She'd missed Papa, but that was a familiar ache, as he'd actually left when Mama had died.

As always, anger wrapped around Francine's grief. She knew it didn't make any sense, but all she wanted to ask was why, why had he hurt her so?

Pierre stepped through the arch and it collapsed before they could say anything else.

Francine had never seen an arch fold in on itself that way.

She was going to have to ask Pierre to show her that later.

If Pierre still wanted to be teach Francine anything; if he would trust her that much ever again.

"We need to get someplace safe," Pierre told them.

"Lady Melisandra's?" Francine asked, remembering the strength of her safe haven in the backyard.

Papa jerked his attention back to Francine, his expression unreadable.

"No, though that's a good second choice. She might help us—help you," Pierre said with a pointed stare at Francine.

Francine nodded. Just 'cause Pierre would help didn't mean any of the other Seelie would.

"But I was thinking Brooks and Jacque's place," Pierre continued. "They're living here now, trying to keep order with the queen gone."

"Why there?" Papa asked. "Why would Brooks help?"

Francine heard the unspoken, "Why would he help *me*?" There had to be some awful history there if Papa hesitated, as tired as he looked.

"They owe her a debt," Pierre explained.

"Really?" Uncle Rene said, sounding surprised.

Papa also cocked an eyebrow in question.

Francine nodded. "When their bubble world was collapsing."

"That was you?" Papa sounded angry, folding his arms across his chest.

"Yes," Francine snapped, ready to match his rage.

"They were my..." She paused, the anger leaving as quickly as it had appeared. They weren't her friends, not really, though they'd been friendly enough.

"It wasn't right," Francine continued quietly.

"Just leaving them to be, I don't know, reabsorbed."

Papa looked to the side, not meeting Francine's gaze.

"You could have been hurt," he said softly.

Uncle Rene gave a loud, dramatic sigh.

Both Francine and Papa looked at him.

"Would ya'll stop dancing around each other like you're concerned strangers and just admit that you're flawed family?"

Francine's look turned into a glare. Out of the corner of her eye she saw Papa had done the same. A quick glance showed her that she and her papa stood the exact same way, with their hands fisted on their waists, chins out, necks strained. She bet if she had a mirror, it would show they both wore the same expression.

Papa looked at Francine, then bit his lips together.

Francine recognized the gesture—he was trying not to laugh.

It still hurt that Mama wasn't there to help them see each other. That they had no mirror there to reflect off of. But maybe they could learn to do that without her, now.

Francine dropped her arms at the same time Papa did. They turned to face each other.

"I missed you," Papa finally said.

"Oh, Papa," Francine choked out as she crossed to where he was and flung her arms around him.

"My baby girl," Papa murmured, pulling Francine closer.

"My number-one girl."

Something crashed nearby: a limb falling, or something worse, like a wild boar *Fée* on the hunt for more Seelie?

Both Francine and Papa jumped.

"We have to go," Pierre repeated.

"The woods aren't safe."

Francine let herself be hurried along the path, but she kept looking back to make sure Papa followed.

She wasn't going to lose him again.

* * *

Gator eyes greeted Francine as the door swung open. She steeled herself from taking a step back. It didn't matter if Brooks hated her now; he had to help her papa.

Brooks' stern eyes looked from one to another in the group before he said, "Ya'll are like a bad penny, always coming back. Get in here."

He stepped to the side as they shuffled in, then turned and walked straight back through his house after he closed the door, expecting them to follow.

Francine caught a glimpse of an empty living room and pale, bare walls, as if no one lived there. The kitchen was a homey contrast, a white-and-black tiled floor running into checked walls with a similar pattern. It could have been dizzying, but the bright red chair rail and shelves broke the pattern just enough.

It looked like the kind of kitchen Aunt Lavine would have loved.

It didn't surprise Francine that the back of Brooks' house looked like the field from his bubble world, with long green grass and spots of tall reeds. A faded blue rug lay along one side, and Jacque looked at them from it.

"Look what the cat dragged in," he drawled.

Jacque sounded friendly enough, but his smile didn't meet his eyes.

"You rescue them, too?" Brooks asked as Francine as her papa got Uncle Rene settled on the rug.

Francine nodded, something tight and hard hurting inside at how Uncle Rene still worked to catch his breath after running through the woods.

Jacque looked at Brooks, who nodded. Jacque disappeared inside the house for a brief moment before returning with moon wine.

"This will help," he told Uncle Rene, his fingers wrapped around his wrist to hold it steady as he sipped.

When Papa took over, Jacque went in and came out with glasses for everyone.

"This gonna be a habit of yours?" Brooks asked, his voice as hard as his eyes.

Francine nodded.

"Or maybe I just need to see if the third time's the charm."

"Oh?" Brooks asked, not looking at Francine, his posture stiff, as if tensing for a blow.

"We have to rescue the queen."

* * *

"So what are ya'll intending, exactly?" Brooks asked as they all settled down on the blanket for a "war council." Stars shone coldly above, barely burning through the dark. The woods were quiet, every creature hidden away. The wind barely whispered above them.

"I saw where they buried Queen Yvette. I know where she is," Francine declared.

"So?" Brooks asked, challenging her.

"We can go get her back."

Brooks and Jacque exchanged a quick glance.

"How do I know it's not a trick?" Brooks asked.

Francine looked down at the rug and picked at a loose thread.

"The Unseelie—they were good to me. But they used me, worse 'en you did."

From across the rug Francine could tell Papa had just sat up stiff and straight. She'd have to talk with him later to make sure Brooks didn't come to an accident.

"They used me," Francine repeated. Now she looked up, staring directly at Brooks, her ready anger rising.

"I won't be used by anyone anymore."

Brooks met her eyes for a long moment.

Francine couldn't read anything in that golden glare.

Finally, Brooks gave a curt nod.

"I believe you. And I'm willing to work with you. But know that the rest of the court won't be so kind."

He turned and looked at Uncle Rene.

"While you're still welcome to visit, I'm not sure how long you'll be able to stay, now."

Francine swallowed hard against the sudden lump in her throat. Oh God. What if she'd just killed Uncle Rene by rescuing him and Papa?

Uncle Rene reached over and placed his big hand on Francine's knee, giving it a squeeze.

"Don't you fret. I have whatever time I have, and I've enjoyed every minute of it."

The silence strained as Francine struggled to swallow down her tears.

"So, are we going?" Papa asked roughly.

"You're not going anywhere," Francine retorted.

"You need every fighter you have," Papa said.

"I don't care. You're not—you're never going back there," Francine said vehemently.

"But—" Jacque started.

"No!"

Francine glared at them all.

"He might be right," Brooks said with a sigh.

"No. He is not."

Francine knew if she said one more word she'd start shooting flames at all of them.

"I can't deal with all you idiots right now," she said as she stood up, stomping off the rug. The tall grass easily parted for her as she walked further into the yard.

She stopped at the back wall, where the trees started. Without thinking she reached out to touch one, then jerked her hand back.

The moans of Queen Yvette still skittered across her palm, making her skin itch.

"Hey, babe."

Francine turned to see Uncle Rene.

"You should be resting," she scolded, reaching for his hand and drawing him to a clear space between the tree trunks where he could sit down.

"He worried about you every day."

"No, he didn't," Francine said. "He worried about himself."

"Child, I've never seen you be so willfully ignorant before. Just look at him."

Francine grimaced but did as her uncle asked.

At first, it appeared Papa talked with Brook, Jacque, and Pierre. But after a few moments his eyes turned toward her, checking to see where she was. As Francine watched, Papa did it repeatedly, always looking toward her, always checking.

"He never stopped looking for you, waiting for you, not even as the years passed."

"Years?"

Francine's stomach fell and her insides knotted in fear.

"It's been more than five years since you left."

Francine shook her head.

"No. That's wrong. It hasn't been—" she counted in her head "—even eight months yet."

"No, darling. It's been longer than that for him. First

your mama, then you. That sorrow weighing him down."

Where had the time gone? Had it disappeared in the wilds, while she danced with the trees?

"But you both seemed so happy when I saw you," Francine snapped.

"When was that?"

Francine gestured toward Jacque and Brooks.

"You know."

"We were happy to see them," Uncle Rene said slowly.

"And coming here did lift a stone off your papa's heart. But he spent every day expecting to see you, to turn around and have you pop out of a corner somewhere."

Uncle Rene sighed.

"With your mama, it was easier to let go. He knew he'd never see her again. With you, all he knew was that his grandma had sent you away someplace and wouldn't tell him where."

"Lady Melisandra's my great-grandma?"

Uncle Rene rubbed the back of his head and looked down.

"No one explained, did they? Your relations."

"Papa wouldn't talk about them. *You* wouldn't talk about them," Francine accused. She glared first at him, then at her papa across the yard.

Papa met Francine's gaze steadily for a moment before turning away, as he always did.

"Darling, he wouldn't really talk to me either. I don't know what happened. His grandma raised him."

"So Queen Yvette is Lady Melisandra's daughter?"

Uncle Rene gave her a hesitant nod.

"Not directly. Once or twice removed."

"Huh." It didn't make sense, but Francine got the general idea. She looked back at Brooks and Jacque.

Maybe they really were her cousins, two or three times removed.

Then she noted Papa had turned to look at her again.

A soft breeze played with Francine's hair, blowing it across her eyes. *Just try* came the faint words.

Francine would have sworn it was her mama talking.

With a nod, Francine pushed aside her anger and really *looked* at her papa. He did look older; she'd noticed that before. Care wrinkles lined the corners of his eyes, deeper and more downturned than the laugh wrinkles. When he glanced her way again, she finally saw the question in his eyes, the hope that she might care.

"He was pretty mean," Francine said quietly.

"And he's beat himself up about it, too."

"I don't want to lose him again," Francine finally admitted, her voice cracking.

"All you have to do is let him in," Uncle Rene said.

"He'll never let go of you, either."

It sounded so easy.

Francine knew it would be harder than breaking apart oak branches twined together to give him more room in her heart.

"I'd kill him if he got captured again," Francine said. Or she'd kill herself.

Uncle Rene chuckled.

"That's my girl. You show him just how bad it'll be if he's an idiot again."

Francine felt a smile creeping across her face though she tried to deny it. Then Francine turned and looked at Uncle Rene.

"What about you?"

"What about me, darling?"

Francine merely glared at him.

"I've already lived a full life."

Francine's heart caught in her chest and her happiness froze.

"That bad?" was all she could choke out.

She reached out for him, grasping his hand.

"'Fraid so. That's why Charles brought me here again."

"I'm sorry it had to be now—with all this," Francine said, gesturing to the twilight and screaming trees.

"Now's all I got," Uncle Rene said.

"So yeah, I'm going too, to rescue the queen. Because you both need me, and I ain't got nothing better to do."

Uncle Rene squeezed their joined hands.

"Can't be spending my afternoons making hush puppies here," he added mournfully.

With her other hand, Francine pushed away the tears that had welled up.

"Well, if we're all gonna be idiots, we might as well be idiots together. Come on."

Francine stood and helped Uncle Rene back to his feet. They walked arm-in-arm across the yard, back toward the others.

Papa saw them coming and rose to his feet. At first, he looked like he was going to be stubborn, arms crossed across his chest. But seeing how loose and easy Francine walked, he let his arms fall, and looked puzzled.

"Papa, if you get hurt or recaptured, I'm gonna kill you. All right?" Francine said as they drew near.

Papa pressed his lips together as if to stop from smiling, but he nodded.

"Fine by me, darling."

They all sat down again, this time with Francine closer to her papa, leaning into him sometimes as they made their plans.

Later that night, when Francine found she couldn't keep her eyes open anymore, she lay down with her head in Papa's lap.

Just before she slept, she realized how like a tree he felt, how comforting, solid, and strong.

Chapter Fourteen

"But I've never raised a bridge before, let alone a tree," Francine complained.

"Neither have I," Papa admitted quietly.

They still sat in Brooks and Jacque's backyard, the morning finally winding its way through the trees. Birds sang beyond the wall, and a quiet breeze shuffled through the grass. Trails of clouds stretched across the sky, like wisps of dreams.

Francine stubbornly resisted relaxing into the peaceful surroundings. Too much was at risk.

"I have, though. Well, raised bridges. And other things. You can just follow me," Pierre assured them.

Uncle Rene, Francine, and Papa all shared a look at that.

"I see the parallels, I do, Pierre, but I don't know," Francine said, shaking her head.

"It's close to the same. You just gotta find a way there, find that *something* under the ground and raise it up."

Pierre tried to show it with his hands, but ended up shaking them in frustration.

The group stayed silent for a moment.

"You sure you strong enough, boy?" Uncle Rene finally asked.

Pierre sat up stiffly.

"I *have* been the queen's head fiddler for some time."

"That's only since Charles never challenged you," Brooks said quietly. "Or Francine."

Papa looked at Brooks, then bent his head and looked at the ground.

Francine would swear Papa seemed embarrassed, except she'd never seen him ashamed her whole life.

"I was young and stupid," Papa said quietly, finally looking up at Brooks.

Brooks nodded, a smile softening his hard gator eyes.

"And I was even younger and more of an idiot."

Francine suddenly remembered the story Lady Melisandra had told about Papa stripping the clothes off a man. Had it been Brooks? Had that been what had driven him from the court?

"So what do we do?" Jacque asked. "Brooks and I?"

"Nothing," both Papa and Uncle Rene snapped.

"You stay here," Francine added.

She may have lost the battle about her kin coming, but if the only remaining royalty of the Seelie court came with as well, she'd have too many to defend.

Pierre pressed his lips into a thin line.

"I actually need you to hold the arch here."

"Why?" Francine asked sharply.

Why would someone, anyone, have to keep a doorway open? Unless…

"If you don't make it. If you're captured or killed," Francine said softly.

Pierre nodded. "The arch would collapse. And if we're being attacked, ya'll won't have time to form another. If you even can."

"Then let's make sure you stay safe," Francine said.

Though she was never sure how she felt about Pierre, the trees would feel more hollow without him.

"Yes," Papa agreed.

Francine finally voiced her main concern.

"What if the queen won't come? She's bound by honor to stay, you know."

"Not in pain. Not like that," Brooks said firmly.

His eyes abruptly turned white, like his mother's had when Francine had locked the fetters on her wrists.

Jacque bumped Brooks' shoulder deliberately. Brooks glared at him, but his eyes turned back to normal.

As normal as a gator glare would ever be.

* * *

It was daylight in the Unseelie woods as well when they stepped through. Francine didn't know if that was a good thing or not—if more of the court would be awake and around.

Depended on whether they'd had a party the night before.

Francine waited impatiently as the others came through the arch. The air wrapped around her, hot and sticky, making her itch. She glanced around the woods nervously, but all she saw were the trees, all she heard were the normal critters and wind. She didn't think any of the Unseelie were close by, though she didn't dare touch a tree to ask.

Pierre came last. The archway dimmed after he stepped through, as if a dark shawl had been dropped over the opening. It meant the magic had worked, and the arch was being held on the other side.

It also made the doorway obvious, which meant they had even less time.

"Come on," Francine said, leading them toward the Great Hall. They'd arrived at the bottom of the ridge, very close to the sloping hall, in a thicket. The woods only tried to trip her a few times, a twig playfully pulling at her hair. The other suffered more: Pierre started cursing in French as he stumbled along. Even Uncle Rene had some choice words about the branch that tried to rip his shirt.

When they reached the Great Hall, Francine paused, searching.

None of the Unseelie were there.

"Is it a trap?" Papa asked.

He'd grown pale again, being back in Unseelie territory.

Francine didn't know if it was the memories of being a prisoner or something else.

Uncle Rene had the same haggard look.

"I doubt it," Francine said.

Erastus had boasted that they'd hidden the queen. No reason to guard her.

Francine turned to Pierre.

"Do you know what tree she's under?"

"Of course," Pierre scoffed. He pointed at the large oak growing on the side of the hall, its branches draped along the platform where the musicians played.

"There."

"No," Papa said, indicating the tree closest to them. "There."

Uncle Rene pointed to yet a different tree.

"She's under the willow," Francine said, puzzled.

She didn't understand the magic at play here, and neither did any of her companions. Unease coiled in her belly and a small knot of fear lay in her chest.

No one expressed any doubt of Francine's claim, but she saw it in their faces. Stubbornly she walked forward, knowing they'd follow.

The hall hadn't changed as far as Francine could tell. A carpet of kudzu ran across the raised platform. Oaks, cypress, and palms grew boldly along the edges, not in neat lines like in the Seelie court but into the actual hall itself.

The moss on their branches linked their limbs together.

Only after staring for a moment did Francine realize that something had changed: All the trees grew closer together now. Not as if they'd moved, but as if they'd swelled.

"Quickly," Francine told Pierre.

Something didn't feel right.

Pierre directed his tune at the willow.

Francine, Papa, and Uncle Rene joined in, following Pierre's lead: a skipping, light tune that still had a strong structure to it.

Nothing happened.

Pierre continued his melody, merely adding variations.

It still didn't work. Not a branch on the tree so much as twitched.

Papa and Uncle Rene shared Francine's frustration given their anxious looks.

"You gotta try something else!" Francine hissed over the music, poking at Pierre's tune, trying to twist it.

"Not like that," Pierre said between gritted teeth. He wove his melody more strongly around the other musicians, and Francine found herself following though she knew it was wrong.

"Francine."

A voice called to her from beyond the trees.

Julius stood there, alone. He seemed puffed up, his suit barely containing his muscles. His powerful glare moved from Francine to the rest of them, then back to her, now with a sneer.

"That pitiful tune won't raise a thing."

Francine nodded. They'd failed. She should have led them, figured out how to raise a bridge somehow.

Pierre and the others continued playing, but the tune had finally changed. A deliberate thread of defense now mingled with the melody.

Francine started to back away, toward the arch. She was

ready to fling deadly notes at Julius, and he knew it.

Still, Julius followed, eyes boring into Francine.

"They aren't as good as you," he said softly.

"Not even as backup."

A flaming note passed by Francine's ear and grazed Julius' arm.

She didn't have to turn around to know Papa had sent it.

Julius' sneer returned.

"You didn't teach her when you had the chance."

Now it was Francine's turn to toss a flaming note.

"He's still my papa."

"You'll never forget who really mentored you, hon."

"That, son, would be me," Pierre suddenly said, stepping in front of Francine, sawing furiously on his fiddle, driving Julius back.

Movement to the side caught Francine's attention.

Warriors. Lots of them.

"Run!"

Francine took charge of the tune, tumbling them forward toward the gate.

"And the student surpasses the master," Julius snarled.

A quick look confirmed Julius' skin had grown mottled. His eyeteeth curled down and his eyes flamed red, not gold.

Then Francine was too busy fighting warriors to worry about her old friend. She regretted every flaming wound she caused, but she had no choice.

Fortunately, the dark archway loomed behind them.

"Uncle Rene! Now!" Francine shouted.

"Go!" Papa seconded.

Francine staggered under the loss of Uncle Rene's fine accompaniment. He'd laid a strong bass for them to follow, and the tune trembled when he stopped playing.

"You next," Papa said through gritted teeth. He laid a line of fire along the feet of the warriors to his right.

"You go first," Francine shouted, throwing line after line

of swirling dark notes at the warriors on her left, forcing them to dodge and making it impossible for them to come closer.

"Both of you. Now," Pierre ordered.

"I'm not coming back to save either of your asses. Again."

Francine gulped and looked at Papa. The strain showed on his face, his stumbling feet.

"Fine."

"Fine?" Papa asked.

"Three, two, one," Francine said, literally throwing Papa through the gate, herself on his heels.

The arch vanished as soon as Francine stepped into the Seelie woods, making a loud popping sound.

Pierre hadn't even had a chance to step through.

Francine rounded on Jacque, who stood there slack-mouthed.

"What the hell happened? You were supposed to keep it open!"

Jacque shook his head and sank to the ground. He shook his head again, moaning in pain as he lay down on his side, curled in on himself.

"What happened?" Uncle Rene was suddenly kneeling next to the young man, running one of his big hands down Jacque's arm, squeezing his shoulder.

Brooks knelt down as well, a glass of moon wine suddenly in his hand. He lifted Jacque's head, but Jacque barely took a sip.

"Something." Jacque's voice cracked.

He cleared his throat, took another sip of wine, and tried again.

"Something else tried to come through. Not Pierre. Not—*Fée*."

He shivered again, a full body shudder, before he closed his eyes and curled up on his side again.

Francine went back to where the arch had stood.

A twisted, burned tree limb lay across the threshold.

Francine poked at it with her bow. It tried to twist itself around the end of the bow before the limb dissolved into black ash.

The Unseelie trees didn't belong here.

"We have to go back," Francine said, still looking at the limb, her failure also tasting like ashes.

"They'd be waiting for ya'll. You wouldn't get two feet into their woods," Brooks said flatly.

"But Pierre's there! And the queen!"

Francine finally looked up, her rage mixed with sorrow.

Brooks bit his lip.

"Pierre can survive."

"What do you mean?" Francine asked, fear building deep inside her gut.

"He turned himself into a tree, didn't he?" Papa asked.

"He hates doing that," Francine said quietly.

Brooks grimaced.

"No, he hated it when the queen forced him into it. This was his choice."

"It'll be hard for the Unseelie to hurt him, when he's that way," Papa explained. "Plus, ya know, he's in a thicket of trees. If they hurt him, the trees standing beside him will also be hurt. They're all interconnected."

Francine opened her mouth and shut it.

That meant Pierre now also felt the anguish of the queen, beating in time with his heart, and could never escape it.

"How do we rescue him? And the queen?" Francine asked.

"You must wait."

Startled by the new voice, they all turned. Lady Melisandra stood beside them, tall and foreboding.

"The tree that holds Yvette will only rise with the turn of the season," she scolded.

"Why did you think you could trick it?"

Francine's chin raised in defiance.

"We could have done it."

She knew, now, exactly what to play, to trick the tree into thinking winter was there. Carols and hymns, jazz funerals and dirges all came to her mind.

Lady Melisandra chuckled.

"Youth. So impatient. Ya'll need to wait. The wheel turns. It'll be as it should. There's other you need to do. Other bridges to build."

She looked pointedly at Francine, then at Francine's Papa. Then she shook herself and her presence shrank until she was merely another lady of the court, beautiful and perilous, like all the *Fée*.

"Now, who'd like some sweet tea?"

* * *

Trees stood silent in the thicket, their winter-thin branches overlapping. The nearby stream had dried to a trickle, and leaves covered the ground. No birds sang; they'd all gone somewhere else for the winter, abandoned their homes in hope of sunnier places.

Still, Francine stubbornly walked there every morning. It was where Pierre had first tried to teach her, the place where she'd found him and gotten him into this mess.

She walked further up into the woods, to the deepest part of the creek, where the water was at least a foot deep, and started playing. Today she tried dancing tunes, light airy pieces that both Pierre and the queen would have liked.

After a day of playing, the stars rose in the dark of the afternoon, but a bridge never did.

Francine walked back to the Great Hall, stumbling with tiredness. She was surprised to see Papa there, standing on the stage, practicing a quiet country jig.

"Hey, Papa," Francine called out as she came up to him.

"Hey, darling," Papa said. He came over to the edge of

the stage and sat next to Francine.

"How's my best girl?"

"Tired," Francine admitted, resting her head on his shoulder.

"I keep trying, Papa."

"I know," Papa said.

He hesitated, growing stiff.

Francine pulled back in worry. He was gonna do something stupid again, wasn't he? Forbid her from trying?

"I know you been trying to raise a bridge, or something. I—I can try, too, if that's what you want."

"Really, Papa?" Francine asked, surprised.

"Of course." Papa looked off into the trees.

"Sometimes it's better to do things together. Even idiotic, scary things."

"You mean *especially* the idiotic, scary things," Francine teased.

"I don't want to lose you again," Papa said, still looking away.

Francine took one of Papa's big hands in hers.

"I promised I'd always be careful in the woods, Papa. And I am. But I gotta go deep, too. You said I could."

Papa finally looked at Francine.

"I know darling. I do. And I'm proud of you."

He took a deep breath.

"Let's go deep together. Let's find that bridge."

Francine nodded, unable to trust her voice.

It was all she'd ever wanted: her stubborn papa at her side.

* * *

Dark green pines circled the small pond that Papa led Francine to the next morning. Cool gray water reflected the steel-colored clouds above. The frost-covered grass crunched under their boots as they walked.

Francine hummed in quiet anticipation. They had to get this right, today, now. It wouldn't be long before the longest night of the year, when the Unseelie would bring the queen back to the surface and drain away the last of her power.

Papa pulled out his sleek black fiddle that shone like a dark mirror. Francine still had her bone white one, with the golden metal strings.

"Any ideas?" Papa asked as he plucked a few notes with his thumb, trying to get a feel for how they'd sound here.

Francine shrugged.

"I've tried just about everything. Court music, zydeco, jazz—nothing worked."

Papa shrugged.

"Then here goes nothing but the joy of playing with you, darling."

Francine hid her smile as she brought up her fiddle, following his lead.

The song was light and airy, complicated and fey. Francine had never heard it before, but it made her chest warm with joy.

"You wrote that, didn't you?" she asked when they'd finished.

Papa nodded.

"For you. When you were born."

"How come you never played it for me?"

"Because we weren't here."

"Is it a bridge song?" she asked suddenly.

"Were you trying to bridge human and *Féerie*?"

"No, never," Papa said, laughing.

"Your mama was always my bridge. I walked all the way across, too."

"She was our bridge, sometimes," Francine said.

"That she was. She'd be proud of you, you know."

"Proud of us," Francine insisted. An idea tickled at the back of her mind.

"Papa, would you call that court music, what you just played? For the *Féerie*?"

Papa thought for a bit.

"I suppose so. It ain't quite classical, is it? It's just—like here. Fits here."

Francine nodded. The song Papa had played was similar to what Pierre played for the court: a light, complicated dance of notes that echoed the moonlight glitter of the *Fée*.

While Francine's music, like the human boots she still wore, drove a solid beat against the earth.

"Stay there," Francine told her papa. She walked around the pool, not stopping until she stood on the other side.

With a nod, Francine began, starting with a light tune, something Pierre had taught her. She tossed it over to Papa, who picked it up, taking it higher. Francine began laying a more solid line underneath it, a syncopated jazz pulse that made her move her feet and started the water bubbling.

They passed the melody back and forth, each adding elements to it, a zydeco riff from Francine, a fey flourish from Papa.

For the first time, a structure began to form out of the water.

Francine felt her heart catch.

It was *beautiful*.

She couldn't believe they were doing it, finally—bridging the two worlds with their music. She didn't let the tune falter, though. She ran with it, chasing all of Papa's notes up through the clouds to the endless blue sky she knew was waiting for her, then back down the rough tree trunks and into the sweet, rich earth.

The bridge continued to rise. It looked like it was made out of hardened water, clear and gray. The shorings curved like church arches, and the stairs had delicate carvings in the center of each, sprays of flowers and trees, clinging kudzu and delicate butterfly wings.

Without worrying about the consequences, Francine put her full weight on the first step.

Papa grinned and joined her. They matched each other's steps, meeting in the middle as the song finally reached its end.

"Papa, we can save her," Francine said, bopping up and down on her toes. She knew this music would work.

They could build a bridge between the two courts.

"Yes, darling, we can."

Neither of them spoke the other words they both heard clearly: *We can save us, too.*

* * *

Uncle Rene met the pair of them as they walked back to the Great Hall.

"It's time," he told them grimly.

"What do you mean?" Francine asked, though her heart was already sinking below the dirt path they walked along.

"The priests have raised the binding world. If you want to go watch the queen rise, you have to be bound first."

"Bound?" Papa asked, growling.

Francine raised an eyebrow, surprised. Generally he knew all about these court rituals.

"Swear not to hurt the Unseelie while in their court."

"All right," Papa said, looking relieved.

"What?" Francine asked.

"They could have asked for a lot more," he said, shrugging.

"What's to bind the Unseelie from hurting us?" Uncle Rene asked as he fell into step with them.

"They're bound by the traditions of hospitality," Papa explained.

"They have to be good hosts, or the magic would scar them just as badly. But—they're still *Fée*. Don't ask for anything, or your wish might be twisted."

Francine nodded, not surprised by either the bond or the tricksy nature of it.

Only a few of the Seelie court still remained under the growing dusk in the Grand Hall. Francine, Papa, and Uncle Rene rushed to join them.

Gray clouds covered the sky of the world they stepped into. The field before them was filled with dried winter grasses that muffled their steps. No colorful leaves or moss grew on the nude trees. Even the dirt seemed a faded brown.

Francine tried to watch just the Seelie in front of her and not look at the Unseelie surrounding her. But she couldn't help the glance at Julius when he circled around them.

He wore an immaculate three-piece suit, rich brown in color, with subtle gray pinstripes. A cream-colored shirt set off his dark skin, and the points of a yellow handkerchief stuck out of the front breast pocket.

He didn't look at Francine once as he moved to the front of the group.

"Anyone who tries to leave this circle without completing the ceremony is fair game for the warriors," he warned.

The warriors, who now stood in a loose circle all around the Seelie, gave a rumbling growl that sent shivers down Francine's back.

Next the Unseelie priests stepped forward, in their blue robes and heavy ropes of jewels. They chanted something that sounded like French, but older.

Then they switched to the language Lady Melisandra had used, ancient and powerful. Francine listened carefully—could she capture it in a song someday? The priests started spinning out sparkling silver nets of magic, weaving them together with the words. As the priests floated the net higher, they switched back to English, calling on the saints to watch over the proceedings, like Saint Matthias and Saint Isidore, whom Francine had heard of. But also saints she didn't know, like Saint Buford and Saint Odilia.

Francine chanted with the others in the Seelie court, promising no harm through action or inaction. She shivered with the rest when the priests dropped the net on them. It dissolved into cold spiderweb threads on her skin when it touched.

After the ceremony ended, Francine turned with the others to go to the Unseelie court.

Suddenly, Julius was pulling on her arm, his hot hoof scalding her skin. He thrust her in front of an Unseelie priestess.

"Did the magic really work?" he demanded.

"She's not fully *Fée*," he sneered.

"We're all a mixture here," the priestess chided. She looked at Francine, her gaze going slowly from her hair to her toes.

Francine looked back. Instead of blue robes and jewels, this priestess was painted bright blue, with tree limbs crossing her skin, as if someone lay on their back and looked up through the trees on a sunny day.

"She'll obey while she's in our lands," the priestess said slowly. Then she winked.

"She'd never harm the *Fée*, sugar. She's a healer, too."

Julius sighed as if he'd been asked to do something unreasonable.

"All right."

"I'm sorry, Julius," Francine said quietly.

"You sure about that?" Julius asked bitterly.

"Cause I think all you ever cared about, really, was just getting back to him."

He pointed with his chin at Papa, who stood nearby, his arms crossed over his chest, ready to come to her defense.

"You were never in it for the glory of revenge, were you? It really was a puny thing."

He spit, carefully avoiding her boots, then walked away.

Francine swallowed around the sudden lump in her throat, knowing Julius would never understand.

Maybe if she hadn't rescued Papa, maybe if they hadn't started finding a way back to each other, Francine would have only wanted revenge, and it wouldn't have turned out to be such a puny thing, as he called it.

Or maybe revenge *was* puny, would always be puny, in the face of love.

Chapter Fifteen

The full dark of the night was on the Unseelie court by the time Francine stepped through the arch. Red lights shined down on the court from the branches of the still-swollen trees, the only brightness there. The court wore their gowns and silk coats, fancy gloves hiding claws and paws alike.

Francine joined the other Seelie musicians ranging behind the giant willow that still held the queen. Like the others, she plucked at her instrument, a soft tune, nothing like what either the Seelie or the Unseelie were used to hearing from her. She worked at keeping the song simple, understated.

Even those standing closest to her didn't seem to get it, and would look away, not drawn by it at all.

Just as she and Papa had planned.

Erastus came before the court. He wore his white fur cape again. He'd grown darker, his lips fuller, and his teeth and horns sharper. His bare chest glistened in the dark as if it'd been oiled.

When Erastus started to talk, the other musicians stopped their random tunes, but Francine didn't. She wove her song around those closest to her, filling them with peace and calm. Then she slowly pushed out tendrils to the next group, lulling them all, building a base.

The willow groaned as it started to raise its roots.

Francine swayed easily as the ground moved. Papa now joined her, an airy counterpoint, floating above the heads of everyone who heard. They added more melody now, building a song that maybe Mama would have sung.

Papa moved casually to one side of the tree while Francine moved to the other side. They built a bridge of music between them, strong and steady, that lifted the spirits of the few who could hear.

Queen Yvette rose like a flood creek belched out of the side of a mountain. Blood stains spattered across the front of her white dress. Strands of green moss and brown mulch also spoiled its former purity. Twigs and leaves littered her hair, and her dark skin looked as though it had been bleached in ash.

The fetters had turned from black to gray as they'd drained the queen of her power, corrupting the iron until the *Fée* could touch it without pain.

However, the queens eyes were gator gold, and a bright star shone around her neck.

The court murmured, restless.

Francine played a bit louder, calming the *Fée* around her.

Papa joined her, adding layers of lace on top of her firmament.

Erastus glared at Francine, then shook his head.

"The queen is ours! Her power, her light!" he declared, striding up to her.

The queen meekly raised her hands.

Erastus gave her a cruel smile, gathering them in his like a lover.

"Now these are mine."

He tugged out the pin from one shackle, raising it above his head to show to the crowd. The Unseelie court shouted their approval, growls, hoots, and roars shooting toward the sky.

Francine continued her quiet playing, catching Papa's eye. He took a step forward and she mirrored him, sliding up into the upper ranges as he slid down, playfully swapping roles for a few measures before returning.

Erastus let go of the unpinned fetter.

It didn't drop or fall off.

When Erastus touched the first fetter again, a sliver of the darkest ivy twined out from the iron, snaking its way up, wrapping around Erastus' wrist.

"What trick is this?" he asked, dropping the pin.

The court murmured uneasily.

"No trick," Francine said, stepping forward, increasing the tempo of her song, building the bridge with her Papa.

Erastus stood still, entranced by the rapidly spiraling ivy curling up his arm.

The queen took advantage of his distraction and freed her second hand from the fetter.

But it, too, didn't fall, as ivy crept out from it and up the queen's wrist.

"What?" she asked, glaring at Francine, then at her papa.

Francine stepped closer, her tune swelling. She threw all her passion into the song now, the driving beat of zydeco, the slide of jazz, and the cry of the blues.

Papa built on top of everything Francine laid down, adding all the frills of *Féerie*, the glittering moonlight and talkative trees, the healing waters and spiked berries.

The fetters transformed, turning silver in the light of their tune. They shimmered and the light spread across the king and the queen, covering them both in a cloak of healing magic.

Francine and Papa switched roles again, with Francine

bringing all the passion of the Unseelie into the music, while Papa brought the formality of the Seelie: wild dancing with courtly turns, teasing trees with easy paths.

Queen Yvette clawed at the ivy climbing her arm while her feet shuffled to the song Francine and her papa played. Erastus tried to pull away, his body turned one way, while his feet continued to face the queen, moving in time with her. The rest of the court had already started to dance, unable to resist. Eula, the snake-like Unseelie, twirled with Brooks, while Julius stomped with Lady Melisandra.

"You must find a balance," Papa told the queen. "Between the dark and the light. It can't all be one way."

"Charles—" the queen warned.

"You heard me. You must return to the light," he growled.

The queen shuddered, and the shining star around her neck flared. Her gown turned white as the first winter's frost, her skin growing dark and rich again. The king also changed, sharp angles taking over his face, his ears turning pointed and his mouth, cruel.

Francine added some of the sadness she felt as they king transformed. Her friend was gone, though the light of the queen did ease her heart.

She'd never be able to come to the Unseelie court again, regardless of whether they'd welcome her or not.

The king and the queen finally began to dance together, jerkily at first, then with the grace inherent to the *Fée*. They floated through a few turns of a waltz that then sped up to the staccato of zydeco. Leaping up, they spun in the new moon, the magic spiraling out, blessing the crowd, the trees, and the lands. They mirrored each other better now, one dark, one light, one blessed, one not.

From the far side of the Grand Hall, a new fiddler joined in. At first the music sounded out of place and the notes didn't slide together well. But before the next refrain they were well joined as Pierre walked through the dancers.

Pierre gave a wan smile to Francine, his fingers skipping as he relearned playing with extra joints. His shirt echoed the tree bark he'd worn, segmented and mossy. His pants were woven ferns, green and crackling.

Francine poured more joy into the tune, welcoming Pierre, expanding the song to encourage him more.

The low sax of Uncle Rene joined them; then, one by one, the other musicians as well, both the Seelie and the Unseelie playing together for the first time.

Francine kept hold of the rhythm, not letting a single style take over. They needed to mix, to mingle, but also to be pure to themselves, the Seelie, the Unseelie, and the mixed *Fée* that joined them together.

Papa gave Francine the biggest smile she'd seen him wear, at least since Mama had died.

Mama, if she was watching, would have been very proud of them, indeed.

* * *

The trees closest to Francine felt real under her fingers, with rough bark and sweet sap. Buds swelled the branches. Birds hadn't returned yet, but the squirrels had come out, chittering and racing, scrambling and doing death-defying leaps between the branches.

But in the distance, mists wrapped tightly around the trunks, swathing the branches and hiding all the details. It seemed to Francine that she stood at the edge of a watercolor painting. The earth under her human boots felt solid and real. Yet when the trees echoed her music back, it returned high and thin.

The Seelie court woods had changed, losing more of the human elements, become more *Féerie*, less attached, less real.

Francine soaked up as much of the morning as she

could, breathing in the cool air, the taste of moon wine still on her lips.

They were going home: Francine, Papa, and Uncle Rene.

Or, at least, back to the human lands.

Francine had spent the night making music with Pierre, tossing melodies back and forth, capturing the light of the *Fée* with their tunes, then kicking up their heels to Francine's beloved zydeco. They'd made the trees dance and the waters sing. They'd gelled like they had that first night, each of them letting go of their fear.

With the coming light, Pierre had slipped away like the mists, his tune trailing behind him as he went.

It was the best goodbye Francine could expect.

Papa, Uncle Rene, and Queen Yvette waited already in the Grand Hall. The queen shone brightly in the wan morning light, like a star that had fallen. She gave Francine a cool nod of her head but didn't say a word; she hadn't spoken to any of them since they'd forced her to be more balanced.

Papa put his arm over Francine's shoulder when she came up.

Francine rolled her eyes. Papa had let her go spend the night with Pierre, but he was always scared she'd never come back.

He didn't need to worry. She'd always come back, now that there was something to come back to.

The queen formed the arch, flinging the top of it high enough to brush the branches of the trees above them. It stood like a dark curtain in the meadow.

Uncle Rene picked up his sax, then blew a cool, sad riff. He gave the queen a stiff bow, then walked through.

Papa went next. He kissed Francine's cheek, then approached the queen.

Queen Yvette stiffened as Papa neared. Regardless, he leaned down and kissed her cheek as well before turning swiftly and walking though the arch.

For a moment, the queen smiled, sly and thoughtful. Then her face grew blank as Francine approached.

"Thank you," Francine told her. She gave her deepest courtesy. Even Pierre would have been surprised.

"For everything."

"You're welcome, darling," a new voice said.

Startled, Francine looked up.

Lady Melisandra walked across the Grand Hall. The queen glared at her.

"She's too proud to say it, but she'd like to thank you as well," Lady Melisandra said.

"No, I wouldn't," the queen said, addressing Lady Melisandra.

"The child weakened us."

Lady Melisandra gave an unladylike snort.

"Like hell. She helped you become more pure again. But you're young yet yourself."

Then she walked past the queen and came directly up to Francine.

"Goodbye, darling," Lady Melisandra said, giving Francine a very human hug.

"I know you can't come and see us again, but you never know who may come to have tea with you sometime. I've heard your Uncle Rene's biscuits are quite a treat."

"That they are," Francine said. She was looking forward to them.

"You'd be welcome," Francine said. "I can't thank you enough. The trees, my woods—"

"I know, dear. You miss those most, I imagine. They'll come visit you in your dreams sometime."

Lady Melisandra kissed Francine's forehead. Warmth blossomed across her skin, filling her with the fizzy energy of glittering moonlight.

For a dizzying moment Francine thought about staying,

about going back to her woods, that place of her heart—but she knew she couldn't.

Francine had had enough of fairy magic and tricks.

"Goodbye," Francine said firmly. She picked up the bone-white fiddle and stepped through.

Dry gravel crunched under Francine's boots. The air struck her skin as cool and surprisingly dry. Papa and Uncle Rene waited for her on the side of the crossroads.

Francine blinked, surprised. It all looked so…normal. She'd expected to be jolted, but she wasn't. The sun hadn't quite peeked through the trees. Thin clouds hid the pale blue of the winter sky. Francine took a deep breath, breathing in the dust of the road, the pungent pines and the quiet of the day.

It wasn't the sweetness of *Féerie*.

But it was still good to be home.

* * *

A noise startled Francine out of her studies. She looked up from her books and blinked. The only light was the one shining on her desk—it had grown dark outside and she hadn't realized it.

She stood and stretched, then glanced back down at her books. Two more weeks and she'd be ready for her GEDs. Then she could send the Louisiana music college her application. She already had her audition CD prepared; both Papa and Uncle Rene had helped.

What had disturbed her? She glanced at the clock.

Papa wasn't home yet; he and Uncle Rene had started another band and were playing that night.

Francine had wanted to go hear them, but she knew she wouldn't have been content to just listen, and would have spent the night playing when she needed to study. At least Papa was having fun, and Uncle Rene's cancer had stayed in remission. The trip to *Féerie* hadn't cured him, but it had stopped the cancer, at least for a while.

The knock came again.

Not from the door, but from the window.

Francine's first instinct was to pick up her sadly human fiddle, but it could no longer defend her. It had faded to plain wood in the human world, no longer shooting sparks or flames.

Still curious, Francine lifted the shade.

Pierre stood outside, holding his fiddle in one hand, his bow in the other.

"Wanna dance, *ma chérie*?" he asked with a winsome smile.

Francine looked back at her desk. She *should* study. She should finish the next practice test.

Her feet decided for her, and she found herself already drifting to her bed and picking up her fiddle.

"Just for a bit," Francine told Pierre sternly, already sliding open the window and slipping out into the backyard.

"You wound my honor, darling," Pierre told her, giving her a slight bow. "You know we only play as long as you want."

"And you never ask me to stay," Francine said, unsure as always how she felt.

"Neither do you," Pierre said quietly.

Francine nodded. It took two sides to build a bridge, and they were both too firmly rooted in their homes to do more than meet in the center sometimes.

But that was enough.

"Let's play," Francine said with a smile.

And they began to dance.

Author's Notes

Louisiana Music College doesn't exist.

The academy that Francine attends doesn't exist.

Small cell lung cancer, however, does exist, and really is that much of a killer. Average life expectancy after diagnosis is one to two years. There are no stages. There is no reversal or remission. There are treatments to prolong life, but no cure.

A percentage of the profits from this novel will go to the American Lung Association.

Zydeco Queen and the Creole Fairy Courts

About the Author

Leah Cutter's first novel, *Paper Mage* (Roc, 2003), is set in China, during the T'ang dynasty, around 837 A.D. Her second novel, *Caves of Buda* (Roc, 2004), is set in Budapest, with many different time periods, including pre-Christian Hungarian mythology, Roman magic, World War II, and 1957, when the Russians came back to Hungary. Her third novel, *The Jaguar and the Wolf* (Roc, 2005), is set in the Yucatan peninsula, around 1000 A.D., and explores what would have happened if the Vikings had met the Mayans.

Leah Cutter's fourth novel, *Clockwork Kingdom* (Knotted Road Press, 2012), is a young adult contemporary fantasy, with bloodthirsty steampunk fairies determined to take over the world.

Her short fiction includes fantasy, science fiction, mystery, and horror, and has been published in anthologies and on the web. A collection of her short fiction is available in *Baker's Dozen* (Knotted Road Press, 2011).

Read more stories by this author at:
www.KnottedRoadPress.com
Follow this author's blog at:
 www.LeahCutter.com

www.ingramcontent.com/pod-product-compliance
Lightning Source LLC
LaVergne TN
LVHW021654060526
838200LV00050B/2353